T0304915

THE BONE HUNTERS

JOANNE BURN

S

SPHERE

SPHERE

First published in Great Britain in 2024 by Sphere

1 3 5 7 9 10 8 6 4 2

Copyright © Joanne Burn 2024
Illustrations by Persephone Blaxhall

The moral right of the author has been asserted.

A CIP catalogue record for this book
is available from the British Library.

ISBN: 978-1-4087-2651-8

Typeset in Garamond 3 by M Rules
Printed and bound in Great Britain by
Clays Ltd, Elcograf S.p.A.

Papers used by Sphere are from well-managed forests
and other responsible sources.

MIX
Supporting
responsible forestry
FSC® C104740

Sphere
An imprint of
Little, Brown Book Group
Carmelite House
50 Victoria Embankment
London EC4Y 0DZ

An Hachette UK Company
www.hachette.co.uk

www.littlebrown.co.uk

For Jack, with love.

I have wished to keep my reader in the company of flesh and blood.

Preface to the *Lyrical Ballads*,
WILLIAM WORDSWORTH

The House of the Geological Society,
No. 20 Bedford Street,
Covent Garden,
London.

17ᵗʰ August, 1824

Miss Ada Winters, Broad Ledge,
Lyme Regis, Dorsetshire

We acknowledge receipt of your request, but regret to
inform you that our society is for gentlemen only.

Yours respectfully,

Charles Lyell,
Corresponding Secretary

CHAPTER ONE

Lyme Regis

AUGUST 1824

*L*yme crowds a narrow combe, caught between hunched hills. In the shipyard to the west, beyond warehouses and timberyards, within spitting distance of the customs house, amongst the clatter of mallets and hoarse insults from heckling throats, rocks are crushed for ballast. To the east, on the foreshore, sea masons quarry. And stonemasons tucked away in dusty workshops chip at lintels and fireplaces, finials and corbels.

On the distant horizon, Portland, from where stone is daily chiselled for the grandest halls and houses, slumps stony-faced, the colour of a bruise. And in the quiet of the woods far above the town, water purls over pebbles in the River Lim before plunging for the Waterside Factory and the fulling mill, Old

Factory and Town Mill. It murmurs, stealthy, past the back entrance of the Kings Arms and under Buddle Bridge (where smugglers flit, swift as bats), trembling at last upon the beach, thirsty for salt and the clean sea breeze.

In the harbour, a customs official throws tobacco onto the king's pipe, and fishwives mend nets upon the beach, waiting for the men to return, wondering if this is the day they won't. The waters are a fisherman's nightmare, but the better sorts know nothing of that. When they tire of the frivolities of Bath they flock to Lyme on the new roads built especially for them, to fill their bellies with Purbeck oysters, Newfoundland cod in butter sauce and shrimp pink as their rosy cheeks. Those reliant on parish charity make do with clams, or mackerel if they're quick to help with hauling in the catch when the cow horn sounds. And a scattering of those folk, in the pale dawn light, now skirt the boats and tangled nets and lobster pots, looking for nuggets of coal, for anything dropped. Above them, graves like jagged teeth line the top of Church Cliffs: crooked stones and monoliths that teeter where the earth is wont to crumble, threatening to bring down those interred, tumbling bones of the long deceased onto the doorstep of the cottage below. It has happened before, this calamity. When Ada Winters was small and curdle-haired. When her father was alive and her mother was happy. When Gramfer perched all hours between nuncheon and supper on his stool by the range: milky-eyed, twitchy as a tin of crickets, speaking tales of piskey-folk and sea buccas and the *wild wolf woman of Lyme*. Tales as ancient as the town itself.

Ada swings her pickaxe into the cliff, rocks tumbling to her feet. She passes for a man at a distance: tall, and bold enough to wear her dead father's breeches and working smock. Hewn from hard graft and the four winds, she keeps her sun-weathered, freckled face shaded by a wide-brimmed black hat. No flimsy mobcap, no bonnet with ribbons. Beneath the smears of grey clay, she has the colouring of a lion, all fawn and gold – but that is something of a secret.

Soft in the head, Lyme folk say.

But Ada isn't soft. She carries a stone in the pit of her belly and sometimes in her throat, which gets in the way of eating as frequently as lack of coin. Her mother says if her smile weren't quite so stony then maybe she'd be married by now. Hag stones line her pockets, not for protection from witches, but because there's nothing so pleasing as plunging one's finger into the middle of a stone and out the other side.

Sweat prickles her face and armpits as she rummages in the fallen earth. Her mouth is dry and her belly rumbles, but she won't return home for breakfast until she's found something to prove to herself she's worthy of a place in their society.

Their society.

Her bitterness is gritty as the shingle beneath her feet.

The crisp cream paper had looked so incongruous in her muddy hands, although that sense of oddity was only evidence that she *is* what they say she cannot be.

She is a geologist.

Church Cliffs seem to think so. Black Ven, too – its dark, forbidding crag face looming high above her, and stretching eastwards in the direction of Charmouth. These ancient tombs give up their treasure to her in a way they don't give it up to others: tooth and skull, rib and claw.

She had hoped to strike up a correspondence, at the very least. She'd gone so far as to imagine hosting those men of science on this very beach, where she knows better than anyone what is what.

She should have listened to her mother, who'd been tamping down Ada's hopes with her quiet disregard, saying only one thing on the matter: 'They won't 'ave ye.' Ada had protested, sensibly and logically, that the society exists *for the purpose of making geologists acquainted with each other, of stimulating zeal, of facilitating the communications of new facts.*

'It don't matter,' said Edith. 'They still won't 'ave ye.'

Josiah and Annie Fountain, owners of Fountain's Muse: Binder & Bookseller, had all along been telling Ada much the same – that she was wasting her ink and paper (*their* ink and paper, in truth, not to mention the tuppence for postage).

Along with her letter, Ada had sent a slim volume of her ammonite drawings, bound in cloth by Josiah, describing what she knows to be two new species. She'd made sure to tell the society that she's been reading their transactions for the past thirteen years, since they were first published in 1811. Since I was eleven, she told them. Josiah and Annie suggested leaving that detail out. 'They'll probably not believe it,' they said.

But it's true, so she included it.

She swings her pick again, plunging it into the crumbly black earth, pulling it out. She growls with the effort, her neck as tight and knotted as it was yesterday when the postboy proffered the letter and she felt her hope, quick as a hare, kicking in her chest. She'd cracked the wax seal where she stood, pausing briefly to consider the man who had written out her name so carefully; observing the precision of his hand, that he dipped his nib at regular intervals and didn't let his pen run dry. Then she unfolded the single sheet of paper, and all hope was dashed.

'Is that *all*?' she muttered. 'What about my drawings?'

Her pickaxe now leans against her leg like a tired child. She licks her lip, tasting salt, rolling her aching shoulders, gazing upwards.

What she notices then is straight as a finger bone, flaring out into a knuckle. It's ten feet off the ground in the cliff face, beneath a grass-strewn ledge. She scrambles towards it, pulls away a loose tangle of grass, brushes at the dirt and follows the line of the fossil with her fingertips. She digs it out, turns it over, brushes it free of mud. It's too long for a human finger bone, but that's what it resembles, laying there across her palm, pointing at her heart.

CHAPTER TWO

*A*da startles at the rapping on the door, irked that their landlady's regular Saturday-evening visit still makes her nerves jangle so. She longs for the courage to ask Mrs Hooke whether she really must hammer at the door with her brass-tipped walking stick – the cottage is small and they're not hard of hearing. If she had the nerve she'd ask why she even feels the need to come at all; surely it's beneath her, to traipse her silk and furs through the grey mud that clings to the pebbles this side of town?

Ada looks to her mother, not long back from the mill. Strands of damp hair have escaped her mobcap and exhaustion drifts from her as tangibly as the smell of soap and wool-grease. Her arms are raw from her week of washing fleeces, florid from fingertip to elbow, and she inhales slowly and deeply, as if strength can be found that way. Ada gives her a little nod, then turns away, breath hitching as she lifts the latch.

Every week without fail, Mrs Hooke allows Edith only the time she needs to collect her weekly wages (six shillings and six pence), pay the grocer what she owes on her way past, and

8

make it home to eat her evening meal before counting out every coin in the house. And here she looms in the doorway in her narrow-waisted, full-skirted gown; the black silk flashing a beetle-like, iridescent green. The fur stole she always wears, no matter the season, is draped about her neck. She pushes past Ada into the house, rustling as she goes, like the scurry of so many chitinous feet on the stone floor.

She casts her cold appraisal about the room, letting it slide across the birds' nests, and the feathers pasted to one wall with bluebell glue: undulations of blacks and browns so the effect is of dark rolling waves tipped foamy-white. She glances, too, at the collections of shells separated into species, and further separated along lines of patterning and hue. There are blanched skulls of stoat, rabbit, vole and hare. And there is seaweed drying on the table: slender wart weed, egg wrack, Irish moss and wireweed. Mrs Hooke wrinkles her nose, but, in truth, there is something intriguing about it all – something that brings to mind the cabinets of curiosities to be found in the drawing rooms of some of her friends (those better travelled and à la mode than Mrs Hooke). Of course, Ada's collection lacks objets d'art, ivory and ebony; she has only what she can forage for herself.

'A mess, then, as always,' Mrs Hooke says.

This is how they conduct themselves each week: Ada putting herself as best she can between Mrs Hooke and Edith, steeling herself to look Mrs Hooke in the eye and do whatever talking needs to be done because Edith can never find her words in the presence of their landlady (cannot truly find her words in the presence of anyone but Ada and Pastor Durrant).

'Your rent is going up,' says Mrs Hooke, swaying slightly, as if they are together at sea. She plants her feet wide, leans forward on her cane.

Ada swallows down a rush of nausea.

'How much?'

'An extra shilling a week.'

Mrs Hooke shrugs, as if shillings are pennies.

Ada shakes her head. 'That's too much.'

'Everything's on the up.'

'But it isn't worth that.' Ada gestures to the floorboards where the water's coming in, the damp rising up the walls like dark shadows. 'And the roof still leaks.'

'I sent a man.'

'I keep telling you, he didn't come. You can see from the outside that the roof is bowed, the slates are loose.'

'I'll send him again.'

Ada wants to say that it isn't good enough, that it isn't fair, but she isn't *so* bold to risk a fight with Mrs Hooke.

Edith is busy at the drawer where they keep their coin in a small wooden box, and when Ada drags her gaze from Mrs Hooke's painted face, it comes to rest on the hunched figure of her mother. Her backbone is visible through her clothing and Ada cannot take her eyes from it – has she always been so thin? As Edith counts pennies and farthings, and Ada counts her mother's vertebrae, Mrs Hooke's gloved fingers reach for the reticule dangling from her arm. She unties it, and holds the fabric open for Edith's handful of coins (four shillings in all). Ada watches the money gobbled up and the throat of the reticule pulled tight once more.

Before the clock strikes for midnight, Mrs Hooke loses those four shillings at the assembly rooms on the roll of the dice. And as she throws that money away, an old crone watches idly from the dark beach, water lapping at her bare feet.

The great bay window of the assembly rooms looks out to the restless sea but, of course, once the night closes in, from within those rooms one can see nothing of the outside world. To stand in the mizzle, however, out in the darkness, gazing in, everything is illuminated – the young women in flowing chemise-dresses, diaphanous petticoats shimmering beneath flimsy muslin, pink coral beads nestling against their throats; the men in frock coats with fur-trimmed lapels (some of those coats turned inside out for good luck at the carding tables), white shirts fastened at the cuffs with gold, cravats of coloured silk. They are silent players on a stage, and that suits the old crone just fine; she has no interest in their conversations. They discuss the cost of housebuilding and canal-building and whether Lyme needs yet more hotels. They don't speak about the cost of a loaf, but talk about the labourer riots and what can be done to snuff them out. There is always much gabble about steam engines and the wonders of electricity, and sure as eggs are eggs, any gentleman who still favours breeches and stockings will fall eventually into the old tattered talk of Waterloo and La Belle Alliance. Arrangements are made to meet the following day for tea or to take the waters. And beneath the oak beams of the cellar and the limestone foundations, below four feet of sullen earth and clay, in a wet passage cloaked in shadow, three bone-tired smugglers bring twenty kegs of rum, six bales of tea and a dozen geese stuffed with lace into town.

CHAPTER THREE

Edwin

Who would imagine that letting one's young son scrat around in the local quarry could lead to the ruin of everything? It seemed a harmless enough activity at the time, especially for a boy who erred on the side of caution and inactivity. But undeniably it has led to what Edwin's father considers the strangest and most ungodly of obsessions. He ruminates on this day and night, as if the decades can be rolled back and matters altered through sheer magnitude of regret. His son was *so bloody quiet*, as if butter wouldn't melt. Dr Moyle Senior had always harboured a concern about his son's reserved nature, how suspiciously amenable he was. He put on a fine show of falling in line, but all along he evidently had ambitions of his own. Dr Moyle sits on the edge of his bed, looking down at the wasted muscle of his calves, the liver spots and bruises. In a moment, when he has gathered his energy, he will reach for the bell and ring for assistance. And then, once he's dressed in the best of his authority, he'll give Edwin one last talking-to before his only son throws away everything they have worked so hard to achieve.

Edwin looks down at the open trunk, mentally riffling the papers within. What will he need, and does he have it all? The closer he gets to leaving for Dorset, the more Harley Street seems to be crowding in on him; as if the houses themselves have shuffled just that little bit closer together. As if he might drag this final trunk down the stairs only to find that the front door no longer opens – that the house opposite has lifted from its very foundations and lumbered across the road to block his exit. His consulting room has never felt so stuffy, and he flings open a window, rubbing at his temples. At any moment his wife, Christina, will slip in and enquire how he's getting along. His father will soon be up and about and hot on her heels. Between the two of them they will mither and harangue, and he simply doesn't have the energy for it. He reminds himself of his promise to Christina to clear the parlour of his fossils before he leaves; she doesn't appreciate them *scattered everywhere*. They are, in fact, ordered meticulously, but he has ceased pointing that out. He glances around his consulting room, at the many shelves crowded with rocks and fossils in here also: Oxfordshire pound stones, fern leaves, crystal corals, fish skulls and lizard bones. He ponders the troubling possibility of returning to find everything boxed up, and is assailed then by an urgency to pack it all away himself, to protect the careful sequences and classifications. But he still has his books and periodicals to select and wrap. With perfect timing, all around the house, the clocks begin their chiming conversation to mark the passing of the hour – and Edwin's own, inner mainspring tightens incrementally with the loosening of theirs.

He takes a deep, purposeful breath and reminds himself that by the end of the morning he'll be bound for Lyme Regis. The temporary physician who is to run the family practice in his stead will have arrived, and the place will be in safe hands (he finds himself rehearsing this mantra, in preparation for the inevitable quarrel that will occur with his father over breakfast). Their good reputation will *not* suffer. Dr Moyle Senior's impressive rise from Oxfordshire country doctor to one of the most respected physicians in London will *not* have been for naught. And Edwin is coming home in three short months. Goodness, he is not, after all, leaving for ever. Does he not, after seventeen years of attending patients, deserve to attend to himself a little?

CHAPTER FOUR

*S*team rises from the clam broth, and Ada opens the door to watch her mother trudging home – the tired rise and dip of her stiff-hipped walk. Ada sighs, preparing herself for the inevitable conversation. After Mrs Hooke's visit on Saturday night she'd made herself scarce to avoid a difficult exchange with her mother about the increased rent. And yesterday after chapel she went straight to the beach, throwing her energy into the precise area of Black Ven where she'd found the peculiar finger-like fossil. All afternoon and into the evening she'd pulled apart the earth in search of anything more, but to no avail. Today, however, has proved more fruitful. She pushes her hand through her skirt and petticoat and into her pocket, grasping the bones she unearthed a few hours previously, just a few feet from where she found the first. These three almost identical fossils provoke a confusion of questions and, as she moves about the kitchen, they knock in her pocket like finger-nails tapping on a table.

A weary bustle at the door, Edith looks straight into Ada's eyes.

'Wretched girl,' she says, through a half-smile.

Edith grasps the knotted hank of rope that hangs from the doorframe (put there by her own mother the year that Ada was born) and anchors herself against it for a brief moment, resting her forehead wearily against the damp hemp. Then she releases it, and enters the kitchen.

She gives a tug of her head: a silent instruction.

Ada follows her into the parlour, waiting for Edith to ease into her chair and rest: limp as her bedraggled hair. Her mother closes her eyes, and inhales tremulously as if it is the last breath she will ever take. Ada imagines what her mother has previously described – how the mill haunts her body long after leaving it behind at the end of the day, so that she lies in bed at night rocked nauseously by the wet echo of water and wheel.

Ada sits in her chair and waits. Eventually, Edith opens her eyes. Pushing herself upright, picking up her skirt so she can fiddle with its hem, she looks at her daughter.

'We need to discuss it, Ada. I don't know fer how much longer we can make ends meet. A crown a week fer this place! The price of everythin' these days . . .'

Ada looks to the empty hearth, thinking of autumn soon on its way and how they haven't set aside any fuel yet this summer. She wishes she'd made more effort to do so – she'd have been in a better position to reassure Edith about their declining situation if their scuttles were full of coal and the kitchen was piled with drying wood. But she finds it almost impossible to go scavenging fuel when there are fossils to be searched for.

'I can do more selling,' says Ada.

'Yer curios bring in pennies, 'tis not enough.'

'More than that sometimes.'

16

'*Sometimes.*'

'There's broth if you'd like—'

'Don't ye move!'

Ada sighs, leans back in her chair, reaches for the mending basket, snatches out a stocking, a needle, a length of yarn.

'I be workin' hard fer us,' Edith says, 'and ye need to do more.'

Ada bristles, although she only has to look at Edith to be reminded that her mother pays a high price for her lowly job at the mill. She pays not only with her health but with her dignity – to be washing fleeces still, after ten years of labouring hard at it.

'Ye could ask again fer work at the Old Factory,' says Edith.

'There's coin in these cliffs, and you know it.'

'How long since ye spoke to Mr Muir last? He has no complaint with me, I don't put a foot wrong.'

And yet, Ada wants to say, *he promotes every good-for-nothing layabout ahead of you.*

'He might 'ave something fer you now, Ada. And think if we were both bringin' in a regular wage . . .'

'I couldn't . . .' Ada shakes her head. The graft is not beyond her. It's the thought of being shut in all day. Trapped in with all that noise, and so many people. The thrum of all those bodies. Sometimes she stands in the woodland by the river, near the wishing tree, and listens to the drum and rumble of that huge stone building; it is terrifying, even from the outside.

'I have my fetching and carrying.'

It is Edith's turn to bristle; she doesn't approve of Ada helping the smugglers bring their lace into town, even though the rum they pay her puts fish on the table three times a week.

'We've managed these last ten years, and we'll continue to manage,' says Ada.

''Ark at thee! 'Tis easy fer *ye* to say. 'Tis time to sell all this rubbish!' Edith gestures through into the parlour.

'I *am* selling it.'

'No, you be *collecting* it. Pastor Durrant has told me some rich folk would pay a pretty penny fer everythin' ye have in that parlour. It needs to go! We cannot keep on and on. However frugal and industrious we be, 'tis not enough, not with the extra rent to find.'

Ada swallows down the dark horror of what her mother is saying, and the insult of Pastor Durrant's suggestion. She couldn't part with all she has brought into this cottage. These objects *are* the cottage. Just as her father's beautiful cabinets, stretching across the whole back wall, are the cottage. Ada's gaze flickers across the shelving where once upon a time her father's leather-bound volumes leaned one against the other and his periodicals were stacked in neat piles. Science fascinated him, but liberation was his theme. The works of Godwin and Wollstonecraft. Essays by Ben Franklin, John and Abigail Adams, Thomas Jefferson and Thomas Paine. He was more than a cabinetmaker; he was a thinker. She looks from one cabinet to the next, then from drawer to drawer, as if she might find him there. *He* would share her consternation. Why did he teach her to read and write, if not for something better than the tyranny of the mill?

'Ye cannot have it all ways,' says her mother. 'We need bread on the table.'

'I'll think of something.'

''Tis not a matter for thinkin'! Ye need a job, my girl, or a husband. 'Tis not some riddle to be fathomed.'

Ada slaps the arm of her chair.

'Don't peck so!'

Then she leaps to her feet, snapping her apron on her way to the kitchen.

After they've eaten their clams and bread, they sit together darning stockings in silence. All the while, Edith's agitation and disapproval drift from her, until it seems to Ada that the whole room is full of it – like a choking dust. Eventually, when she cannot stand it any longer, she leaves the cottage without saying goodbye and without telling her mother where she's going or when she'll be back. She simply takes up their rusty pail and heads east in the direction of Charmouth. It would be quicker to walk to the well in town, but Ada never heads that way without a pressing reason; she would always choose the littoral peace of an evening beach over the gadding hordes of Lyme.

A handful of fishermen are pulling their nets and pots up above the tideline. They pay her no heed, as if she's not there at all.

She walks half a mile to a meagre rivulet that emerges where the steep cliff gives way to a tumble of gullies and grassy hillocks. Holding her pail to the small gush of water, glancing back the way she came, she remembers her fossil finds of the last few days and the bewilderment they've provoked. All around there are things hidden by time more than man, and knowing that to be true is somehow settling. Ada would hate to live in a world where everything was laid bare upon the surface; it's the mysterious and unfathomable that sustain her.

When the pail is full she leans forward and sups straight from the hillside, rubbing her face afterwards with the cold, fresh water. She drinks down questions and calmer thoughts until the knots of irritation in her stomach have loosened.

Ambling back in the direction of Lyme, she sees a customs

official standing atop Black Ven, glass to eye, and she can't help following the direction in which he looks: out to sea, due south, where a three-masted schooner rests halfway to the horizon.

Waiting for dusk to gather itself, Ada stops several times to press her back to the dark, steeply terraced slopes of Black Ven cliff, feeling the jeopardy as she looks up at the vast layers of crumbling earth that are forever falling upon the beach. Some folk think a landfall is a sign of God's anger, and mutter prayers of protection in response. But Ada is only ever thrilled by the slipping and heaving of the world, scrabbling over the bawdy-bare earth, searching for what treasure has been newly exposed. Her father warned Ada about these cliffs. To watch them carefully; to *know* them. 'Ye will never get the better of them,' he would say to her. But they understand one another, Ada and the cliffs.

'Don't we?' she says, touching her hand to the crumbly rock.

CHAPTER FIVE

*A*s the summer visitors to Lyme are sunk snug in their beds and missing the dawn, hotel staff bustle quietly in kitchens stoking ranges and counting carcasses, fishermen haul thrashing nets from the water, and Ada scrapes clay from beneath her nails with the tip of her penknife. She is meticulous; it takes concentration to do the task properly: to create a pair of hands that look even vaguely presentable. When she's finished, she brushes her hair and secures it in a bun beneath her hat. She pulls on her best pair of stockings, fastens her leather ankle-boots, ties her pockets about her waist. She fetches her hawking basket and brushes from it, testily, every crumble of encrusted mud; she would much rather be returning to Black Ven in her working clothes than going to sell her wares in her Sunday best. But being upon the beach is infinitely better than a job at the mill, so she hurries to her task, looking over the fossils and rocks she has sorted into groups on the table – items she has picked clean with her knife and polished with sweet oil. She knows what appeals to the visitors and chooses the best of her fool's gold, devil's toenails and ammonites.

Realising the Geological Society letter is in her pocket still, she takes it out and stuffs it into the back of a drawer. She'll not confess it to Edith just yet, because she isn't ready for the humiliation of admitting that her mother was right all along. She nearly burned it in the range when she was making the clam broth the other day, but changed her mind at the very last minute. Still now, she isn't sure why. Perhaps because it's her very own name written so carefully on the kind of paper she could never afford. Or perhaps she's simply keeping evidence of the rejection so she might provoke herself by fetching it out and reading it all over again at regular intervals. Perhaps she understands it's not only questions and mysteries that inspire her; it is also a kind of belligerence.

She presses both hands to the smooth oak of the cabinet, pausing for a moment to remember her father, breathing away the loss she still feels at his absence. She pushes back the familiar thought that comes rushing in – that it was only her father who understood her and how different things would be if he were still alive. He wouldn't think her endeavours a waste of time. Sighing, she opens one drawer after another, selecting teeth and vertebrae from the small partitions. Hidden among these specimens are those fossils that she will not sell: the croc-odilian snouts and the vertebrae more than three inches wide. These are also things that she hides from her mother, because Edith cares more for food on the table than rocks in drawers.

She wraps a sprinkling of crinoids in a strip of cloth; they sell well when she explains that these tiny pentagonal frag-ments are ancient fairy coins she traded for her baby teeth one year on May Eve (right here on this very beach). *Was it a fairy who bought the teeth from her?* No, it was an ancient crone with hair so untamed and teeth so pointed that Ada believed for a brief, skittish moment that she was striking a bargain with the wolf woman herself. The children from London and Oxford and Bath know nothing of this wild, unbroken woman. *The wolf witch. The wolf wench.* So Ada makes sure to tell them a tale or two (there's usually an extra penny for her trouble). What she doesn't tell them is how the children of the town used to come flocking to her gramfer for these very same tales whenever they spied him upon the beach; no one told a story better than he did. Those children even knocked upon the kitchen door for him. Ada wouldn't brook being crowded like that – all those grubby fingers fiddling with her hems and buttons. But all the same, she likes the feeling she gets when she shares the tales that came from him. And it makes her wonder, if he could see her now, would he be proud of her? As proud of her as she was of him? '*My* gramfer,' she'd whisper, as a jealous girl: this half-blind man who trailed children behind him.

She slips a stone the size of her palm into her hawking basket, certain it contains an impressive ammonite. If she finds the right customer (one who looks as if they might part with a shilling) then she'll splice it open in front of them. Before she does so, she'll whisper that they're about to see the remains of a fantastical creature long buried and preserved in stone – entombed until this very moment. She'll nestle the sharp blade of her chisel into the crack that runs around the edge of the flat, grey rock. She'll ready her hammer and allow the anticipation to build a little.

It all puts coin in her pocket.

But Ada isn't a hunter of fossils for the sake of impressing the visitors to Lyme. Or even to make a living – not truly. She hunts because she always has. Because she cannot help herself.

Because the objects in her cottage, spread wildly across every surface, make her feel whole, solid and real.

She only has to open the door and the beach is there. The tide is on its way out, and she ambles across the wet sand to see what the water has left behind. Tossed and scattered seaweed, shards of lost pottery, the infinite curvature of clay pipes, tiny pyritised ammonites that shine in her palm like coins. She glances at the fishermen and their upturned boats, the creels of fish being dragged across the pebbles, and beyond all that to a sea of mud-brown and sage-green. And then she looks to the visitors scattered about the place: a small group of women bending for shells at the shoreline; a couple squabbling with their three children; a pair of gentlemen on horseback. Slipping the ammonites into her pocket, she looks towards Gun Cliff (a man-made sea defence and a place of mounted cannons), and beyond that to the Cobb: a curve of harbour wall stretching into the water. The brooding day toys with darkening clouds, threatening rain.

Because Town Beach is always busier, she walks in that direction, readying herself to catch an eye and offer a smile. These are people who do not know her. People who do not care that she lives in a sea-battered house; the only house left on Broad Ledge: a stone's throw from town, but apart from it. These are people who haven't heard the town talk about her father John Winters: a man who wooed wood into beauty and started a riot about the price of bread and was killed by God himself as he agitated the angry crowd. These are people who do not know the tittle-tattle (mute mother, troublemaking father, *peculiar* daughter – grubbing about in the mud in her dead father's clothes), and so judge Ada only for her poverty. It's because of this that Ada, although ill at ease with the beach so busy and the steep narrow streets of Lyme teeming with carriages, finds some comfort in her dealings with the incomers. As she speaks to them about her fossils, as the words spill from her mouth like a landslide, she forgets everything except the curiosities she holds in her palm.

But sometimes Ada knows before it even begins that she'll have a dull day. That people will avoid returning her smile. That they'll turn away with their families to watch the fishing folk at work instead. It's during these mornings that Ada feels the heavy tread of boredom sidle up close, tugging at her elbow.

And it's one such morning.

Rumbles of thunder mimic her discontent. She, too, feels like growling. Her Sunday best is a little too warm for the summer weather, her dress and knitted stockings a little too thick. Sweat prickles the nape of her neck and she longs to scratch, but knows what people will think if she does.

The grass-strewn ledge at Black Ven calls to her, whispering enticements and not-quite-promises. She presses her hand to her pocket, reminding herself of the shape and solidity of the three strange fossils, ruminating all over again on what exactly they are. She'll give the visitors another hour before going home for something to eat, for a change of clothes, for her pickaxe and hammer.

She is dragged from her reverie by the hollering of a group of lads, and she looks towards them, knowing the familiar shape of their gangly limbs, the tallest one with a mop of black hair, a pair of tiny children trailing behind. They're heading for her, she realises, sighing. But she's not afraid of them, and to make sure they know this she turns to face them, putting a hand on her hip. They're not afraid of her either, and come swaggering onwards, whooping and cheering like their fathers after a night at the inn.

'Hawking yer pearly, are ye, Miss?' says the tallest lad, the ringleader.

'You watch your mouth,' Ada warns.

They circle her, feigning interest in her basket and its contents. She lifts it above her head, and they knock and jostle her in their jumping up for it.

'Get away,' she snaps.

The tallest lad grasps her wrist and pulls on it, reaching up with his other hand to take hold of the basket. Ada resists him, stretching higher than he can reach, making the most of her height.

'But we're lookin' to buy what yer sellin',' he says, and his followers stagger about, clutching their sides at his wit.

He takes another swipe for the basket and knocks half its contents across the pebbles. Ada grabs his arm, twisting it hard. And then she pushes him, forcefully, so that he stumbles and falls. He jumps up, eyes narrowed, mouth twisting.

'Ye scabby bitch!' he says, coming towards her. 'Look at the state o' yer!'

He spits in her face, snatches a handful of fossils from her basket and throws them into the terraces of muddy shale and stone. Then he turns tail and runs. Ada makes chase, but only half-heartedly; already her thoughts are with her polished treasures, now scattered across the beach and slumping cliff. She clenches her jaw as she thinks of the lost time, the lost shillings. Watching the lads scarpering, wiping her face, shuddering at the ghostly feeling of a hand tightened about her wrist, tears sting at her eyes and anger rises up in her like vomit. She bends for a pebble to hurl after them (she's a good shot because her father made sure of it: *choose a stone, choose a target*), but the lads have left behind a small ragamuffin, bedraggled and hungry looking, and he's staring at her with tired, gammy eyes. Ada sighs, lets her pebble drop.

She knows all these boys; she's watched them grow. And there would be no point taking it any further by seeking their parents in town. They'd give her short shrift, ballyragging *her* rather than their sons. Ada has learned this the hard way.

She smiles at the small child, but he doesn't smile back. She goes to her basket and picks a sea urchin fossil from it – its five petals perfect. She holds it out, crouching down in front of him. He takes it from her without looking at it.

'No,' she says. 'Look here at the pattern. See?'

He watches her trace the curves with her finger. Then she stands, and with a sigh brings her attention to rescuing her things.

She's always had an eye for finding fossils; looking at the beach and seeing things that others don't. She has an affinity with shapes and patterns; they demand her attention. And so, casting her gaze across the stones and pebbles, it's not so difficult to find her scattered specimens. Over and over she bends and straightens, plucking her things, which are not really *her* things at all (she knows this, and feels guilty sometimes for selling them). She scours this little area of the beach, searching the stone and shale for the things that blasted ramshacklum flung away.

CHAPTER SIX

Edwin

*H*is wife's letter arrives so soon after settling into his rooms, that it seems the post must have chased him all the way from London. He sits at his desk, bracing himself.

She hadn't wanted to trouble him as he was preparing to leave, she tells him, but she wanted him to know that she's not menstruated now for six weeks.

I feel differently, this time!

She has underlined this.

Edwin's heart sinks. He knows this pregnancy – if there is a pregnancy at all – will come to nothing. There is no reason to think otherwise. Christina is thirty-three, and for fifteen years the story has been the same. He has tried to suggest it is time for a *new* story, but his wife sees things differently. And when he returns home, she will, no doubt, be drifting round the house like a spectre, full of grief.

He sighs, rubs his brow.

Perhaps it will be different this time.

'Good Lord, please no,' he mutters.

He thinks of the cold cruelty of his own childhood. How the beatings came from nowhere – no matter how scarce he made himself, no matter how small and quiet. At times, in fact, it seemed that the quietness might have been the problem. But other times the opposite was true. He was perpetually flummoxed as to where he was going wrong; what he had *done* exactly to warrant the belt, the strap, the cane. He would rack his brains, fretting at possible misdemeanours and failures of character, knowing his father would demand an explanation as to why Edwin himself thought he deserved the sting of something sharp across his soft, bare skin. But most of the time he had no idea. Uncertainty was not an option in the Moyle household, however. Having an opinion was paramount. *Understanding* was essential. And sometimes Edwin would go so far as to fabricate some sin or other.

The confusion of childhood is not a suffering that he wishes to inflict on another being. So, no, he does not wish to be a father.

He shakes away his thoughts, and neatens his books and papers. He picks up his knife and sharpens a pencil, then walks across the room to throw the shavings into the grate.

On his return he stops at the window and watches the sea for a moment, saying a silent prayer to the town. If anywhere can help him create a new story for himself, it is Lyme. Geology is Edwin's passion, not medicine. And there is nowhere in Britain more enticing for a geologist than this briny little corner of England.

CHAPTER SEVEN

*O*n each of his monthly visits, Pastor James Durrant
brings more than a jar of beeswax balm and a paper-
twist of tea leaves. He brings a weightiness, as if the cottage has
let down its anchor. When he steps into the kitchen Ada feels
the air thicken, warm and syrupy. It's not exactly unpleasant,
and as Edith is always at pains to point out, *ye know where ye be,
with Pastor Durrant.*

He sets the small brown jar onto the table, giving it the
tiniest of pats. Ada watches for this little habit of his: the slow,
thoughtful *tap, tap.*

His face is well scrubbed – cheeks shiny pink against pale,
unlined skin. He's neat in his black coat and pantaloons, and
his white linen cravat is spotless, nestled high beneath his chin.
The velvet buttons of his coat are black, and match his velvet
collar; no splash of colour anywhere about his person, no frippery.
Sombre looking as a bear, measured in his movements and tone
of voice and the expression of his thoughts – regretful even, as if
forever on the cusp of offering his condolences. He has the countenance of a man of fifty, yet cannot be more than thirty-five.

He keeps the tea leaves in the inside pocket of his jacket until they've exchanged pleasantries.

'Shall we?' he says then, slipping his hand between coat and shirt, conjuring that careful twist of paper so they might together partake in civilised refreshment while they talk around the unseemliest of subjects: seashells embedded in the rock of the highest mountains; plant life petrified within coal; the fish fossils found beneath layers of rock containing the bones of land animals; the chaos inherent in all this, and what it means for the word of Moses and for Archbishop Ussher's accepted chronology of the earth's age (5,828 years, thirty-nine weeks and six days). What they speak of over tea is seen by some as a threat to morality, plain and simple. And Durrant's Congregational flock are ebbing away because of it. They do not have to defect to St Michael's if an Anglican church is a stretch too far; there's the Baptist chapel that will welcome them with open arms. *It's no skin off our noses*, they tell him. On some Sundays just recently (since Durrant sent a letter to the *Dorset County Chronicle* positing that the story of creation might be better seen as a metaphor) the Congregational chapel has hosted less than a dozen parishioners for its Sunday service. Ada and Edith are fastidious regulars, which is less a matter of religious devotion and more that missing church (even though it's only the Congregational chapel) really would be the end of things for them in Lyme.

'I heard back from London,' Ada says, as Edith boils water in the kitchen. She brings her letter from the drawer.

'Here.' She thrusts the correspondence at him.

And then she sits down, leans back and waits for him to reach inside his coat for his eye-glass. Positioning it carefully, slowly, he takes the letter from his lap and unfolds it, holds it up at arm's length. After only a second or two, with it aloft still, he looks at Ada and says, 'Ahh.'

'It makes no sense,' says Ada. 'I have so much to contribute.'

Pastor Durrant raises one dark, spidery eyebrow.

'I don't doubt it,' he says. 'But it's the way of the world. I did warn you.'

'If I only had the opportunity to talk to them, to share my thoughts and my collections. I might not have the means to travel the globe conducting research, but where else on earth boasts better fossils than here? Who can say they've found more fossils than I? It's not fair to shut me out because I'm a woman. Do they wish to advance the science, or not?'

Pastor Durrant considers her, but says nothing.

'It is not *right*,' she says, reaching out for the letter and returning it to the cabinet drawer. She looks at him expectantly, but he only offers an apologetic half-smile.

Ada sits down again, slumps forwards, elbows on her knees. 'Please don't mention it to Mother; I haven't told her yet.'

He nods, quickly, conspiratorially – pleased, Ada realises, for the two of them to be sharing some secret.

After he has left, Edith turns to Ada.

'He do be sweet on ye,' she says.

Ada acts as if she hasn't heard, thinking that perhaps if she says nothing then Edith will say nothing too – after all, Edith prefers silence above all else. Her mother picks up the jar of balm, unscrewing the lid. She sits down at the kitchen table talking of the pastor and his virtues, smoothing the beeswax into the cracked skin of her hands, rubbing it in carefully, easing it up her arms.

'Suitors don't be queuing up for ye, Ada, and ye be *four and twenty.*' She leans in and whispers this, as if it's the most terrible secret. 'Ye wouldn't be foolish, if it came to it?'

Her gaze is questioning, but accusatory, too. Their hazel eyes are identical, and their hair is the very same colour again, as if their creator painted them with one quick dash of a brush. Edith's eyes are red-raw, though, these days; her hair streaked with skeins of grey, her face lined with worry.

'He'd be a good husband,' says Edith.

'I don't want a husband.'

Ada doesn't even like the *word*, husband. She never has.

In her mind it's fused to other words she dislikes equally; words that make her think of lambs pulled in slimy cauls from their mothers' bodies. Bleating, mewling, suckling words. Clammy words that want to touch and feel. Words that make her think of specimens in jars: dead things preserved.

CHAPTER EIGHT

*F*ountain's Muse: Binder and Bookseller is down a narrow
twisting alley, a wooden finger on Combe Street pointing customers in the right direction. The door is heavy, well
varnished, and as Ada steps into the shop she breathes in the
pungent smell of leather and vellum, of ink and glue.

Her father has always remained here, in the walnut bookcases
that stretch from floor to ceiling, in the desk that squats against
the far wall and in the glass-fronted cabinet that displays
mounted taxidermy from a specialist workshop in Piccadilly:
an Irish white stoat with a shocked expression, a rather dishev-
elled brown hare and a tawny owl with piercing, judgemental
eyes (Ada could never bring herself to meet its gaze when she
was a child). She glances now, not at the stuffed creatures but
at the narrow panel of inlaid floral marquetry her father placed
between the two glass doors; it must surely be admired by
every customer who steps foot in the shop: it's a work of art.

'Ada!' exclaim Josiah and Annie.

Speaking in unison is a habit of theirs; a peculiarity so frequent and so bizarre that Ada has wondered if it's something

they practise (although concluding that impossible). She goes first, as she always does, to the cabinet: touches her hand to the marquetry as Josiah and Annie exchange glances. Her father became friends with the two of them while fitting the book-shelves and cabinets in their newly purchased shop. After the work was completed they took to sharing a brandy on Saturday evenings as well as a pew in chapel on Sundays. Josiah and Annie stopped attending chapel a long time ago. They don't go to church at all any longer, and don't seem to have suffered for it. Even their childlessness doesn't seem to be held against them by those who see a woman's barrenness as some indication of the state of her heart. But Ada cannot be sure of this; she isn't privy to Lyme gossip, being the subject of it. It might be, after all, not so much that the Fountains are immune to tittle-tattle, but that they're impervious to it: blithe as the children they dreamed of bringing into the world.

'Busy day?' asks Ada.

They nod.

'Summer visitors ...' says Annie, twisting a loose curl of silver hair in her fingers.

'They always keep us busy,' says Josiah. He too has silver hair – frizzy curls that stick up in wild tufts.

Ada is shades of brown in their presence: plain, grubby, smelling of clay. And she is only too aware of it. Annie's flower-print gown, all pinks and reds, edged with lace and tied beneath her breasts with ribbons, has been spritzed with lavender water – Ada can smell it six paces away. Josiah's white shirt is impeccably clean. His light green waistcoat peeks from beneath his dark green jacket, and his cravat is a rash of red spots. They dress to impress the visitors, of course they do. But they have kind and open hearts, and are thinkers too, which is why her father loved them. His books now sit upon their shelves; Annie bought them from Ada a few years ago, during one particularly harsh winter when Ada and her mother couldn't afford to light a fire. Those books are not for sale down here in the shop, but are kept in the parlour upstairs; all of them well thumbed and waiting for the day when Ada might be able to buy them back. Annie and Josiah may dress for the visitors, but they shared beliefs in common with her father: *all creatures of the same species are equal; a husband should have no more power over his wife's life, than she has over his; daughters have the right to an education too.*

'I've come about a fossil,' says Ada.

'Be our guest!' says Annie, flicking a hand towards the sub-scription library books at the far end of the shop. Neither of them asks her for specifics. Annie and Josiah have an interest in many subjects, but have never followed Ada's explanations regarding anatomy – order, family, genus. It's all just bones to them. They like the pretty ammonites, the anemone fossils, or the delicacy of fossilised fish, but their interest ends with the admiration of tiny details, whorls and repeating patterns. They do their best to conceal it, but Ada knows that they don't entirely approve of her scratting around in the mud and clay quite so much. 'It's your right to have benefited from an education,' Josiah once told her, 'but in this day and age it's also a privilege.' He'd looked at her expectantly, as if he was making perfect sense. Later on, she'd realised what he meant: Ada should be doing something better with her time. But it has always seemed to Ada that this place where she lives, this very spot where she was born, has something to say. And it's clearly something that others cannot hear, which makes the burden all the greater. Even those that come for the rocks and fossils, for the fascination of a shifting landscape. They love the curios. But once they have been found or bought, and put into a cabinet to be glanced at occasionally, they cease to really matter. They provoke wonder momentarily, but they don't nettle and niggle as they do for Ada.

'Oh, by the way,' says Annie, 'a young man came in yesterday, interested in folk tales. Collecting them, apparently, from all around Dorset. He burst forth into raptures of delight when I told him about the wolf woman of Lyme. I wondered if I might send him down to you?'

Ada looks into Annie's pale blue eyes, thinking it through, then shakes her head.

'Do you really not want to hear about him? He was extremely friendly . . . '

'Entirely unaffected!' Josiah and Annie announce together, turning to smile at one another, bursting into laughter.

'Don't send him my way,' says Ada.

'Haven't you . . . ?' begins Josiah, looking to his wife.

'It matters not,' says Annie, singing the words and turning away.

Ada takes all five volumes of Georges Cuvier's *Lessons in Comparative Anatomy* down from the shelf. She brings them to the table in front of the window, sun streaking through the twists of glass, turning the table into glistening honey. Her stomach rumbles. Retrieving the three strange bones from her pocket, she gazes at them.

What are you?

Opening the first volume to check the contents page, she begins her search.

CHAPTER NINE

Edwin

*E*very evening, rather than going down to the hotel res-
taurant, Edwin requests the plainest thing on the menu
and takes his meal in his room. The hotelier has asked three
times whether Edwin is feeling ill, and he has done his best
to convince the fellow that he is quite all right. Despite others
finding it hard to believe, eating bread and ham alone in his
room is something of a luxury, although he wouldn't attempt
to explain exactly why.

Since gaining his medical degree, Edwin has assisted over
six hundred women in childbirth, has amputated thirty-seven
limbs, removed eighty-two kidney stones. He has sewn torn
skin, and set broken bones. He has scraped putrid flesh from
open wounds.

Perhaps unsurprisingly, he has lost all appetite for liver, rare
beef, or oozing-soft cheese. He can tolerate, in fact, nothing

fusty or ripe. Delicacies are the worst culprits when it comes to this affliction of taste (oysters, snails, offal and the like), and the dinner table of every wealthy friend proves the most formidable challenge. Usually, by the time he's heading home with Christina, their carriage jolting over the cobbles, his constitution is unsettled and his brow damp with perspiration.

He is similarly challenged in the marital bed. He's heard men speak of how a woman's natural aroma pushes them to the very edges of desire. But Edwin finds it entirely off-putting. He cares for his wife, but is more at ease with the perfumed, powdered bodies of the women at Rosie's Emporium of Delights. He likes them with their clothes on: brief glimpses of wobbling flesh and the sudden, surprising heat of their cunny beneath their skirts, all adorned with lace and satin; rolls of the stuff so he's near-tangled in a bustle of fabric.

He is one of the gentlemen the women talk about before doors open, measuring his virtues and the likelihood of him taking one of them to keep; that he wouldn't be so bad: courteous, steady, predictable. He likes what he likes, and his proclivities are not distasteful. The worst they might say about Edwin is that he's unimaginative; before he left for Lyme he gave his favourite, Clara, a pyritised snakestone as a parting gift.

'A creature made of gold and stone,' she told the others. 'It's an ugly thing, though, ain't it? And an awful strange gift, too, if you think about it. For a girl, I mean.'

CHAPTER TEN

*A*fter chapel on Sunday, Ada goes out upon the blustery beach, tying her leather pockets about her waist over her father's breeches, pulling his brown linen smock-frock over her head. She takes her basket, pick-hammer, trowel and penknife. If she were at all God-fearing she might presume the wind and black clouds and distant rumbling were a sign she ought to be in her parlour with a Bible in her lap (it's the Lord's day, after all). But without a shred of doubt in her heart, Ada walks directly to Black Ven. There, she scrabbles up to the damp, muddy ledge that has gifted her the mysterious bones.

All the way home from chapel Edith pestered Ada about a job at the mill, telling her how she'd spoken on Friday to Mr Muir on Ada's behalf. Fat raindrops fell sporadically, wetting Ada's face like giant tears. Edith wouldn't let the subject drop and Ada was so anxious by the time they sat to eat their lunch that she couldn't stomach a single mouthful. Her throat-stone had returned, and still now it sits there, threatening any moment to choke her. She tries to swallow it away, but it will not shift.

The beach will help, she tells herself.

The beach will help.

She lied to Edith on her way out, saying she was away to find curios for the visitors – the untruths stacking up between them.

'We don't *need* more curios,' snapped Edith. 'We need a buyer fer what ye have already!'

Ada's answer had been to slam the door behind her.

Back upon her knees, as if in prayer, she rummages in the belly of Black Ven, only a few feet from where she found the finger-like fossils. For the first hour of searching she finds only nodules that she breaks apart with deft, desultory blows of her hammer. She finds a fish within one, and although it's a perfect specimen she casts it into her basket without the wonder she usually feels: *I'm the first to lay eyes upon this long-dead creature.* The objects she finds are as familiar to her as shells, and she's irritated with them today because of this.

After a while, she returns to the precise place where she found the first fossil, an area she has twice searched meticulously. She has that first fossil, and the next two she found, tucked in her pocket like some kind of charm, and as she starts to dig, deeper than previously, she sees straight away that her stumbling luck has found its feet. She unearths a fourth fossil. Right beside it, there is another. By the time she has cleared the clay, she's looking down at something vaguely reminiscent of a human hand – albeit giant, elongated, other-worldly. It is the length of her arm.

'You *see?*' she whispers.

Whatever waits within this cliff has called to her, day after day, and she has been back and forth to it like the tide, itching with anticipation. And now she knows why – the thrill of what she's uncovering rushing through her like cold blood. *This is not all*, she thinks. *There is more, yet.* It's as if the earth speaks to her, real as the church bell ringing in the distance. Sometimes she isn't sure what speaks most persuasively — the future or the past, the living or the dead.

She scrapes away more of the earth, looking down at the multitude of bones in neat rows of five, then rows of four, then rows of three, then two, tapering to a delicate tip. It is a paddle, she thinks, of some aquatic creature, and she has seen no fossils like it previously, not in the ground and not in the journals. Her heart kicks hard in her chest, for laid at her feet is a mystery. And Ada likes nothing more than a question in need of an answer.

Gradually, she lifts the fossils from the earth and puts them in her basket. She continues searching, certain of finding more, although, in the end, finding nothing.

Now she is hungry (throat-stone gone), and she thinks of home. The urge to continue digging is strong, but she's tired and weak, and in need of something to eat and drink. She stands, stretching her aching body, looking up at Black Ven rising above her. She can't help smiling up at it, thanking it, and feeling herself at some turning point. *This creature*, she thinks. She conjures an article, and imagines her name in the society transactions. These fossils are going to change things for her — she's sure of it.

She touches her fingertips to the cliff face.

'Please let me have it,' she says, beneath her breath, telling Black Ven that she'd give up every fossil she has in return for this mysterious creature.

'Take it all,' she offers, bartering with her meagre life. 'Take it all, but give me this.' She thinks of her collections, and Edith's insistence that they ought to be sold. Is this the bargain? Would she sell everything in the cottage in exchange for the rest of this skeleton?

'Take it all, but give me this,' she says again, realising she means it.

She feels a sliver of embarrassment at the thought of her father hearing her commune with the earth in this way – bargaining with it. This part of her is her mother's fey way of things. Her gramfer's, too. And it's the kind of thing her father warned her about.

It is threatening rain, but despite the gathering winds and darkening clouds, there are bathers in the sea among the boats, children playing at the shoreline, women collecting shells, and a group of men in the distance examining Church Cliffs. She watches those men in-between packing up her basket, then walks in their direction.

As she gets closer she sees they're not tourists hunting curios; these are gentlemen with an interest in geology; they have satchels and notebooks and pencils.

'... it is comprised of layers of shale and limestone, and you'll notice the blueish tint to the shale, and how against the limestone it creates quite distinctive stripes. This is the Blue Lias that you've heard about, and within this cliff can be found the finest ammonites in the region.'

Ada comes closer, the words tripping across her tongue.

'The greatest number come from Church Cliffs,' she says. 'But the finest ammonites are found further along in Black Ven, and high up too. You'd want to clamber up ...'

The five men have turned to look at her. They're a bustle of waistcoats and shirtsleeves, of cravats and half-beards, the pages of their notebooks fluttering in the wind. A distant rumble of thunder breaks the silence, and from the furthest reaches of her mind comes the knowledge (pressed upon her repeatedly) that she ought never to speak to a gentleman unless he addresses her first. She pauses, considering this, then says:

'. . . that's where the largest specimens are found, and a great variety of species.'

The man who was speaking is tall and willowy, bones jutting from the folds of his elderly face. He regards Ada, seemingly dumbstruck, blinking frantically as if blinded by the sun. It's hard to know whether she has impressed, offended or confounded him. Edith has always insisted that folk don't like to be engaged with without an introduction first; that it doesn't do to shake hands with perfect strangers. That *rank may not matter to ye, Ada, but it matters to the rest o' the world.*

Eventually he recovers himself, and nods at Ada's basket. 'You have your curios there, do you?'

'You're not from Lyme,' she says.

'Indeed, we're not.'

'Are you from London?'

The men exchange glances.

'Oxford also,' says the elderly man.

'I live here on Broad Ledge.' Ada points towards her cottage. 'Are you from the university? Geologists? Mineralogists?'

There are raised eyebrows at this, the shuffle of paper, and two of the group turn back to the cliff face, starting a conversation between themselves.

'Well . . . one could say that we're all together a jumble of those things,' says the man. 'And we are busy acquainting our new friend here, who has never been to Lyme, with the wonders of these cliffs.'

'Are you members of the Geological Society?' Ada asks.

The man gives a quick nod, and then gestures to a stocky, middle-aged gentleman with greying hair and a clean-shaven face. He wears buff-coloured pantaloons, knee-length black leather boots with their tops turned down, and has been tapping the tip of his cane idly against a rock ever since Ada interrupted them: *tat, tat, tat.*

'Dr Moyle here was an early member of the prestigious society of which you speak.'

Ada turns to face him.

'Sir, I sent a selection of ammonite drawings with a letter ... I was hoping to be accepted as a member, or to at least engage in some correspondence,' says Ada. 'I'm not just a collector of curios, I'm a fossilist. I've been a student of the science of geology since I was a child. In fact, my father had all the journals – the transactions of the Royal Society as well as the Geological. I've studied them all, as well as everything in the subscription library at Fountain's Muse: *Theory of the Earth* and *Organic Remains of a Former World* and *Research on the Fossil Bones of Quadrupeds.* And it might interest you to know that Josiah Fountain's cousin is married to William Smith whose stratigraphical maps have informed some of your own colleagues' work.'

Dr Moyle's gaze falls from Ada's face to her over-sized, filthy linen smock-frock. And then, even though he doesn't smile, the whole of his face flutters with amusement; it capers about his eyes and cheeks, bold as anything.

'Well,' he says. 'It is not an *open* society, though.'

'But why were my drawings not returned? I've discovered two new species.'

'It is a club for gentlemen only.'

'That hardly answers my question.'

He laughs. 'I can only presume your drawings were in some way overlooked or misplaced. I imagine you have copies?'

He doesn't believe me, thinks Ada. *He'd take greater interest if he really thought I'd discovered something new.* The group is drifting away, examining the cliff face up close, pressing shale between their fingertips. Rain begins to pour, bouncing from the wide rim of Ada's hat. The men thrust notebooks into satchels, button up their coats, put up their umbrellas.

'There is something else,' she says, desperate to keep their attention. It is too good an opportunity to miss, and every vein in her body seems to be pulsing with the urgency of that understanding.

'I can show you something!' They are turning away from her now. 'A paddle from a new species of aquatic beast!'

Even after this astonishing claim, they don't turn back to her. She pulls off her hat, then her smock-frock and lays it down, emptying her basket onto it.

'Look here!' she calls after them.

She crouches to position the bones into five, long, drifting fingers. Water pours down upon her, soaking her hair and shift. She looks at her find, struck by the beauty of it, the lump in her throat returning. Perhaps this is what people feel when they look at their new-born infant: a fulsome mix of awe and pride.

The men are scurrying away, huddled beneath two umbrellas.

She calls out again, jumps up and runs after them.

'Please!' she says, as she draws close.

The thin, elderly man turns towards her, briefly, and gestures something of an apology. Everything about him is limp, as if he might dissolve in the rain.

She watches them go, transfixed by the sight of them, and by the odious sense they have left behind. The deluge has soaked right through her breeches and shift, and she feels it running down her chest and stomach, soaking into her drawers, trickling in rivulets down her legs.

CHAPTER ELEVEN

*V*exed by Edith's constant fretting about the rent, Ada has escaped the house and come to the Cobb. She'd hoped Edith would take some comfort from the news that Ada now intends to sell her fossil collections. Perhaps she'd even hoped for a little gratitude from her mother, but that hasn't been forthcoming. Disgruntled, she sits on the curve of harbour wall, the quarantine hospital four-square behind her.

The windows are grimy, too small to be climbed through and the door is riddled with locks. Within its damp walls there are pallid sailors wasted with typhoid, plagued with leprosy. One of those men comes to stare from the window, contemplating days now vanished. He regards Ada, watching her rearrange her hat, kick at the wall with the heels of her boots. He stares at her for so long that eventually she turns and looks straight at him. He presses his palm to the small windowpane, and she raises her hand in answer.

*

She watches the blur of pale face until it turns away and fades into the blackness of that desolate building. Unsettled by the thought of him and all the other men he shares the hospital with, she stands and walks a little way back towards the beach. It's the rag-end of the afternoon, and families are drifting slowly home, dispersing through Cockmoile Square and making their way up the narrow combe through which Lyme tumbles down: its steep winding streets like arteries and veins, narrow and twisting, flowing one from the other.

Distracted by shouts – both threats and enticements – Ada turns for a moment to watch a reluctant pony pulling a bathing machine down the beach and into the shallow waves. She imagines the woman inside that wooden hut, equally reluctant. Any moment she'll emerge to dunk herself in the frigid water. This is what they come for: cures for the convalescents, nourishment for the fatigued, entertainment for the wealthy.

Ada thinks of her grammer and gramfer – folk who had no fondness for the sea, no matter that they lived upon it and listened daily to its whispers and taunts. Her gramfer would dip a finger in the water, bring it to his mouth and swear blind it tasted of blood. French blood, English blood, pirate blood, smuggler blood. The ocean roads, he said, were the devil's roads, watched over by ill-wishing water spirits, by mermen, by an eel-skinned sea bucca with weeds for hair. It was only fishermen who put to sea with honest intentions, and their bodies washed up upon the beach too often for comfort, so doesn't that tell you a thing or two? Her grandparents prised mussels from rocks, collected seaweed for the pot, bought fish straight from the boat. And that was close enough to the water for them. What would they make of the town-dwellers who flock to the shore now, languishing half-dressed in the midday sun and plunging themselves into the heaving sea? What would they make of Ada, swimming at night when the beach is empty and the sky is lit with stars? What madness would they suppose had come to Lyme?

Her mother has told her, on more than one occasion, that her parents offended the ocean. 'Ye mussen live upon the shore and loathe the water,' she said. She told Ada how the sea came for them, affronted. Five years on the trot, starting when Edith was a young girl, the sea raised a storm on a spring tide and flooded the house. 'It knew what it were doing,' said Gramfer. ''Tis true,' said Edith. Ada never knew if the sea had really come for them, because Edith and Gramfer said that it had (that it could choose like a person might choose), but her father insisted it hadn't. He'd look her straight in the eye and say, 'What do *you* believe?' This was their question; the thing they passed between the two of them, like love. But sometimes Ada just didn't know what she believed, because she believed them all, and they all told her different things about the world.

When she was a little older, not long before he died, John Winters confessed to his daughter his lack of faith. His promise to Edith had always been that he'd pretend some belief in that direction to give Ada the chance of knowing God. He'd conceded that being seen to believe can help with employment and good standing and such like, so his atheism wasn't something he'd discuss with just anyone. 'And I 'ave never wanted to tell ye exactly what to think, Ada. So I'm not tellin' ye that there be no God. Only that I do not hear him, I do not feel him, I do not perceive him at work 'ere in Lyme.'

Her father, of course, didn't believe in water sprites or mermaids either. He believed in bread for all, and a fair day's wage for a fair day's work.

She's so busy thinking of her father that she doesn't notice Dr Moyle until he's right beside her, wishing her a good afternoon. She looks up into his green eyes that are crinkled round the edges, much friendlier today than yesterday.

'You remember me,' she says, instantly flinching at her foolishness (at times she speaks before she's even aware of the thought or sentiment).

'She who sells seashells . . . ' he says, and Ada startles at those soft, sighing words, hung together like a string of pearls. She savours the unexpected gift of them beneath her breath. He smiles, his face igniting with amusement, just as it had when she confronted him about her drawings. She'd felt diminished then, but today she feels something else. *He* has approached her this time, after all; he has chosen to speak to her.

'We weren't formally introduced, if I remember rightly,' he says. 'I'm Dr Edwin Moyle.' He doesn't hold out his hand, but claps it to his heart.

'Miss Ada Winters,' she says, scrutinising him, thinking, *You don't want to be seen shaking my hand.*

'It was unfortunate,' he says, 'that my friends and I needed to hurry away. The weather wasn't on our side.'

She glances at his clean coat, his spotless cuffs. He carries no pouch, no trowel, no gloves.

'You're not out collecting, then?'

'I'm out surveying my new home.' And he gestures like a player introducing his troupe – a theatrical sweep of his arm.

'Home?'

'Temporary,' he says. 'I'm staying at the Angel Inn until the beginning of December, to conduct some research.' He looks east, in the direction of Black Ven.

It is ridiculous to, but Ada rashly believes – in a wild,

gulping leap of imagination – that he's about to ask her to assist him. And she conjures that scenario in her mind's eye: showing him what to look for and how to look for it. Most people simply cannot see what's there in front of them when it comes to hunting fossils. They know their books, and they know a specimen all cleaned up. But seeing it in the field is a different thing entirely.

'It's brave of you . . . ' he says then, turning to look at her.

The breeze shifts, sweet with the scent of his fragrance. He smells like something from the bakery at Christmas – warmly enticing – and she takes a small step away from him.

' . . . doing what you do,' he says, as if that clarifies matters.

She wonders what he refers to exactly, but she won't ask, for fear of seeming like a simpleton. There are a multitude of reasons why a person might say such a thing, and she watches his face as if she can fathom something from it. Brave, because the rocks might fall upon her head? Because scrabbling about in the mud is no way to make a living? Brave to pursue a thing without truly knowing what it is she pursues? To be searching for understanding but settling at every turn for something *so far* from understanding? Night after night to look for the moon, but to hardly glimpse it for the clouds?

'To be out on the beach,' he says. 'It's no place for a lady to be alone.'

Ahh, so he speaks of respectability and reputation. These are the risks he thinks about, first and foremost. That she might attract the wrong kind of attention. That people may talk. She can't help but smile at that; at how little he understands.

'You mock me,' she says. 'We both know I'm no lady . . . '

He laughs quietly, looking askance at her, tapping his cane against his boot again.

52

'I've been considering the fossils you spoke about yesterday, and I'd appreciate a look, if you're willing?'

'My ammonites?'

'Well, perhaps those as well. But you said something about a new species of aquatic beast.'

His gaze is piercing, and his presence looms larger than the body that contains him; she feels it so strongly that she finds herself taking another step backwards.

'Oh,' she says, surprised. 'There was I believing my announcement had fallen on deaf ears.' She's not intending to be petulant; it's simply perplexing. 'I don't understand then, why you chose to ignore me. If I were any of you, and I met a person upon the beach who was offering to show me what they thought was some part of a new creature, I'd suffer any amount of rain to see the thing for myself.'

'I'm not sure any of the others *did* hear you,' says Dr Moyle. 'None of them mentioned it, and we didn't discuss you afterwards. For my part, I confess, I thought it unlikely that you'd discovered anything so exciting as a new species. There are plenty of ichthyosaur paddles that have been found here in Lyme.'

'It's not an ichthyosaur paddle.'

'Well, we can take a look at that. I'm simply explaining why I didn't seem keener to take a look at the time. It was ghastly weather, after all. More than just a little rain!'

He searches out her gaze, smiling.

'It's *not* an ichthyosaur paddle, though,' she says.

He surrenders with a slow, conciliatory nod.

'Very well, it is not an ichthyosaur paddle. You seem convinced you have something interesting, and you clearly know your subject, so let's investigate the matter together.

Mr Mottershaw, another member of our society, would, I'm sure, also be very keen to take a look. He wasn't on the beach with the rest of our party, but I'd appreciate the opportunity to bring him along to meet you. I'm sure he'll be fascinated to look at your find and also to peruse what you have for sale. We both will.'

'She who sells seashells . . . '

Perhaps these men are the gentlemen collectors she's been waiting for. She wonders if this is her opportunity to prove to Edith – and to Black Ven – that she's willing to let go of her collections. It would be gratifying, of course, to be able to make good on her promise to her mother. But even so, it's certainly not what she hopes for most from this encounter. How strange, she thinks, that just yesterday she was chasing these men in the rain, and here is one of them now seeking her out.

She nods her agreement, unwilling to let her full enthusiasm show. *He thinks I know my subject.* She understands already that she likely knows as much as this man and his friends. That there's every chance of her enlightening them, as much as of them enlightening her. And not just in matters of mud, but in matters of theory. So, it grates that the gratitude is all hers, and that she'll be required to ingratiate herself (she knows she will, and feels the inclination already). These men, along with the famous Cuvier in Paris, are the purveyors of geological truth. They publish the hypotheses and conclusions they believe worthy of publication. They scrutinise, and they dismiss. They decide among themselves what has value.

But there's nothing to gain from being churlish about it. This man who has come to see her – who has sought her out especially – is someone with influence. A month ago, she was awaiting correspondence from his very society, knowing there was every chance the letter wouldn't come at all. And here now is flesh and blood, suggesting her finds are worth a look. It is, in truth, quite beyond anything she could have allowed herself to hope for.

They walk together to Cockmoile Square, discussing Lyme and all it has to offer. Once there, they begin their goodbyes outside the assembly rooms. Already Ada feels the curious eyes of the town upon her: Jane Smith from the bakery is peering through dusty windows to nosy what Ada is up to, not caring to disguise her interest. Ada prickles at the attention, knowing the flimsy tittle-tattle that is the grist of Lyme gossip. It doesn't make sense to Ada, and it never has. All those years ago, after Sunday school lessons, walking home with the other girls, Ada could never get excited about their secrets and confessions; couldn't feign interest or fake the camaraderie. *Would you not rather look for ammonites?* she would want to say. But even then she knew that they wouldn't rather; even then she understood that anything appealing to her would be quite perplexing to another girl her age. And it's been no better since – the mysteries of female friendship like a language nobody thought to teach her.

'Mr Mottershaw and I will pay our visit when your mother's home,' says Dr Moyle. 'In the late afternoon tomorrow?'

And then Ada is striding out beneath Gun Cliff. Feeling fortunate isn't something she's accustomed to, and she doesn't know whether to believe in it. Her world is tipping, opening to reveal itself anew as it does after a storm, when everything familiar has been whipped about.

CHAPTER TWELVE

When Dr Moyle arrives the following afternoon, he arrives alone.

Stood upon the doorstep he's taller than Ada remembers. Balanced on the flat of his palm is a paper package. In his other hand is his cane, and she wonders if he ever goes anywhere without it.

'It's a long way to have walked such,' says Ada, thinking the package looks precarious – one gust and it might have blown away.

'A gift,' he says, holding it up. 'Strawberry tarts and clotted cream.'

'I've—'

She stops before the words can escape and reveal something she suddenly wishes to keep private – that she has never eaten a strawberry tart with clotted cream before. She has, of course, picked strawberries, made savoury pastry with lard, scooped cream from the top of the milk. But she has never eaten a strawberry tart. She has eaten pound cake from Annie Fountain at Christmas, and the sugar cookies that Pastor

Durrant occasionally brings. But she has never enjoyed this particular luxury.

The knotted rope that hangs in the doorway has caught on the shoulder of his coat, settled there like a hand placed in welcome. He tries to shrug it off.

'Sorry,' she says, flicking it away.

'What is it?' he asks, stepping aside, wrinkling his nose like a child who doesn't want to eat his soup.

She shakes her head. 'It's nothing.'

How can she tell him about women who sell the wind?

'I don't believe you.'

'It's a silly thing – a superstition.'

'And I should like to hear about it.'

'Very well ... it was once full of knots, but they've been untied over the years to ward off calamity when my grandparents felt threatened by the sea.'

'Witchcraft, then?'

Ada shrugs. 'Well, we don't believe in witches, do we?'

'Just the one left?'

He's looking at the knot at the bottom of the wet hank of rope.

She nods, unwilling to explain that the last one is never for loosening, for the last knot, when untied, releases the fury of all the storms pacified by the charm. She's always brushed away the superstition, but all the same she would never release that last knot. In idle moments she ruminates on all it keeps safe – every storm it has captured.

As he steps across the threshold, the house seems to shrink around him, and she doesn't know where to put herself; wherever she stands it feels too close to him. He passes her the tarts, and her mouth fills instantly with saliva. The rest of her fills with an awkwardness as she realises she does not know what to do with the gift – whether to open it now and offer him some, or to save it till later? Putting the package onto the kitchen table, she delays the decision in the hope it will somehow resolve itself.

He shuts the door and turns to face her. Reaching into his pocket he pulls out a packet of tea. Not a paper twist of leaves, but a whole packet of finest hyson.

'And ...' Reaching into his other pocket, he pulls out another packet. 'Sugar,' he tells her.

Ada knows that this will be white sugar, not the hardened brown lumps she and her mother are grateful for.

'It's too much,' she says. 'You didn't need to bring all this.'

She prickles at the thought he felt the need to.

'My mother is ...' Ada gestures vaguely behind her.

Edith is hiding in the bedroom, probably abed, and will feign a headache if Ada tries to fetch her. She told her mother that a gentleman collector is interested in purchasing some of her fossils, understanding very well that Edith would make herself scarce – that she'd have no interest in meeting the man, no matter that polite society might expect it. It's rather convenient for Ada, as she's yet to tell Edith about her discovery.

'She's feeling badly,' says Ada. 'A headache from the noise in the mill.'

'How unfortunate, for her. Poor Mr Mottershaw is doing no better – confined to bed with a badly sprained ankle. He ventured over the cliffs and came a cropper. In fact, it is partly your doing. I told him what you advised about where to find the best ammonites, and without a moment's hesitation the man was stumbling around up there. More stumbling than anything else, it would seem.'

He smiles at his own joke, places the tea and sugar onto the table, then rubs his hands together. She prepares the pot using the last of their own leaves, adds the dark crystalline sugar to their cracked, stained cups. Her father comes to mind, and she tries not to care what Dr Moyle thinks of their kitchen, their crockery, the quality of their sugar. She tries to be the person her father would want her to be.

When it's ready, she passes Dr Moyle his cup and they go through into the parlour. She knows it's all wrong; he ought to have been seated, and then she ought to have brought a tray with everything laid out upon it, and then she should have poured for him as he sat and waited. She *does* wish to impress him, and she understands there are certain rituals, but she also knows it would be ridiculous to try to pretend. The distance between them is too great – it is a vast, sweeping escarpment, dizzying if one regards it for too long.

He does not, anyway, seem at all uncomfortable with the lack of social niceties. He is transfixed by the crowded shelves of rocks and fossils, the multitude of feathers, the birds' skulls boiled white, the eggs and nests. His face twitches with obvious surprise, eyebrows raised. He opens his mouth as if to speak, but changes his mind. He puts his cup of tea on a small table covered in fossils, takes a belemnite and turns it over, rubs at it with his thumb. He looks to the cabinet stretching across the far wall, his gaze skimming its drawers and glass-fronted compartments. He goes to it, running his fingers across the polished wood.

'He was the best cabinetmaker in Dorset,' she says.

Dr Moyle touches the edge of a drawer, lifts the handle, lets it drop.

'I can see that is probably true,' he says, reaching up onto a shelf and lifting a box down.

'It *is* true.'

He twists to look at her.

'Yes, I didn't mean ...'

He gestures with the box. 'May I?' he asks, and when Ada nods he lifts its lid, finding another box within: a puzzle.

'You have to try to open it,' she says.

She takes a sip of tea and lowers herself into her chair, watching him prise and peer at all sides of the polished box. It is Ada's most treasured possession. More treasured than the eagle stone her father gave her, or the crinoids she found in the River Lim. It is treasured not only because her father made it, but because it's so very clever. She knows her guest will fail to open it, although he looks like the kind of man who might keep trying.

While he's pushing and pulling at the puzzle box, she fetches the fossils from the highest cupboard in the cabinet (the cupboard that Edith cannot reach), and spreads them out on the floor, in front of the fire, between the two chairs. He gives up on the puzzle and comes to stand over her. She feels the rain on her neck again, as if she's back on the beach in the foul weather, so keen for Dr Moyle and his colleagues to see these fossils for what they are: extraordinary. She notices her fingers trembling, and curses herself.

She looks up at him.

'Goodness,' he says, bending to touch the fossils. She feels a rush of pride.

'You see?'

'I *do* see. How wonderful! And I would agree, not an ichthyosaur. But I'm not convinced that what you have here is a new species. It could be a turtle, perhaps.'

'A *gigantic* turtle?'

'It's possible.'

She shakes her head.

'I just don't think so. I've been consulting Cuvier's *Lessons*, studying every entry on turtle anatomy. I'm sure it isn't a turtle.'

Dr Moyle takes a deep breath, stands back and lowers himself into Edith's chair. He rubs a palm against his cheek – the sound like sandpaper on wood.

'It's tempting,' he says, 'to believe this is something entirely new. I *want* to believe it. But we must be cautious; too often geologists get carried away.'

Ada holds back from saying any more. There's part of her that doesn't mind waiting. When she's found the rest of the creature – and she will find the rest of the creature – she will not have to prove anything to anyone. She folds the fossils away in their piece of linen, and all the while she can feel Dr Moyle's gaze rough against the side of her face.

'I have a proposition for you,' he says.

She looks up at him, pushes herself to standing.

'Why don't we continue searching the cliff together, for more of whatever this is?'

'You want to help me?'

'I want us to help each other. I have three months in this little corner of the world, and then I must return to my life as a physician. Surely two of us is better than one?'

A proprietorial flicker ignites within her, and for a moment she wants to refuse him. Already she thinks of the creature as hers, and is greedy for its bones. But if there's one thing wrong with the world, her father always told her, it is greed. *There is plenty for all*, was his hymn; enough of everything for everyone. *Together* is better than apart, better than against.

'Very well,' she says. 'Two of us is better than one.'

Dr Moyle suggests tea and tarts to celebrate, and Ada goes

through into the kitchen. She sets the kettle to boil and takes the packet of tea, toying with the idea of not opening it and reusing instead the steeped leaves at the bottom of the teapot; Edith would use them at least another two times. Ada also knows her mother would be grateful for unopened packets of finest hyson tea and white sugar (she'd exchange them sharpish for a whole basketful of more practical groceries). But Ada knows there is only one option, and she makes fresh tea by opening Dr Moyle's gifts. The leaves are pungent, and the sugar crystals impossibly white on the tip of her finger. The tarts are nestled together like fledglings in a nest – bright red strawberries topped with yellow clotted cream.

When it comes to it, Ada eats her tart as if this rich, crumbly, sweet treat is an everyday occurrence. Gobbling it in three mouthfuls, it is gone too quickly. But that doesn't matter; there are more in the kitchen and she'll learn the different ways of eating a strawberry tart when she is alone.

Dr Moyle only nibbles at his (because it's not the most delicious thing he's ever tasted, and he earlier consumed a rather excessive afternoon tea).

'By the way, I intend to enquire about the drawings you sent,' he says to her, putting his hardly touched tart down onto the little table. 'I know the man to speak to, and I'll make it a priority. We'll have them returned to you. No doubt they're languishing in some pile of papers that our secretary has overlooked. I think you probably understand there's nothing I can do about our rules of membership. These kinds of societies cannot function sensibly with members of the fairer sex attending, although I understand the purpose of sending your letter, and you've probably achieved your ambition – to have been noted.'

He takes a sip of tea.

'And if I may be permitted to borrow these particular fossils, I'd very much like to show them to my colleague, Mr Mottershaw, invalid that he is. I'm sure he'll be delighted to give us his opinion on them. What do you say?'

Ada hesitates, awash with uncertainty; she doesn't want to let them go. It seems to her that they are better kept here in the cottage, close to the beach where they were found. But this is the world she wishes to enter – a world of facts and evidence, of discussion and debate. It is not a world of hiding things in the back of drawers.

'They'll come back to me?' she says, though, still doubting.

Dr Moyle throws up his hands.

'I am not a thief! You will have them back within the week.'

CHAPTER THIRTEEN

Edwin

O nce back at his rooms, Edwin spreads the fossils out on his desk. He considers going straight for Mr Mottershaw, but thinks better of it. He would like, he realises, to go to his colleague with a theory, not a question. He then consults every book he has to hand that contains even a passing reference to turtle and whale anatomy.

He ruminates for so long that he misses dinner, ringing down eventually for some soup and a bottle of wine. Then he continues to muse on the matter until the rest of the hotel slumbers (until even the cook is fast asleep and dreaming of the miller's wife).

By the time the night is dark, stippled with stars, Edwin concludes that Miss Winters is on to something. There is every chance these bones form the paddle of a new aquatic species. He folds the fossils away into the linen, his heart startling.

But what to do now?

He feels protective, all of a sudden. Jealous even, as he looks down at the parcel in his arms (cradled like a new-born). He finds, with a little surprise, that he has absolutely no desire whatsoever to share this find with any of his colleagues – Mr Mottershaw especially. Thomas can be a fussy man, slow to make decisions and long to ponder. His colleague corresponds regularly with Mr Cuvier, the famed anatomist in Paris, and would no doubt straightaway be writing letters and sending samples to France. But is this what Edwin wants? He has already had one of his quarry finds – a huge molar that he was certain belonged to a gigantic herbivorous reptile – dismissed by Cuvier as nothing more than the tooth of a hippopotamus. He cannot risk a similar humiliation with these bones.

He nibbles on his bread, thinking it through.

They must begin a proper search of the cliffs where the bones were found as soon as possible; time is not on his side, after all. Miss Winters is clearly not afraid of getting her hands dirty, but still it seems sensible to hire a man or two to help. How, though, might they begin such an extensive excavation without attracting the attention of his fellow geologists in Lyme? He takes a deep breath, pondering the dilemma, thick with indecision. He will need to be discreet, and he will need to be cunning. It is fortunate, then, he thinks, that his father has made him so well practised at these things.

CHAPTER FOURTEEN

The clouds are pressing down and out at sea, far off, rain falls. Stretching into the distance past Charmouth, towards Seatown, the cliffs are orange-tipped with clay, and atop them are terraced fields – stubbled, recently scythed. Last week those fields rustled with ripe oats swaying in the wind. Now they rustle with mice that fill their bellies with scattered kernels, and weasels that fill their bellies with mice.

Dr Moyle seems like a different man to Ada when he appears on her doorstep in his working clothes. He's still smarter than Ada ever looks, even in her Sunday best, but he has his tools in a bag slung across his shoulder and he wears an old, scuffed pair of leather wellington boots. He chooses not to step inside, but waits for her to grab her basket.

She'd told him they should make an early start, but she had also told him not to come to the house until Edith had left for the mill. His punctuality lays bare his keenness; Ada saw him making his way along the beach only moments after Edith disappeared from view.

They walk together past Church Cliffs, towards Black Ven.

'See how the water sifts the stones into ribbons along the shore,' says Ada, pointing. The tide has not long gone out. She bends and picks up a stone that looks like a tiny brown mushroom and holds it out for him to look at. Moyle takes it from her and she gestures at the pebbles beneath their feet.

'Where you see lots of this, you'll also find the pyritised ammonites.'

Ada crouches and scrabbles through the wet gritty pebbles until she finds a tiny golden ammonite.

'You see?'

He holds out a gloved hand and Ada drops the fossil into it. He inspects it for a moment before passing it back to her.

'Shouldn't we . . . ?'

He gestures towards Black Ven and she nods.

'I'm considering hiring some labourers,' Moyle says, as they walk, navigating the boulders, stepping cautiously on the larger rocks that shift and tip beneath their feet. 'To help us find this creature.'

Ada's mind races, imagining careless men who don't know how to look, who don't know what tentative means.

'Perhaps,' she says. 'If it's absolutely necessary. My father and I hired a stonemason once, to help lift an ichthyosaur from the foreshore. It was embedded in the limestone, and could only be removed by lifting slabs of the stone itself.'

'How large an ichthyosaur?'

'Fifteen feet. Its head was more than three feet long; the vertebrae were three inches wide, sixty of them, neat as peas in a pod.'

'Great Caesar's ghost!'

'It's one of the finest ichthyosaurs to have been found on this coast.'

'And where is it now?'

'My father sold it for twenty-three pounds to Lord Henry Hoste Henley. To pay off a debt.' Ada can still summon the regret she felt at the sale, no matter that the money was sorely needed. And that regret is intertwined with the grief of losing her father because the two events were separated by a matter of months. In the aftermath of putting John Winters into the ground, if Edith was not blaming her husband directly for his own death, then she was blaming *the monster*. It didn't wish to be taken from its watery grave and put into a fusty library, she insisted. 'It 'as wreaked its havoc.' Her mother had been wild back then, refusing to eat, refusing to speak in front of anyone but Ada. Even Pastor Durrant had been unable to reason with her, to calm her down, to settle her. She refused the tinctures he brought, and the sugar biscuits he tried to tempt her with.

'It were ungodly,' she kept saying, to Ada. 'Ye had no business messin' with it.'

Ada looks at the familiar cliff as they draw close, wondering what Dr Moyle sees when he looks at it. Its great height, surely. The black tongues of mudstone that have slipped upon the beach. The vegetation that rambles and crawls across the exposed ledges and plateaus. He won't see the drinking water flowing down onto the beach a little further on. He won't see the smugglers' hole hidden by sharp reeds and leafy brassicas. He won't see those brassicas as welcome food.

'You see the Blue Lias?' Ada asks.

And they begin to talk of lias clay and mudstone, limestone and shale.

Ada shows him the area where she uncovered the paddle bones. They discuss in which direction to explore next and then set to work, crouching together, their hands in the clay.

'How did you learn about fossils,' Ada asks, 'living in London?'

'I spent my childhood just outside Oxford,' he tells her. 'Near Stonesfield Quarry.'

He describes the day he found a thigh bone of a quadruped, quite by chance, as a lad, and how that discovery had been like Pandora's box – awakening something within him that refused thereafter to settle.

'The rocks stared me in the face; they wooed and caressed me, saying at every turn, *Pray, pray, be a geologist!*'

Ada laughs, nodding, delighted by his passion, recognising it.

He describes the quarrymen at Stonesfield pulling the oolite slate from the ground; not a slate at all, but a limestone destined for cottage roofs. How the quarrymen found an abundance of fossils as they worked: pterodactyls and crocodiles, cirripedes and starfish. How they would ease these creatures' remains from the stone, clean them up and place them in their cottage windows. How academics from the universities would visit at the weekends to peruse these workers' windows for specimens.

He tells her that he studied to become a physician because that was his father's wish, but his heart remained bewitched by geology. Listening to his story of discovery and longing, she begins to forget all that separates them and puts aside what her father would have said about the likes of Edwin Moyle.

He asks her about her father, about the fossils they had hunted for together. And she tells him that John Winters had been a self-educated man with an interest in the world. She explains how keen he had been for Ada to read – and to read widely. She recounts how he brought her volumes from the circulating library, bought all the periodicals he could afford and borrowed everything newly published on the subject of geology from Annie and Josiah, even books not strictly for loaning. She doesn't say that he was an agitator. And she doesn't mention the nature of his demise, only that he has passed.

After a few hours of searching, and finding nothing, Dr Moyle suggests they try again the following day.

'I like to go to the whist club, at the rooms at three,' he tells her. 'Do you play?'

She shakes her head, gathering her things.

He takes a leather water canteen from his bag and offers some to her, although only after drinking from it himself.

They walk back towards the cottage, discussing arrangements for the following day.

'It'll be raining tomorrow, more than likely,' she tells him.

'It will?'

'Not enough to trouble us,' she says.

'I shall be here, rain or shine, at the same time tomorrow after your mother has left for the mill.'

Ada nods her agreement, and they walk together in silence.

'It seems our endeavours are provoking in both of us a desire for secrecy,' says Dr Moyle, after a moment or two.

'What do you mean?'

'You seem keen to keep your mother in the dark, and I have realised that I feel similarly with regard to my geologist colleagues. So if we feel our excavation warrants some added manpower, then I will arrange that,' he says. 'But I will make no moves in that direction until my colleagues have left Lyme in a week or so.'

Ada glances at him, curious.

'I think we might have something of interest here, Miss Winters. And I rather think we should be judicious. We should keep it quiet, until we know what's what.'

Ada understands what he feels – the fear of losing something that they do not yet have. The fear of someone else coming to steal their dream.

'So two is better than one, and also better than three?' she asks, smiling.

'I fear it wouldn't be three, but a multitude. Too many cooks, Miss Winters. Early on, at least. Let us understand what we're dealing with before we disclose anything to anyone.'

'So you didn't show the paddle to your Mr Mottershaw?'

'I decided not to.'

He looks around at her and they regard one another briefly, before Ada looks away. It would seem then that she has a colleague, and between them they have a scheme. The certainty she has felt about this creature – that the cliff must relinquish it, that it will, surely, because she feels it in her own bones – seems all of a sudden well justified.

Take it all, but give me this.

CHAPTER FIFTEEN

When Dr Moyle returns the following morning he brings with him the paddle bones in their folds of linen. He steps inside the kitchen to place them down upon the table, and Ada notices how gentle he is, that he rests his hand upon the parcel briefly.

They go straight to Black Ven to resume their digging, and all the while a misty rain falls, water dripping from their hat brims.

They eat their lunch in the mizzle, and then they continue their search. The weather is kinder as the day progresses, and eventually Ada removes her hat to let the breeze dry her dampened hair. Deep in the afternoon, she wants to remind him that she needs to be home before Edith returns from work. But she can feel Dr Moyle's frustration emanating from him. *What about your whist club?* she wants to say.

It has been the same all day – wanting to speak, but feeling unable. Mainly she wishes to tell him that he needs to be patient; *that* is how fossils are found. *You have to get your eye in. Don't try so hard.* But there's something about his agitation that has put her on edge. She wishes to soothe him – an impulse from living with Edith – but doesn't know how. And so she has retreated into silence; focusing only on the mud and rock, on looking from her eyes' edges.

When she realises that she cannot wait any longer, she begins collecting her things into her basket.

'I'm going to rinse my hands,' she says.

He grunts, not looking up.

As she's making her way down the beach, she notices a young man approaching, from Charmouth way. He raises a hand in her direction to get her attention, striding purposefully. Then he breaks into a quick run, raising his hand again. He wears a white shirt that ripples and billows in the breeze, soft as silk. She glances at Moyle, who is digging still, almost frantically.

'Miss Winters?' the young man says, still ten paces away, but already holding out his hand for Ada to shake. She is startled by his face: his nose and lip are twisted to one side, a thick red scar running between them; she tries not to stare. He's barefoot, but obviously not a fisherman. He wears corduroy trousers, but is clearly no labourer.

Ada shows her mud-caked hand, to put him off, but he reaches for it anyway, shaking it enthusiastically. His face is tanned, but his nails are neat, his skin clean. His cuffs, she notices, are spattered with paint.

'Miss Winters,' he says. 'Isaac Berryman. The Fountains sent me your way; friends of yours, I believe.'

Ada regards him without saying anything. She doesn't consider herself to have any friends. There is Pastor Durrant: family confidante and fellow fossilist. And Annie and Josiah were, strictly speaking, her father's friends.

Isaac is gabbling about the wolf woman and his wish to hear her stories, speaking so fast that Ada can hardly keep up – *yoppin'*, her gramfer would have said. His sandy-coloured hair whips about his face, falling in front of his eyes so he has to keep brushing it away.

Ada points to Dr Moyle.

'I'm busy,' she says.

Isaac falls silent, fiddles with the cuff of his shirt, gazing down at his hands. His withdrawal into himself, quick as a startled crab, floods her with feeling. He will know ridicule and rejection, she realises, and the thought of it is like a netting needle between the ribs. He will also know pity, and will surely detest it as much as she does.

I told Annie not to give him my name, she thinks. The permission Annie sought to send him her way had been refused. *Don't send him to me*, had been the instruction. This request of his has been thrust upon her and it wouldn't, therefore, be unfair to send him packing.

'It's just not a good time . . . ' she says.

'Then let us meet another day.'

Ada shakes her head. 'I have something occupying me; I'll be busy with it for a while.'

He nods.

'All right,' he says.

She wants him to leave, because she needs to rinse her hands and get home. Because she needs to say farewell to Dr Moyle and make an arrangement for tomorrow. But the wolf woman runs through her mind, scattering her thoughts, howling to be heard.

'I'll come by again,' he says.

But Ada shakes her head.

'Just to see,' he says. 'It doesn't matter if you're busy.'

A wave rushes almost to their feet, catching them unawares. Ada turns away from Isaac and follows the water as it retreats, crouching to rinse the awkwardness from her hands.

CHAPTER SIXTEEN

The following morning, after Edith has left for the mill,
taking her sullenness with her, a pain deep in Ada's
belly causes her to catch her breath. She leans on the windowsill
momentarily, waiting for the spasm to pass. She can see Moyle
through the smeary glass – swinging his cane as he walks.
Quickly, she runs upstairs to the press, takes out a napkin and
finds her belt.

Downstairs again, she kicks off her slipped shoes and pulls
on her boots. She throws a heel of bread into her basket along
with her hammer and trowel.

She meets him at the door just as it starts to rain.

'You brought it with you,' she says, and he laughs.

She's pleased to see that he has cheered.

At the cliff face they get to work, and once they've settled
into a rhythm, Ada asks tentatively about the Geological
Society. She wants to hear about their meetings – how exactly
they're conducted.

But Moyle doesn't seem interested in disseminating
the details.

'I would make it all sound very dull, if I tried to tell you. At times there are ten men with so little to say that it hardly seems worth the effort of being there.'

'I don't believe you.'

'It's true.'

So they end up speaking about stratigraphy and the twenty-one strata of rock: from chalk to coal. They speak of how one sandstone is indistinguishable from another, without fossils as a guide. They talk order: limestone to clay to shale. Edwin delivers an ode to oolite. What would Bath be without it? he asks. Or the Cotswolds? This stone that stores up the sun's rays and glows bright with them. And then he speaks of Bath, as if Ada is familiar with the town and its environs: steep cliffs and quarries, unconformities, outcrops and faults. He speaks also of the entertainment and the water: the heat of it and how foul it tastes. He tells her that he's not one for dancing, although his wife insists upon it.

But as the morning passes they fall into silence, and Ada feels Moyle's energy waning. He goes at the mud with ever increasing fervour, but defeat hangs about him like a cloud of flies. Ada makes sure to show interest in the small fossils they find, feeling strangely responsible for keeping him buoyant.

When the rain eventually stops and the sun flares hot from behind scattered clouds, he doesn't cheer at all, and it's a relief when he suggests, shortly after they've eaten their lunch, that they should stop for the day. He mumbles something about his whist club, although Ada has already noted that it starts daily at three; they have plenty of time yet.

'Don't lose heart,' she tells him. 'The earth moves so much in these parts.'

'Which surely makes it ridiculous to think we could ever find the rest of the skeleton.'

'Not ridiculous at all. We just have to keep exploring.'

He doesn't reply, but busies himself with packing his tools into his bag.

'Let's meet again tomorrow at the same time,' says Ada.

He nods, slinging his bag over his shoulder and tucking his cane beneath his arm. When he's only a few strides away she sits down upon a rock that's warm from the sun. Suddenly tired, she pauses for a few moments, leaning back against the cliff, aware of the dark ache settling in her belly and the blood that flows from her. With the first warm trickle of blood each month Ada always thinks of the wolf woman – how she was suckled by a wolf when her shepherd father left her in the hollow of an ash tree as he worked. How, when she grew into a woman and bled for the first time her human skin fell away to reveal the rippling fur of a wolf. For seven days and nights she was freed from her cumbersome human form. And every month afterwards, during her bleeding time, she'd run with her wolf kin, breathless across the moors.

Now she's alone with her own thoughts, Ada ruminates on last night and the fight she had with Edith. The memory is at once sharp and heavy, like her pain. She wishes to forget it, but it won't be pushed away. Replaying the scene – their familiar argument about money – she feels her inner world slumping. She has no desire to return to the cottage to scrape together a meagre meal that will be so inadequate that her mother's pleas ('Ye need to do more!') will seem entirely justified.

She considers telling Edith about Dr Moyle, and about their work together. Telling her about their hopes – that something valuable waits for them in this cliff and that together they're going to find it. That Ada *will* get her membership of the Geological Society of London, and Edith will have roast beef on

Sundays and rest easier in her bed at night. But after the ichthyosaur and her father's death, Edith is hardly going to approve of some long-dead beast saving them from poverty. And Ada feels too tired today for another fight with her mother – who may be small and frail-looking, but can also be fierce.

She'll never rest easy, anyway, thinks Ada. Her mother is like a frightened bird; has always been like a frightened bird. She's been afraid of the world for as long as Ada can remember. It's certainly been worse since her father's death, but Edith's grief was not the beginning of her fretting. So why should a little money in her purse change anything? Edith looks at the world as if it is in some way deeply wrong: unfathomable and unfixable. Ada would have to dig for a very long time to find a cure for her mother's worry.

CHAPTER SEVENTEEN

*O*n Saturday, the weather is so foul when Dr Moyle arrives that Ada invites him inside for a few moments while they wait for the worst of the downpour to pass. Water flows from his closed umbrella, making a puddle at his feet, and he fills the kitchen with a humid fragrance – the warm spice of his perfume and the faint aroma of tobacco. She wonders what the cottage smells like to him, and whether he finds it unpleasant. She tries not to care, one way or the other.

'I've something to show you,' she says.

She beckons him through into the parlour, where straight-away he picks up the puzzle box and troubles himself with solving the mystery. Ada brings some copies of the Geological Society transactions to the table, opening them out, proffering them.

'I imagine you know Mr Conybeare of Bristol?' she says.

'I know him well; he helped establish The British Philosophical Institute.'

'Do you remember the partial skull he found in Somerset a few years ago? Along with some vertebrae?'

He looks up from the box, nodding vaguely, as if he doesn't remember at all.

'It came back to me last night,' she says. 'And I've found the articles. Look here at the drawings.'

She passes him the papers and waits for him to study the sketches.

'A lower jaw and eleven unusually shaped cervical vertebrae,' says Ada. 'Unusual enough for him to surmise that he has in his collection a new fossil animal.'

Dr Moyle takes the article and begins to read.

'He was terribly excited about the whole thing,' he says, 'if I remember rightly.'

'The vertebrae suggested a remarkably long neck.'

'That's right, and he called it a sea dragon!' says Moyle.

'It sounds as if people laughed at him?'

'The whole thing was cobbled together – the fossils were from different locations. It's been rather discredited, I'm afraid.'

'It says the vertebrae were from a collection kept in William Bullock's Museum of Natural Curiosities, in the Bristol Philosophical Institute. So presumably the vertebrae were from the same location? I understand the skull came from Street in Somerset. Regardless, the vertebrae are quite distinct from ichthyosaur vertebrae, and are fossils yet to be identified as belonging to a known creature. The interesting thing is that his partial skull and vertebrae were found in locations where ichthyosaurs have also been found. It makes me wonder whether our paddle might be another piece of Conybeare's sea dragon?'

'Forgive me, but I hope not!'

'But why?'

'I am hoping, Miss Winters, that what we have is a new species entirely; a creature as yet undiscovered.'

'His sea dragon *is* undiscovered. He hypothesised it, that's all. He has no certainty and hasn't named it. It's all still for the taking.'

'The skull of his creature is only four inches long,' says Moyle. 'The paddle we have is more than thirty inches. *Our* creature is a beast!'

'And perhaps what he has is a juvenile.'

Moyle pushes the papers away.

'It's exciting,' says Ada, 'to think that perhaps our creature's skull looks like this.'

Ada traces a fingertip along the inky curves.

'It may excite *you*, Miss Winters, but we'll need something more to excite the geological world.'

'I'm certain some geologists *would* be excited by our paddle,' says Ada. 'We are excited by it, after all!'

His bright green eyes look straight into hers, and for a moment he says nothing, a smile tinkering at the corners of his mouth. Ada is confused, the air thickening between them. He holds out the puzzle box and as she takes it from him, she sees that he has solved it; the small drawer is open, the miniature key now revealed.

'Is that the key to your heart?' he asks, laughing.

She tries to laugh too, but the sound catches in her throat. Turning away, she returns the box to its shelf, pushing down a rising embarrassment.

'So you don't think we should announce what we *do* have?' Ada asks, keen to return to their discussion. 'Are you not tempted to write a letter to your colleagues? Our paddle is a first; you know it is. No other creature has digits with ten bones.'

'I have learned that at times what might seem incredible to

an individual can be entirely dismissed by so-called experts. A few years ago, I found a tooth in Stonesfield Quarry that I believed to be from a giant herbivorous reptile. But Cuvier dismissed this suggestion as preposterous. Since then, however, the Iguanodon has been identified, and its teeth prove my earlier hypothesis correct. However, no one is interested in my single fossil tooth now – it is too late. So, whilst we must not dally, we must not be overly hasty either. We do not want *Monsieur Cuvier* dismissing it, for then everyone else will dismiss it also.'

'You don't like the man?'

'I do not like that he's so often given the last word. He claims, in his principle of the correlation of parts, to be able to deduce from a single bone whether the creature in question is a bird, a reptile or a mammal.'

'All limbs and organs are interdependent,' says Ada.

'But to ascertain order, family and genus from that same bone also? To me that's ludicrous. People revere the man, and I don't quite understand it. He's yet to prove himself as far as I'm concerned.'

'And you are yet to prove *yourself.*'

It's only once the words are out and hanging in the air between them that she hears them for what they are. But if he's insulted, he does a good job of hiding it. He chuckles, and says, 'Now you sound like my father.'

'Don't forget,' she says, 'I'm trying to prove myself too. I'm not deemed worthy to even sit around your table.'

He regards her stolidly.

'You have a masculine intelligence, Miss Winters, and perhaps you would not be so out of place at our table.'

It's a compliment and an insult all at once.

'I expect you think I should feel honoured by your assessment,' she says, bending down to tie her boot laces.

'You really should.'

She focuses on what she's doing so she doesn't have to look up at him.

Her father always said that the wealthy didn't possess the moral capacity to discern the shape and variety of their transgressions. And Ada has noticed that it's too often the same with men.

'The rain has stopped,' she says curtly, glancing out of the window. 'Let us stop our chatter and put ourselves to use.'

She leads him back to Black Ven and sets to work with her trowel without discussion. Despite her own prickly mood, she doesn't welcome his when it swirls between them like a cold mist. Throughout the day it thickens. She wishes to tell him that this place is her home – the cliff, the shale, the clay. This is where she comes to settle her mind, not aggravate it. She wishes to tell him to stop hacking at the earth as if it's a person he detests.

'Dr Moyle! Be more careful!'

He sits back on his haunches, beads of sweat dribbling down his face.

'Don't speak to me like that,' he says, not looking at her.

'You're behaving like a crousty child. You've been out here for less than a week; you must be more patient.'

Greedy, she wants to say. *You're being so greedy.*

But Ada also knows greed, and doesn't want to be a hypocrite.

He pushes himself to standing, throws his tools into his bag and walks away. Ada is left to stare after him, dumbfounded. Despite being cross with him, fear suffuses her as she watches him diminishing. She thinks of running after him, for reassurance that she hasn't ruined everything.

As she prevaricates, Isaac appears at her back, startling her. She turns, caught in the warmth of his gaze, wrong-footed by his dark brown eyes that are so full of concern.

'I have nothing!' she says, glaring at him accusingly. 'Nothing at all for you!'

And she walks away from him, hot with tears and anger.

CHAPTER EIGHTEEN

Edwin

*H*ow dare she speak to him in such a manner? He can hardly countenance her impertinence. It is very well for her – with nothing to lose, and all the time in the world to waste upon the beach.

Christina's letter lays upon his desk; her neat, curled hand aggravating him to distraction. In many ways she is the perfect wife, but he knows she'll have nothing to say that will soothe his nerves. She'll tell him either that she is still with child or that she isn't. Neither will bring him any relief.

It is much later, after half a bottle of wine, that he finally opens her letter. *I am coming to Lyme.* She wants to reassure him that the news is good. She would merely like some sea air, and to take the waters and to enjoy the shellfish that are always at their best when eaten on the coast. It is not only Christina coming, however, but his father also. Edwin throws the letter down when he reads that particular morsel. Apparently, Dr Moyle Senior has taken it upon himself to arrange lodgings for all three of them and suggests that Edwin quit his hotel and join them in their cottage on Mill Green.

You may as well, writes Christina. *To save on the expense.*

They will arrive on Monday and he thinks about his work with Miss Winters and how he doesn't wish for Christina and his father to know about it. It wouldn't do for Edwin's family to be in full possession of the facts – that he's been digging around in the mud with an almost-destitute young woman who wears a dead man's breeches. They would think he has lost his mind.

CHAPTER NINETEEN

*T*he next morning, beneath a milk and pewter sky, Ada returns to the cliff after chapel, and is disappointed when she sees no sign of Dr Moyle. Her thoughts are biting fleas, and she scratches at them. They all return to the same conclusion: *You should not have spoken out of turn.*

As she glances casually at the area where Dr Moyle had been digging, that has since been rinsed by the tide, she notices irregular undulations in the clay that hint at something hidden. She falls to the ground, scraping a fingernail across a particularly pronounced protrusion. Prising it out she identifies it straightaway as another paddle bone. Running her palm across the exposed clay, over the just-covered multitude of fossils, her joy is like an ocean swell, lifting her, as this ancient creature presses up to greet her hand.

She uses her pick to excavate a graceful, curved limb. Her heart beats to meet its edges – from its delicate tip all the way up to its broadest part, with five bones across, and then, incredibly, onwards to a tibia, an ilium and femur. A pubis and three vertebrae. She can hardly believe it: a second paddle and connecting bones. She thinks of running all the way to the Angel Inn, hammering upon Moyle's door and mending everything.

Selecting a vertebra, she rubs at it and cleans it up, her own spine tingling as she does so. It's the same unusual vertebra described in the article she showed to Dr Moyle: Conybeare's ridiculed sea dragon. She pictures a long graceful neck, curved like a swan. And remembers the description of its teeth in the lower jaw: long and sharp, spaced widely enough to interlock when clamping down upon its prey.

A spark in the centre of her being, like the crackle of electricity, expands and jumps, running outwards along all four of her limbs. She looks up, in the direction of Lyme, but there's no one on the beach at all. As if the world has deserted her.

As she digs further outwards she finds nothing more. And for some reason, she feels no urgency. They don't need the whole of this creature for a letter to the Geological Society. *This* is enough. Staring down at the fossils in situ, she contemplates covering it up again. If Dr Moyle returns – and she tries to believe that he will – then their spat will be more easily put behind them if she gives him this gift. To be truly part of the discovery of this creature is something he clearly and sorely needs.

Might the mudstone be replaced and heeled in convincingly? She mauls the idea, weighing up its merits. On the one hand it's ridiculous to reward the childish streak she observed in him yesterday. On the other hand it would undoubtedly bring some harmony, and assure Ada of Moyle's continued commitment to their shared endeavour. Without his voice to speak for them both, she's nothing but a local fossilist who has chanced upon something special. Her words won't be published in their society papers and her name won't be mentioned at their meetings.

Just as a cloud blots the sun and the wind ripples chill against her skin, she hears the sound of footsteps on the pebbles.

His face is thunder. Even from this distance she can tell that his mood has worsened overnight. But he is here, at least, she thinks, steeling herself, tamping down a rising – unhelpful – indignation. *Who does he think he is?* His confident stride, the swing of his cane. These little traits are suddenly, somehow, quite repugnant to her. And she's pleased she didn't cover the bones over again. She *does* want Dr Moyle as a colleague. She *needs* him. But she won't pander to the man.

'Before you say a thing,' she says, pointing at the ground.

He arrives at her side: tall, scented, warm from his walk.

'Great Caesar's ghost,' he says, placing his cane upon the pebbles and dropping to his knees. 'This is where I was yesterday.'

'It is.'

'Good grief, good grief! I had it!'

They stare down at it in silence, Moyle running his hand across the bones.

'A rear paddle,' she says.

'You should have waited,' he said. 'This was mine.'

'I didn't know you were coming back.'

'Why would I *not* be coming back?'

'You stormed away; what was I supposed to think?'

He stands and turns to her. Smiling, he places his palms to her upper arms, squeezing them.

'Let's not fight,' he says. 'Look at what we've done!'

She returns his smile, although steps away, extricating herself from his grasp.

'It's incredible,' she says.

Her body still crackles with the wonder of what they have, and the promise of what's to come. Sinking to it, she shows him where she has continued digging, and then she passes him the vertebra.

'Do you recognise it?'

'The vertebrae from William Bullock's museum?'

'Conybeare's sea dragon.'

She wonders whether he'll be disappointed by this, but he doesn't seem to be. He reaches to his bag, opens it, retrieves a trowel and begins prising the fossils one by one from the earth.

'I will take them to show my wife,' he says, glancing round at Ada.

'In *London*?'

'She's visiting with my father – arriving tomorrow. Bloody inconvenient, but there's nothing to be done. I shall need to attend to them. I'm sure you understand.'

'We could still find time to meet, though, couldn't we? Early mornings, perhaps?'

He searches Ada's face briefly, before shaking his head.

'I'd rather not, to be truthful. Let's just wait for a week or so and see what happens. It will do us both good, don't you think? To rest a little?'

Edwin turns back to his task.

'Might we announce what we have now, to the Geological Society?' she asks.

'Let me consider it,' he says. 'Although isn't it tantalising to think of going to them with the creature complete? Imagine their awe? And the rest of it simply must be here!'

He gestures at the blackened ground, his face full of excitement.

'Let's get these out,' he says. 'And then I'll collect the other paddle, too, if that's all right with you.'

Do you really need them both? she wants to say. But of course he does. She would take both paddles if she were hoping to impress somebody. Even a person entirely ignorant about geology could not fail to be awestruck by these great, drifting limbs. Like wings, she thinks. As if this dragon flew through the sea.

CHAPTER TWENTY

Edwin

When Edwin enters the Angel Inn he brings two dirty sacks with him, and plenty of curious glances.

'Exciting fossils,' he tells the hotelier on his way through the lobby, although he does not stop to court questions of any kind.

He prickles with pride; only he knows quite how exciting these fossils are.

It is the very same room that he left that morning, but it seems now completely altered. How homely and welcoming it is – the freshly made bed and the carafe of wine that has been left on his desk with a glass, ready for him to settle down for the evening.

He really is in excellent spirits, and no longer at all troubled by the imminent arrival of his wife and father. If anything, he's excited by the thought of finally showing them what his hopes and dreams are all about. They might not have it within themselves to marvel at his collection of dusty old rocks at home. But they surely cannot fail to be impressed by the wings of a sea dragon!

When he goes down to order his evening meal, he informs the hotelier that he'll be vacating his room tomorrow after breakfast. He's decided that a change of scenery will do him no harm at all. And the notion of a whole week away from the claggy clay is something of a relief. There is no great rush to find the rest of the beast; it has lain in the mudstone for longer than any human mind can possibly imagine, so will surely wait another week.

He arranges for jugs of water and towels to be brought to his room, and rinses the fossils at the washstand in the corner – feeling no guilt at all about the mess he makes. Afterwards, he gathers the bones upon his desk and begins the arduous task of picking them clean with his penknife.

While working, he ruminates on the matter of announcing his find. He thinks one thing, and then the opposite, frustrated by his lack of certainty.

It is dark outside now, well past midnight, and with the lamp drawn close to his hands, the fossil and his fingers and the blade of his knife are all lit bright, casting restive shadows onto the tabletop. The scene speaks to him of secrecy – of the need to continue being cunning and discreet. Alone, he tells himself, is the only sensible way to proceed. He thinks about Miss Winters and concedes that obviously she must be considered. But when it comes to the world of geological study, he doesn't have the time to conduct himself any other way but singularly. He doesn't have the luxury of his colleagues' landed lives, their leisure time and abundant resources. He has three short months to make his mark in the geological world and to show his father that there's more than one way to plough one's furrow.

Drying the last fossil and placing it down, he nods to himself, quite satisfied. He leans back against the comfortable cushions to enjoy that deep, steady feeling he gets when he's sure about something. As if his belly has been filled with ballast.

He tells himself to go to bed, but his excitement refuses to settle. He knows that ahead of him is a night of tossing and turning, so he goes to his bag, retrieves a vial of laudanum and takes two drops straight onto his tongue. At his desk, he pours the last of the wine into his glass and takes it to the window. He looks out onto the velvet night, swaying gently, enjoying the sensation. Contented, sure of himself, he waits for the embrace he knows is coming.

Lyme lies quietly in shadow, not a lamp lit anywhere. But beyond the town, on a watery horizon, the moon hangs full and bright, the broken surface of the sea rippling silver – like the glisten of undulating scales, rising and falling.

CHAPTER TWENTY-ONE

*P*astor Durrant breaks with his sacrosanct routine and pays an unannounced visit to Edith and Ada late in the afternoon on Tuesday. Answering the door to him, Ada prickles all over; she can tell by his expression that something is troubling him and, all of a rush, she knows that what is left of the day is about to be stolen away from her.

'You're a fortnight early,' she says, only half joking, regarding him there on the doorstep. She appreciates the predictability of their routine as much as Pastor Durrant does; she usually finds she's ready to welcome the man by the time the last Sunday of the month comes around. There is always something to talk about after the full moon has come and gone and the tide has washed the beach aplenty. One of them will have read an article worth discussion, and Ada will usually have dug something from the clay that she will put on the table between them. But despite having discovered something astonishing since his last visit, she's not inclined to welcome him. Today is not the last Sunday of the month. What is more, it is looking like a perfect September evening – the sun warmly beckoning her.

Perhaps it seems to Edith that Ada is about to send him away, for she grabs the door and opens it wide. Pastor Durrant brings himself into the kitchen, smiling glumly, patting at his pockets as if he has forgotten something.

'Only nine at chapel this week,' he says, before he's even taken a seat.

Ahh, thinks Ada, this is how we will spend our time.

It's true that it was a particularly poor turnout at chapel; Ada and Edith had each been doing their best to mentally conjure a handful more through the door. They, better than anyone, know the effect it has on the minister when he's preaching to so many empty pews.

'It's really quite dire, and I've decided that something must be done. I deserve better than this. If people don't like my opinions – and they are, at the end of the day, nothing more than exploratory – then they can go elsewhere!'

'Which is precisely what they're doing,' mumbles Ada. It irritates her when people speak of what they deserve; it's perfectly obvious that getting what one deserves is not how life works.

'God made the earth, and all that's in it. The mysteries buried all across this land pose questions that must be answered. This is clearly an invitation by God himself. It makes no logical sense to deny what's there. All I'm trying to do – all *we* are trying to do, Ada – is find answers to the questions posed by God himself. Could there be a more holy endeavour? Am I going mad?' He throws up his hands. 'What is *their* explanation for these skeletons in the rocks? They are not from creatures still walking the earth, and yet they don't like any of the suggestions that explain the existence of these fossils. Our love of God isn't diluted by our enquiry! Goodness me, why are people so blinkered? So black and white about everything?'

Ada hears the words break in his throat, and is taken aback by this uncharacteristic show of emotion. She feels a rush of affection for him as he tries to compose himself, tears shining treacherously in his eyes. She knows what it feels like to be shunned, and to have the tide turn against you. He rubs his face, as if trying to brush away the emotion. But then, very quietly, he says, 'I'm sick of grasping, and of trying to persuade people of my worth. And I'm so sick of feeling ... well, of feeling *alone*.'

He fusses with his pockets again, and his eyes flicker to Ada's, holding her gaze until she looks away from him. Edith makes in the direction of the parlour and Ada reaches out for her petticoat, tugging her back.

'Why not make some tea, Mother?'

Edith clenches her jaw, but doesn't argue.

If Pastor Durrant were just a little braver he might ask Edith directly if he could speak with Ada alone. But he's never been the bravest of men when it comes to matters of the heart (he has let several women slip through his fingers over the years as a result of pure procrastination). He steals another glance at Ada, and sees something strange in her gaze (those hazel eyes, flecked molten gold!) as she looks towards the salt-smeared window. He knows that he keeps her from the beach, and supposes that would always be the case. A life with Ada would be a tussle, but it's a compromise he's willing to make.

'There's something I haven't told you,' Ada says.

It's her best attempt at a distraction; she doesn't wish for Pastor Durrant's loneliness to sit there between them all on the table, open for further discussion. And neither does she wish to maul the conversations the three of them tend to circle around on a monthly basis: the Congregational chapel dwindling in popularity; the ecclesiastical world believing the science of geology an affront to morality; and how the decent folk of Lyme are so frequently besmirched by the less than decent.

She searches for the right words, wondering momentarily whether she really *does*, after all, want to share the secret of the sea beast. She hadn't prepared herself to divulge the details and feels a little wrong-footed.

Pastor Durrant lifts himself up in his chair, his focus entirely hers, and she realises that it's too late to back out now.

'It must be kept quiet for the time being,' she says, 'but I've found the most incredible fossils.'

Quickly, she weighs up whether to mention Dr Moyle.

'Lord Bless me!' says Pastor Durrant, looking about the room as if her finds might be lying upon the range or the sideboard. 'Can I see them? What kind of fossils exactly?'

She cannot help the smile that spreads across her face.

'I believe them to be from a sea creature as yet undiscovered.'

'You really do?'

'Two rear paddles, each as long as my arm.'

Edith spoons sugar into their cups, while Pastor Durrant asks Ada a string of increasingly excitable questions. She responds with details about Conybeare and his hypothesis, about the fragment of a lower jaw found in Street, about its sharp interlocking teeth.

'Where are these finds of yours?' Durrant asks. 'May I see them?'

'They're not here.'

'Where *are* they then?'

'I've been working with another geologist,' she says.

Pastor Durrant looks at her aghast. 'You have relinquished them to someone?'

'I chanced upon a group of men on the beach, and one of them has shown quite the interest in me.'

'Are you jesting?' he asks, hopefully.

'I'm quite serious.'

'You could have come to me with them.'

'Dr Moyle has been a member of the Geological Society of London since its very early days. Can you believe it? After their dismissive letter?'

'Ada,' says Edith, falling to her stool, wringing her hands upon the tabletop, 'is this another monster yer speakin' about?'

'Of course not a *monster*. For goodness' sake, they're paddles – like the fins of a fish!'

Edith looks doubtful, and Ada softens, reaching out across the table for her hands. She looks deep into her mother's eyes.

'Don't think of it like that,' she tells her. 'It isn't a monster at all.'

'Then why didn't ye tell me? Why do ye be keepin' it from me?'

'You don't care about the fossils like I do, Mother. You have no interest. It's the curios I can sell that you're interested in, but these fossils are not for sale.'

'Why *not* sell them, then?' says Edith.

'You'd sell *me* if you could.'

Edith tuts, rolls her eyes.

Ada looks at Pastor Durrant. 'You're no better,' she says accusingly.

He lifts his palms from the table in a conciliatory gesture.

'Apparently, some collector would pay a pretty penny for everything in my parlour.'

'I was trying to help.'

'She's agreed to sell it all anyway,' says Edith triumphantly. She turns and holds up the packet of hyson tea. 'A gentleman came to nosy at it all. Brought tea and sugar for no good reason. That's how rich he be – coin to waste.'

'Really?' Pastor Durrant asks, looking to Ada. 'You're really going to let it all go?'

He looks disbelieving, and it makes her doubt herself. She doesn't know quite how to explain it to him.

'I was going to speak to you about it,' she says, when she finds herself otherwise lost for words. 'Perhaps you know someone who might be interested.'

'What about this gentleman who brought you tea?'

Ada shakes her head, rubs the tired feeling from her eyes.

'He's not a buyer as such ... he's ... this Dr Moyle I mentioned.'

'I see,' says Durrant, taking a deep breath that is undeniably tinged with disappointment.

'I've said Ada should try the Ol' Factory again,' says Edith.

Now it's Ada's turn to sigh.

'A job at the mill won't kill 'er,' says her mother.

She's clearly hoping Pastor Durrant will add some weight to this suggestion, and the minister looks between mother and daughter as if unsure which thread of the conversation to pick up.

'Pastor,' Ada says, waiting until she has his full attention. 'The rest of it is in the cliff, I'm sure of it. It must be fifteen feet, and a new species. My name will be in the museum and we'll sell it for a fortune!'

'So it *is* another monster?' says Edith, fear writ across her features.

101

'You're being ridiculous! Tell her!' says Ada, turning to Pastor Durrant.

'Ada's right,' he says. 'Your fears really are unfounded. There's no reason to be afraid of an animal that lived thousands of years ago. What Ada's discovered is a scientific marvel, and it'll put money into your purse. So perhaps, for now, it's a better prospect than her working in the mill. Your daughter has a talent; let her make use of it.'

'The British Museum pays handsomely for complete specimens,' says Ada.

'And in the meantime,' says Pastor Durrant, 'let me help by finding a buyer for Ada's collections.'

He turns to Ada, his face shining and flushed, and slides his hand across the tabletop in a gesture which Ada can do nothing to prevent. She tries not to flinch when he makes contact, tries not to show the discomfort she feels; but it is *all* she feels. She pulls slowly away and balls her hands in her lap. Edith has fixed her with a stare, although her gaze soon drifts to Pastor Durrant, and then to his hand, which is still stretched across the tabletop, his fingers pointing in Ada's direction. *Everything* seems to be pointing in her direction, and she feels suddenly hot under the scrutiny.

'We would make a good partnership,' he says, withdrawing his hand, touching his cravat, fiddling with the folds of white silk. 'Don't you think?'

'We *do* make a good partnership,' says Ada. 'Our conversations are good for us both, and at times a source of comfort. I'm grateful for them.'

She stands and goes to the teapot, pours the tea, all the while feeling her mother's agitation like the prickle of needles against her skin.

*

Ada can't get out upon the beach quickly enough after Pastor Durrant leaves. But Edith follows. Church Cliffs are to the left as they stride towards Charmouth, the sea fretting to the right: waves likes frills, spilling like strewn lace.

'Do not say it!' says Ada.

''Tis not fair fer ye to be so stubborn, while I work my fingers to the bone.'

'I work too. Every day I'm out upon this beach, in all weathers. I don't sit by the fire in the winter – I'm *here*, collecting.'

'It's ye with the power to lift us out of poverty and allow us to move from this godforsaken beach.'

'Godforsaken?!' Ada stops, and turns to look at her mother. 'This is my home.'

'That were more or less a proposal, Ada, and ye are goading me to madness!'

'Will you stop pecking me? It was not a proposal.'

Edith starts to cry – silent tears and shuddering breaths.

Ada sighs, closing her eyes, turning to her mother and pulling her into her arms.

'Don't cry,' she pleads. 'Things will change for us, I promise. Give me a little time, and I'll show you. You have to trust me. These fossils I've found are something extraordinary. I'm good at what I do, and I'm going to find the rest of this creature, Mother. It'll pay the rent for a long time to come.'

'We'll soon be back to scrattin' around.'

'No, we won't. This is different.'

''Tis not just about the money. People would look at us differently if you were a pastor's wife.'

Ada thinks of Pastor Durrant's dwindling congregation and is unsure about Edith's logic. *He only wants me because no one else will have him*, she wants to say.

Edith fidgets with her apron, worrying at it. And Ada thinks that if she could exchange half her life to give her mother some rest from her own anxiety then she would do so. Of course Ada isn't at ease with their reputation; she doesn't like how they're looked at, and what people say. But she can, somehow, some of the time, see through it and beyond it: it isn't *everything* that matters. But to Edith it is north and south, east and west. It's everywhere she looks, and all that she sees. Edith hopes to recover their reputation and to be accepted again, like they were before Ada's father died.

After his death, which was witnessed by hundreds, townsfolk went so far as to burn John's creations – hauling chests and sideboards and presses out into the streets, gathering a crowd, making a spectacle as they struck the match. Quick as anything Edith was sacked from her job as a quiller at the Waterside Factory in Uplyme and Ada was spat at in the marketplace every time she went. After Pastor Durrant and Josiah Fountain spoke on Edith's behalf, she was offered a living as a scourer at the Old Factory on Mill Green.

''Tis better than nothin',' is what Edith says about that job. 'It keeps the wolf from the door.'

John Winters has been immortalised by tittle-tattle, by stories embellished (as if his death was not dramatic enough). He'll never be forgotten.

'And we,' Edith always says, 'will never be free o' the remembering.'

CHAPTER TWENTY-TWO

*I*t has always been a place for bartering. Wool for wine. Crestcloth for saffron. Salt and wax for Flanders tiles. Bow staves, canvas, resin and pitch. Figs, raisins and sweet potatoes. Vessels sail in and sail out, their weather-beaten crew hollering and muttering or sturdy silent: foul-tempered from too many weeks with the same stinking bodies. On the water, and across the harbour, and in the town itself, pacts are made and deals brokered. Some in broad daylight, and some only in the quiet of the night. Some in back rooms, or openly in smart offices, on the pathway behind the Ship Inn, or upon the cobbles of Gosling Bridge. There are compromises signed in ink. And grudging agreements sealed with a glob of spit. Customs officials press silver into the palms of boys who feel themselves instantly transformed into men. And husbands promise wives all manner of things in the bedrooms of every steep, winding street of Lyme. It has always been a place for bartering.

Ada tells her mother this: if she hasn't found the skeleton of this strange sea creature by the end of September, then she'll relent on the matter of Pastor Durrant and his oblique proposal.

All deals demand astute attention to the terms, and so Edith presses Ada on her definition of *relent*. They're peeling potatoes together at the time, and Ada pauses, stares out of the window, calculating the risk if she promises too much. Such is her confidence, she turns to Edith and smiles.

'I'll definitely consider the matter seriously,' she promises.

Edith only rolls her eyes at that.

Every morning, Ada digs at Black Ven. With the passing days she feels the creature slipping away from her. It's a feeling made only worse because she doesn't have the paddles to marvel at. At times it seems as if she dreamed them.

Her throat-stone is back, and she has no appetite. But all the same, she tries to be patient and to keep an open mind; she mustn't fight with the cliffs. She mustn't be greedy like Dr Moyle was greedy. How unattractive it was to witness it in another.

Although it's not what she's searching for, she finds an ammonite the size of a human skull. It is pristine, and will sell for a crown – a week's rent.

'Coin in them cliffs,' says Ada, when Edith comes in at the end of the day. She nods to the kitchen table, and Edith goes straight to run her red-sore fingers across the coils and curves of the fossil.

'Tis beautiful,' her mother says, rubbing at the rough, white-grey crystals. 'Nothin' else yet, though?' she asks.

'Not yet,' Ada concedes.

'And that gentleman friend of yers, he been back with yer fossils?'

Ada shakes her head, and hopes that it comes across as nonchalant. It's been nearly two weeks, and she's not seen or heard from Moyle. Just two days ago she found her courage and asked after him at the Angel Inn. She was told that he had left – knowledge that filled her insides with ice. But she was also told that he's taken up new lodgings elsewhere. 'So, he has not left Lyme?' she asked, her words soaked with desperation. The hotelier, through a quavering smirk, assured her that no, Dr Moyle has not left Lyme. He is merely staying elsewhere – *with his wife.*

Ada frets every day about the time passing and what it means. About the fact that she now has no address for him – no way of seeking him out. Her father rears up, telling her that men like him are not to be trusted, for they only know how to think about themselves. But Ada feels sure it is not as black and white as all that.

It would be humiliating to go from hotel to guest house in search of him. She would be laughed at and chased away. So for now all she can do is hope that her parcel of fossils is safe in his lodgings and that his intentions are honest. It will be a room with a view, she thinks, and she imagines him there at his casement, gazing out at the water from somewhere up on the hill. He will like the sea best from there – somewhat at a distance, with so much mortared brick between him and it. Whatever they think they come for, the visitors never choose to get too close to the sea. They might take the water for a brief spell, and they'll amble along its edge with a dish of ice-cream if the weather is fair and the sea amiable. But they look aghast at Ada's cottage on Broad Ledge, only just beyond the reach of a high spring tide. It sits where the sea encroaches: lapping and licking, spitting seaweed from its gnashing teeth, pawing at the cottage door and snorting at the casements.

CHAPTER TWENTY-THREE

*I*t is the earth itself that soothes her. For as long as she can remember, during balmy summer nights Ada has conducted an affair with the beach. During the winter it tests her love as if it knows only rejection, but by the time the summer solstice has come and gone Ada is back to whispering words of adoration and making oaths – she'll never give herself to anything or anyone like she gives herself to this salty, sandy, weed-strewn shore.

She has the decorum to wait until the visitors have drifted away and the fishermen have finished mending their nets and sorting their tackle. There may be a lone cutter out there on the water, slicing through the waves on the lookout for smugglers. But the visitors will be gathered in the hotel lounges and the assembly rooms. Edith will be fast asleep. And Ada will sit in nothing but a shift, her hair loose and drifting at her waist. She might walk into the sea and slip beneath its slate-grey skin, relishing the cold caress of the water between her legs. Or she might sit where the water plays, each gentle wave creeping further up her thighs. She might touch herself in the darkness, lost in a rolling pleasure, wet and oblivious, lapped at and loved.

Today she sits fully clothed watching the dusk leeching light from the sky. She sits for so long that the rocks on the beach are no longer rocks, but the taut haunches of hunched creatures. Even when the darkness comes, sudden and stark, Ada finds that she doesn't wish to go home to bed. The moon is a meagre sliver in the sky, and she meanders slowly along the beach, towards the town that's so full of light – the night yet young and eager. She doesn't venture into town in the evenings, but likes to skirt its edges, witnessing and weighing up, contemplating how it is that people go about their living. So she continues to walk, and the cormorants continue to fly in the near-dark: hungry souls circling, lithe and emaciated.

Before she reaches Town Beach, and just as she approaches Gun Cliff, half-illuminated by a gas lamp above, there is movement: the shift and bustle of human form. She isn't sure what she hears, but it makes her skin prickle. From the gloom of the beach she watches the dark, grappling figure of a man, and the light, luminous fabric of a gown flowing about his legs. For a moment Ada averts her eyes and turns to leave. But then she hears the appeal – 'Please, I beg of you' – and hears clearly the anguish in the woman's words. She stops, returning her gaze to a situation she now understands differently.

'*Please,*' the woman says.

Ada steps towards them, the crunching of pebbles beneath her feet surely loud enough for the couple to hear. They seem oblivious to her, although *she* can discern the low, insistent murmur of the man. His voice deepens, growls louder as the woman's voice lifts and breaks. He's pulling at her gown, hitching it upwards as the woman grasps at it also, trying to wrestle it out of his grasp.

'You *cannot!*' the woman says, and his only answer is to shove her back against the wall. She tries to twist away from him, and for a moment Ada thinks he is going to let her go. The women half-falls, makes to run away, but he's a good foot taller than she and easily catches hold of her with just one hand: a cat playing with a mouse.

By day, people stand atop Gun Cliff, between the cannons, leaning against the railings, looking out to sea. By night, young men with pots of beer in hand stand at those railings and urinate down onto the beach. Ada wills one such man to appear now, and she looks up hopefully. But there is only the gas lamp in the gloaming, the sound of revellers in the distance, the empty beach. Even the sea has ebbed away. They are entirely alone, the three of them, and Ada feels the woman's fear as it floats towards her on the breeze.

She hears the tearing of fabric, and the woman's cry.

Ada reaches into the leather pocket that hangs from her waist, withdrawing a piece of coprolite. Heart cantering, she fingers it. She hears her father's voice: *Choose a stone, choose a target.*

'You fuckin' footlin'!' she shouts.

And as the man turns towards her she throws the fossil. He shouts, stumbling backwards, cradling his face. Ada stands rooted to the spot, and for a moment it's as if the woman is rooted too. They stare at one another in the half-light (the ostrich feathers which protrude from the woman's turban flutter in the breeze, her bright auburn ringlets framing her face). But then the woman flees, and Ada follows her example. Her pocket of stones bounces hard against her thigh and she grapples for it, grasping it tightly. Running blind – pebbles sliding beneath her too-loose boots, boulders tripping her, rock pools wetting her – she is nearing her cottage when she realises she's being pursued. Despite fleeing, despite her need to get away from him, she hadn't expected this. She hadn't thought that a gentleman caught out in such a manner would come chasing after her. *Is he not ashamed of himself?* She'd imagined him skulking away with his tail between his legs. She'd presumed that little piece of fossil shit would be the end of the matter – like a bucket of water thrown across two fighting dogs. But as her gramfer often said: *The end of one thing is usually just the beginning of something else.*

Ada snatches a look behind, panic gripping her. She can't lead him back to her cottage so she runs past it, continuing on in the direction of Black Ven, and Golden Cap and Charmouth – all cloaked now in shadow.

She veers left towards the cliffs, runs alongside them, picking up her slip-shod feet as best she can, for the rocks are bigger here and she stumbles over them. Heart pounding, she clutches her petticoats, lifting them, desperation rising.

When she reaches the gulley of fresh water that trickles out of the hillside, she throws herself down onto the grassy scrubland, feeling her way on hands and knees. Her stockings catch and tear on the undergrowth as she feels her way blindly in the dark, hands and face scratched at by thorns.

'Come on!' she demands and, just as it seems he'll surely be upon her, she feels the mass of reeds and branches give way into an empty space and she falls into the smugglers' hideaway. It is far from silent, with the heaving of her breath and thumping of blood in her ears. She dare not try to rearrange all the plant-matter she's disturbed, and simply stares into the darkness around her, wondering what is earth and what is branch and what is the black sky beyond? Her eyes can make no sense of it, and they conjure stars instead – pinpricks of light that pulse there even when she squeezes her eyes tightly shut. She hugs her

knees to her chest, trying hard not to think of whether he's out there just beyond the reeds and thorns, sniffing her out like a hound. And trying hard, too, not to think about this hole in the hillside, and how like a grave it is.

CHAPTER TWENTY-FOUR

Edwin

As soon as he delivered the fossils to the artist (a fellow in a tiny studio at the back of a furniture shop on Silver Street), Edwin began to feel unsettled. He has been troubled since, almost every night, by dreams of being lost on a lonely, unforgiving road. There are potholes and dented wheels. There are flooded ditches to be navigated and often a dead driver slumped there in his seat, the rooks eyeing him from the trees above. It's always the early hours when he wakes, tangled in his sheets, damp in his nightshirt. And although he tries to settle himself again, more often than not he's forced to resort to a light sleeping draught – a few drops in a finger of brandy. It means he sleeps again, but wakes later than he would like, with stiffened joints and aching muscles. He then passes the morning in a tetchy mood (the housekeeper and chambermaid giving him a wide berth).

He believes that he shan't have a good night's sleep until the fossils are back in his possession; another week, then! He's confident the artist will do a fine job; his work was remarkable: watercolours, ink drawings, etchings and lithographs. It was all very impressive for a young man working in a small town. The artist had initially insisted that he wouldn't be able to undertake the commission for three months at least, but Edwin had implored him – spinning some tale about travelling abroad and an ailing friend. In the end, for a rather eye-watering sum, they agreed just three weeks for both an ink drawing and a copper etching ready for printing. Edwin paid half the fee upfront, and made sure to let the young man know he'd be dropping by each week to check on progress.

In the meantime, he has been penning his article for the Geological Society. He'll not divulge precisely where the fossils were found. He will, though, on reflection, make the link with Conybeare's supposed sea dragon, which he sees now will attract significant interest. His change of heart on the matter of announcing the find felt entirely right when he woke one morning convinced of it. His father and Christina had been surprisingly enthusiastic about his discovery, and couldn't understand why he didn't want to share it with the world straight away.

'Get in there, my boy!' was his father's advice. 'Spread a little more canvas!'

No sooner was Edwin in agreement, than he was plagued by a sense of urgency and agitation. While he waits for the artist to complete his commission, he does everything within his power to progress the matter by editing and polishing his article. His Geological Society colleagues, all of whom have now quit Lyme, are none the wiser about his discovery, and he

frequently permits himself the thrill of imagining their surprise when they hear of it; how the news will ripple through his
community, envy following hot on its heels. He can hardly bear
the anticipation – felt as excitement at times, dread at others.

Miss Winters is also on his mind; how to negotiate what he
needs from her. He is in the middle of writing her a note, apolo-
gising for the delay in returning the fossils. He doesn't mention
the drawing and etching, or that he's decided to announce the
discovery. He simply explains he has been caught up for longer
than intended with his wife and father. He'll not delay much
longer, he promises, but will pay a visit within the week.

He will ask one of the stable lads to run the note down to
Miss Winters' cottage, rather than go himself. He folds the
paper and seals it, musing as he does so on the likelihood of
her parting with the fossils willingly. He *is* going to need them,
after all. Whether now or later, she'll need to relinquish them
to him on a more permanent basis. He's quite prepared to pay,
and wonders what he'll need to offer. She is clearly passionate,
certainly feisty, but is she shrewd? In the end almost everyone
has a price that will turn them. And he wonders what Miss
Winters' price will be.

CHAPTER TWENTY-FIVE

*I*n the dead of night, hours after throwing herself into it, Ada emerges shivering from the smugglers' hole. It's not just the cold in her stiff limbs that provokes her trembling, but the dregs of her fear. And as she walks along the beach thinking, *Witching hour,* that fear flares like a struck match when an owl swoops low from the cliff in front of her.

She cries out and then claps a hand to her mouth, appalled at the sound, imagining eyelids peeling open, a nocturnal bristling of attention.

Her pocket of stones is bruising against her thigh, weighing her down. Her clothes are wet, and her teeth are chattering, thoughts leaping. She imagines Edith's reaction when she sees the state of her. What if she has woken and found Ada missing? But she tells herself that her mother will be abed and fast asleep; a fretful mind and six days a week at the mill is an exhausting way to live.

When Ada arrives home she considers lighting a candle to inspect her mud-covered clothing and to see how badly her stockings are torn; whether they'll be saved at all or whether she has explaining to do. But she's too weary to think about it all now. She simply rinses her hands with a ladle of fresh water, and steps across the threshold into the cottage. She welcomes its familiar smell, the aroma of woodsmoke and carded wool. It's such a comfort that she feels a sudden urge to cry. But then she thinks of Edith, and the feeling drains away. If her mother finds out what has occurred, she will demand to know *why*? *Why do ye be involving yerself in what's none of yer business? Why do ye be so reckless with yer own reputation?* Her mother cannot bear it when Ada interferes in matters that don't concern her. What Ada might think is her concern is usually quite at odds with Edith's views on the matter. Ada is lost in thought for a moment. Then she bolts the door and heads through to the parlour and upstairs to bed.

It is only a few hours later, after sleep has alluded her, that Ada finds herself standing once more beneath Gun Cliff. She remembered something, and it lured her back. The dawn sky merges with the tranquil sea: ribbons of palest blue and delicate pink, striped and bleeding like gutted mackerel.

It feels like a memory, this thing she's grasping for. Although she's also wondering if it's nothing more than a confused half-dream. *Did* she see something drop during the tussle, as the woman tried to struggle away? There had been no time to think about it last night; she had been reaching for that little piece of coprolite, calling out and taking aim. But as she turned upon her pillow (for the umpteenth time, dawn approaching), Ada remembered: a little flash in the darkness, like the far-off flicker of lightning over the water.

Here now she searches the pebbles and sand. The tide is coming in, reaching foamy fingers for the wall. Ada squats down and rummages in the stones. She looks from left to right, the water breaking against her boots. She stands, takes a step away, concluding that she must have imagined it. But as she turns in the direction of home, there, right in front of her, shimmering beneath the water is a gold locket.

She bends for it, feeling it weighty in her hand. It is engraved with the initials S.P., and decorated with elaborate filigree work, both front and back. Water drips from its insides, and Ada prises it open, revealing a lock of sodden blonde hair. She lets the water drain away before closing it up and slipping it into her pocket.

CHAPTER TWENTY-SIX

*A*da tears herself away from Black Ven, and runs all the way home. Rain drenches her, but she doesn't care. Her feet squelch in her waterlogged boots. Hair is plastered to her face and she swipes it away. She plunges into the cottage, as if diving into the sea, and perhaps her expression says it all, for Edith is on her feet and stepping to meet her in an instant.

'I've found the rest of it.'

Edith grasps Ada's upper arms, looking at her straight and absorbing her excitement. The women smile at one another, and Ada is delighted at her mother's pleasure. Despite Pastor Durrant's reassurances about there being nothing to fear, Ada hadn't been sure that Edith would share – even tentatively – the joy of finding more of this creature. She reaches for her mother's hands, feeling them chapped and dry in her own.

'Thank you,' she says, her wild smile enduring (her face aches with it).

She doesn't say it, but she thinks, *Thank you for not fearing this creature; for not dismissing it.* She looks down at their well-worn, well-wrung hands.

'Things are going to change, Mother.'

'Ye be soakin',' says Edith, laughing, pulling at Ada's clothes as if she were a child who needs undressing.

'And I'll be soaked again in no time. You must come and see it, though, rain or no.'

'Ye've had nothin' since breakfast. Let's have a bit-an'-drap: I 'ave it all ready.'

They've been eating well since Ada sold the skull-sized ammonite, and on the table there are slices of ham and cheese, as well as fresh bread and butter. A Sunday feast.

Ada realises how hungry she is and sits.

'And then you must come with me and see,' she says, reaching for the bread.

Edith joins her at the table and they eat how they always eat when there's good food on their plates – full of confidence that by the time they finish they'll be satisfied. Eating like this brings a cheer to the table that's difficult to find at other times. When food is scarce there's constant negotiation, with each of them insisting they're really not that hungry after all, that the other should have the larger portion or the last crust of bread (their kindnesses underlaid with irritation; it's impossible not to gripe when your stomach has nothing to digest but itself).

It's good to eat in this way, but Ada isn't at ease. There's part of her waiting at the cliff, still, digging at the curves of bone. Her insides tremble at the thought of it, and her longing tugs at her.

'Might someone else fetch it out?' Edith asks, as if she too, has ambled along in her mind to Black Ven.

Ada shakes her head.

'There's hardly anyone out, the weather's awful. People won't see it,' she says.

'What about your geologist gentleman?'

'He seems to have given up on the beach,' says Ada, looking down at the last of the ham and bread on her plate.

'If he's even 'ere in Lyme still.'

'I'm sure he is, Mother.'

'How can ye be sure? Seems queer to me, to have kept away fer so long. They be *yer* fossils, Ada. I hope he remembers that.'

'His note explained things; he's been busy with his family. He'll be here this week, you see.'

'I just hope he be a man of his word,' says Edith.

'He'll bring them back, I know he will.'

But, in truth, she's beginning to doubt it.

Stood face to face with the waterlogged cliff, Ada isn't sure her mother sees what's there, even as she points it out. The rain falls relentlessly and the beach is deserted.

'These are the edges of vertebrae, you see? And they run, one after the other, horizontally, right along here.'

Ada traces her finger from one fossil to the next: three astonishing yards of vertebrae. Incredible not only because *there they are*, so very obvious: a curve and dimple, repeated splendidly. But because at one end is a jawbone and at the other is a clavicle and scapula. These bones are not a spine, but an impossibly long neck. She'll be the fossilist who makes a truth of Conybeare's fantastical sea dragon. She can hardly believe it and, despite being drenched, her mouth is dry; she is somehow parched. She and Edith stand either end of the exposed bones, four yards between them. Her mother looks from the vertebra that she fingers to Ada.

'You see it, Mother?'

Edith nods. 'I do, I see it.'

They smile at one another, feeling their fortunes shift.

'Clever girl,' says Edith.

And Ada laughs.

The rush of happiness she feels is as bright and pure as a silver charm. As powerful as the waves that break behind her. She hears them roar; she hears them cheer. Even the rain is holy water – surely a blessing.

Edith leans forward and rubs at the earth covering one of the vertebrae. Has she ever been so interested in a fossil? Ada cannot help but laugh at the sight of her mother inspecting the shape of this long-buried bone. Water is seeping from the sodden cliff, trickling over Edith's hand, oozing from the slumping clay. Then something leaps from that clay, slipping from the sullen face of Black Ven. It falls upon Edith like a predator and swallows her whole – she is gone, quick as that.

Ada cries out, falling backwards. She looks to the pile of earth where her mother was stood, but the cliff is still tumbling towards her, and her instinct has her staggering backwards, horrified as she watches the earth settle anew, the landscape changed.

'*No,*' she whispers.

But she *knows* what this is, and how hard it will be to dig her way through it. She screams for help, but it's tea time, and the visitors are drinking their Ceylon and Darjeeling, they are eating their scones and tarts.

Where are the fishermen?

She throws herself upon the great mound of earth covering Edith and claws at the ground, scooping and digging with bare hands. She shouts as loudly as she can, and whimpers in-between. She prays to a God she has no faith in. She calls upon her father and her gramfer. She begs the earth itself for help.

Beside her then is Isaac.

'My mother,' pleads Ada.

He kneels in the mud and scoops clay as if his life depends upon it. They do not speak, but dig and dig until Ada feels that she can dig no more.

'I could go and get help,' he says softly, and Ada turns to look at him.

She'd forgotten his face and it surprises her anew. She shakes her head.

'I'm sorry,' he replies, holding her gaze, tears streaming down his cheeks. 'I'm so sorry.'

And then they turn back to the earth, digging and clawing and pulling until Ada finds a stockinged leg. They go at the ground with renewed energy, as if they might find her alive, but Ada can feel how still Edith's body is. They pull her free and wipe the mud from her face. And Ada shakes her and slaps her and shouts at her in fury, demanding that she breathe.

CHAPTER TWENTY-SEVEN

*E*dith is like a doll, smaller now than she ever
seemed before.

Isaac is sitting beside Ada, the afternoon shifting uneasily
around them. The rain continues to pour, keeping the beach
empty. He's gently asked a few times now whether he ought to
fetch Josiah and Annie, but she hasn't answered him.

It's strange, she thinks, crying in the rain. And fitting that
the whole of Lyme is nothing but a torrent of tears. She cradles
her mother in her arms, wiping continually at her face and neck,
letting the rain wash the worst of the mud away.

'Come back to me, Mother,' she pleads, and Isaac hangs his
head in solidarity, as if wishing and praying for Edith to open
her eyes and take a deep, shuddering breath. Indeed, it seems
to both of them that she might – that she hasn't yet travelled
so far that she cannot return. *Just now*, Ada thinks. *Were we
not eating ham and cheese just now?* Already she knows it was a
lifetime ago.

Edith's mobcap has been lost and her hair fans out across
the pebbles in the shape of a cockle shell. Protruding between

clumps of her mother's hair is a vertebra. Ada doesn't reach for it, but looks beyond it, just a few inches away, to another vertebra. She only has to glance from left to right to realise they are, the three of them, surrounded by fossilised bones. And not just vertebrae, but coracoids and humeri.

'Take it all,' Ada whispers, remembering how she bartered with Black Ven. She can hardly breathe at the thought of it: that this is *her* doing.

Take it all, but give me this.

Isn't that what she said? Didn't she ask for this very thing?

'What was it you said?' Isaac asks, and Ada turns to look at him. It seems that he has read her mind – that he knows of her guilt. He's leaning towards her earnestly, his fair hair plastered to his face, his loose white shirt clinging to his skin.

'You said something,' he clarifies. 'I missed it.'

Ada shakes her head, closes her eyes.

'I'll go and find someone to help us,' says Isaac, rising to his feet, wiping his filthy hands hopelessly on his equally filthy pantaloons.

'If not the Fountains, then fetch Pastor Durrant from the Congregational chapel,' she says.

Isaac nods, before running away down the beach. He's sure to attract attention, she thinks, running like that, with his fine clothes covered in mud.

And sure enough, by the time he returns he brings with him not only Pastor Durrant, Annie and Josiah, but a gaggle of townsfolk. She can't bear the thought of all these people – so many eyes upon her and so many wagging tongues – and she lowers her mother's head onto the pebbles and pushes herself to standing. She wavers momentarily, dizzily distracted by the strange sensation of her clothes so heavy with water. Then she walks to meet the crowd, steeling herself. Ignoring Isaac and Pastor Durrant, Josiah and Annie, she shoos the spectators as if fending off a pack of stray dogs.

'Get away! Be gone!'

They take a step or two backwards, but then linger, their attention drifting to Edith's body. Ada cannot let them feast their eyes upon her and trade the details later with folk who care nothing for her mother.

'I tell you, fuck off!'

She runs at them, so they know she's serious, and they hold up palms to placate her, turning away to show that they mean to leave. She follows them a little, until she's certain they've understood.

It has finally stopped raining and the wind has dropped. The beach is quiet still, and everywhere is shrouded in silence. A dead weight, she drops to her knees. Annie is straight away there at her back, all rose water and clean petticoats.

'They'll take her to the cottage,' Annie says.

Other than a quick nod, Ada is motionless, staring out to sea. She hears the murmuring of the men, their voices low and respectful. One of them says that Edith is light as a feather, and so she knows that they have lifted her. She turns to look, and finds to her surprise it is just Isaac carrying her mother's body. Why would he do such a thing?

'Go with them,' she tells Annie.

Annie doesn't move.

'Go *with them!*'

She looks back to the sea, and Annie waits for a moment before moving away, taking the sound of the pebbles with her.

The gulls are wheeling overhead, their plaintive cries breaking the silence. The ocean is a cold stone-grey, and the sky is just as dark. But in the distance a break in the clouds lets the sunlight through, spilling a bloom of liquid gold upon the water. Ada watches it – the waves aflame. Then the clouds close and the light is gone.

CHAPTER TWENTY-EIGHT

Edwin

*H*aving received news from home that Christina is no longer with child, it dawns on Edwin that he'd sleep a whole lot better if he found himself a Clara-in-Lyme. He fetches the pamphlet he procured from a discreet bar-keep at the assembly rooms, and peruses it, contemplating the women on offer (considerably less varied than those in London, it would seem). He is a creature of habit and he misses his Clara; she knows what he likes and never fails to provide him with exactly that. She appreciates him: always adoring. And, most importantly, she asks nothing of him. He doubts he'll find a true replacement, but Miss Mary Morrison sounds suitable enough: *Her pouting lips, delicate shape, love-sparkling eyes (which are dark), regular set of teeth, together with a tempting leg and foot compose the principal attractions of this goddess of pleasure. This offspring of delight is*

indebted to eighteen summers for the attainment of such charms,
which the reader may, for the compliment of two guineas, be in
full possession of.

CHAPTER TWENTY-NINE

When Ada returns to the cottage the men tell her they have laid Edith upon the bed. Despite their scrutiny she goes to the cabinet at the far end of the parlour and folds herself across it. Chest filled with stone, weighing her down.

The moment hangs heavy and dreadful between them; Ada feels it like another person in the room: a person twice as large as any of them, thickset and stinking like he's never washed.

Eventually Josiah comes to stand beside her, stroking trembling fingers across the buttery oak of the cabinet.

'I'm so dreadfully sorry for your loss,' he says, and Ada wonders whether he, too, thinks not only of what has happened today but also of her father.

Does *he* think: *You are all alone now.*

'It's quite the tragedy God has asked you to bear witness to . . .' says Pastor Durrant.

Ada straightens, turns, and looks through into the kitchen: to the door she left ajar. She wants to run to the woods, or to the sea. To be anywhere but here. She glances at Isaac, who tries to smile, eyes glassy with tears. Neither of them have washed their hands and the mud has dried silver-grey right up to their elbows. Isaac's shirt hangs in filthy folds and his dark blond hair is matted.

Josiah and Annie begin several sentences that they cannot finish and Ada wants to say that it's quite all right; none of them needs to speak.

'The Lord is near to the broken hearted,' says Pastor Durrant, taking a deep breath. 'Blessed are they that mourn, for they shall be comforted.'

He blooms like a funeral lily, scattering his prayers until Ada interrupts him.

'I need to see to her,' she says.

'I'll stay and help you,' says Annie, gesturing that the men should take their leave.

'I'll attend the funeral, if I may,' says Isaac, pressing his hand to his heart. 'And if I can help with anything in the meantime, please just come and fetch me.'

Ada nods, turning away towards the window.

'Thank you,' she says, throwing the words over her shoulder.

She listens to the murmur of their quiet conversations as they make arrangements between themselves.

'I'll return this evening to keep vigil,' Pastor Durrant says, before pulling the door closed. She could have told him that she doesn't want that, but perhaps his company will be welcome when it comes to the longest hours of the night.

With some considerable trouble Ada and Annie remove Edith's clothing. Her boots are full of mud and suck tightly at her feet. The knots of her apron and stays are hardened with drying mud and they have to dig with their nails to loosen them. The damp cotton of her shift clings to her skin as Ada and Annie try to peel it away, and they have to lift her from her bolsters to manage it – her head lolling backwards.

Her eyes peel open, no matter how many times Annie presses them closed.

Once she is naked, they soap her body. Annie seems expert at the task, not at all abashed. And once she's clean, they position her so her hair can be washed in the bucket that Annie has placed on the floor at the foot of the bed.

Edith's skin is pallid grey, mottled purple in places. Her flesh is firm and strangely thickened; her limbs unpliable and awkward. Her hair, though, is completely unchanged and slips through Ada's fingers in the water, shockingly glossy and as full of life as a bucket of eels.

They pat her dry with a linen towel and dress her in a nightshift. She doesn't look at all as if she's sleeping, which Ada has heard people say about the dead. But there's no sign of the cliff upon her any more and Ada feels a soft, aching relief at that.

'It jumped at her,' she whispers, the memory ever sharper as the hours pass.

Black Ven attacked her, she wants to say. She knows it can't be true, but all the same, when she thinks of that ravening cliff she feels betrayed. Then she thinks of the bones of the sea creature scattered across the beach. She thinks of the tide on its way back in and is ashamed of the tug and pull she feels.

They cover Edith with a sheet and coverlet, and Ada pulls up a chair to sit beside her.

'Do you have candles for later?' asks Annie.

Ada shakes her head.

'Then I'll fetch some; we have plenty.'

She reaches out and pats Ada's arm, then withdraws her

hand. The women exchange glances, and Ada feels the loss of something: a drifting away of an opportunity.

'Why don't you get changed before I go, and I'll take your linen for washing?' says Annie.

Ada shakes her head. 'I can manage the washing.'

She can't possibly confess that she still has need of her working clothes today.

Ada listens to Annie making small sounds throughout the cottage as she gathers her things and takes her leave. She hears the snick of the door latch, and the heavy silence that follows.

She lets a few moments pass and then goes downstairs to the parlour window to watch Annie disappearing into the distance. It has started to rain again and the evening is approaching. She thinks of the tide on its way to the bones of the sea creature, and how it'll throw them all across the beach if it reaches them. How it will drag them from the foreshore and into the depths. She calculates that she has two hours at the very most to collect those bones before the tide does. Although less time than that before Annie is back with her candles, and Pastor Durrant with his tea and company.

She pulls on her boots, grabs two sacks and rushes from the cottage, running across the pebbles in the falling light towards Black Ven. She slows to a walk as she draws close and takes in the now-unfamiliar silhouette of the cliffs.

How did this happen?

What a fool she was to ignore her father's warnings. All too well she understood the risk of slippage after heavy rain. The line of bones, newly exposed, had clouded her judgement; she hadn't looked even once for vertical cracks and fissures. But in truth, it's more shameful than that. She has let herself become daft over the years, naïvely entertaining the belief that she possessed some affinity with the land. As if it liked her in a way that the town did not.

No better than Gramfer, with his mithering and superstitions. Believing the cliffs worked in harmony with her. That they gifted her their fossils.

Ada laughs at her stupidity, letting out a battle cry of fury. She spits towards the cliff. It's *herself*, though, that she loathes. Her inability to stay focused. To be sure about what she believes. To be sure what's real.

'The earth moves because that's what it does.'

She says this, sternly, into her clenched fists.

James Hutton has described this so beautifully in *Theory of the Earth*. Everywhere there is change and transformation, whether seen or not. Rivers carry sediment to the sea and the sediment accumulates in layers, compacting into stone on the sea floor. The earth shifts and lifts and folds. It's been this way for longer than it's possible to imagine. *There is no vestige of a beginning*, Hutton has said, *and no prospect of an end.*

Black Ven hasn't betrayed her at all, because Black Ven did not love her. It was gifting her nothing. She cannot lose a thing that was never there. This cliff does not care one way or the other if the sea collects the rest of the fossils before she does. It slumbers. And the sea tumbles closer, one wave at a time.

CHAPTER THIRTY

$\mathcal{T}$hroughout Lyme, the news about Edith spreads. It has happened before, a person snatched by the land, but even so it's a rare occurrence. And so the chatter begins. Another extraordinary death in the Winters family. Already they were tainted, but now this. There's not only John and his wife's demise to talk about, but the peculiarity of their daughter. How bullish and brazen and bookish she is. How coarse, how rude, how strangely kind. How clever she is with her stories for the wee ones, and whether someone ought to put a stop to her mingling. She sees no difference between a coat of arms and a coat of fleas and will talk about her fossils with anyone who cares to listen. Not knowing what to do with Ada Winters is good enough reason to despise her.

Mrs Hooke takes a gin with her son when she hears news of the fall, chewing over the matter. Thick with excitement, she feels herself at the epicentre of this tragedy as if it were a member of her own family who has been taken – but with none of the inconvenience of arrangements to contend with.

The guillemots and cormorants that lost their nests and

ledges in the fall circle the skies in the hope of finding them. They fly in the direction of Uplyme, or far out to sea, returning along the routes they've always used, coming to their home afresh as if *this* time they will find things as they were before. They wait for the world to right itself, crying out in frustration when it refuses.

When Ada wakes the morning after Edith's death, she does so with a rush of urgency. She breaks through the surface of her sleep as if swimming up from the seabed. She gasps for air as her eyes open, aware of the need to speak with her mother about a matter of great importance. But as she emerges into full consciousness, although the urgency remains, she remembers that her mother has gone. Edith lies dead in bed, not six feet away.

'I need ...'

But she cannot say what she needs.

Brittle from just a few hours of sleep, she rises from her pallet and steps towards her mother. The sight of her – this new version – is already so familiar. Ada sat until dawn, watching over her, staring for hours at her waxen face. Pastor Durrant started up praying whenever the silence between them stretched too thin. When the sun began to rise Ada went to the window, and Pastor Durrant took his leave with reassurances that he'd take care of arrangements for the funeral. He supposed it could be tomorrow. He'd speak with Josiah about the cost and they'd sort it out between the two of them. Ada, apparently, is not to give the matter another thought and already she feels the burden of that debt. 'Borrow nothin',' her father used to tell her. 'Borrow nothin' that ye cannot be certain of repayin'.'

Amidst the heavy darkness of death and debt, Ada's thoughts are drawn to the sacks of fossils she ran to collect yesterday evening from the fallen cliff. Those sacks lay hidden now beneath the loose floorboards of the parlour. In the very beginning she'd hoped this sea dragon would put meat on her mother's plate. Now it seems it will pay for her funeral.

When she went for those bones yesterday, fearful of Annie or Pastor Durrant returning and discovering her about the task, she collected only those fossils that required no digging: those specimens scattered about the place where Edith died. She plucked them quickly from the shingle and threw them in her sacks, her intention being to return today when the high tide has rummaged a little more in the mud and exposed anything remaining.

Waiting for the water to do its work, she goes downstairs and sits in her mother's chair in the parlour. She pulls a blanket right up to her chin and listens to the *hush* of the waves in the distance. She continues to listen as the tide brings those waves almost to her door, and she listens as it takes them away.

She's eventually startled out of her stupor by a knocking. She considers not answering, but finds herself drawn through the parlour and into the kitchen, finds herself lifting the latch.

Isaac is almost completely obscured by a great quantity of lavender, rosemary, sage and mint.

'I thought these might be welcome . . . ' he says.

She steps backwards, turning away, permitting him to follow. The herbs will be for Edith, and so Ada takes him straight upstairs. Rolling up her pallet bed she pushes it out of the way. Isaac begins arranging everything, without hesitation or permission. He places a posy into Edith's hands, tucking sprigs beneath the coverlet and on her pillow so they frame her face like a halo. Ada watches him, welcoming the slow transformation of her mother. As if death can be made beautiful.

'My own mother died on All Saints' Day, when I was seventeen,' he says. 'It was a decade ago, but I still grieve for her.'

He continues arranging his herbs and flowers and talking to Ada as if they're already the closest of friends and, although she isn't sure why it seems possible, she lets go of her own thoughts, words pouring from her. He listens as she tells him about the bones in the cliff and how she'd persuaded Edith to go with her and take a look at them. She confides in him what she said to Black Ven all those weeks ago: *Take it all, but give me this.*

'It's a horror!' he says, blotting a tear with his handkerchief.

'When I woke this morning,' she tells him, 'I had the urge to speak to her about something. But then, once I was properly awake, I realised what it was I wanted to speak to her about. All this. Her own death.'

He nods, closing his eyes as if remembering.

After the flowers have been suitably arranged, they return downstairs to the parlour.

'Is this your mother, or you?' Isaac asks, gesturing to the artwork of feathers pasted to the walls.

'She thought it an indulgence, and she was right.'

'Not an indulgence at all. Surely the opposite? Does the making of art not relieve us of our burdens, pointing us towards truth and beauty?'

She shakes her head.

'I have wasted everything,' she says. 'I should have tried again at the Old Factory for a regular wage, and then this wouldn't have happened; we'd have been nowhere near that cliff.'

'But you're an artist, Ada. You need inspiration, fresh air and nature. If you'd stepped foot in that mill, it would've taken all that's good from you.'

'I'm a geologist, not an artist, Isaac.'

As he talks quietly on about contemplating the transcendent, about the holiness of the heart's affections and that man is a house divided, she watches him freely: the strange twist of his upper lip, the shift of his strawberry-blond hair, the way he fidgets with his braces. For a while it feels that she's entered a strange realm where barefoot fairy folk frequent her cottage. Nothing feels quite right, and it's tempting to stay lost in that place. To let Isaac just keep talking. To stay mesmerised by the strange glow he has brought with him. But something else tugs at her – the tide on its way out and the visitors who'll soon be arriving for an afternoon upon the beach. She must get there before they do and search for the fossils she'll have missed last night, and for any newly exposed by the high tide. Her mother may be dead, but finding the rest of this creature doesn't feel any less pressing. If anything, she feels a need for it ever more urgently.

This, though, is something she's not quite prepared to confess to Isaac.

'It's so kind of you to come,' she says, when it seems there's a moment to interrupt his train of thought. 'But there's something I must do before it gets late.'

'Of course,' he says, turning for the door. 'You need some peace.'

She's relieved that he doesn't seem to expect any fussy leave-taking. As quickly as he arrived, he is gone, and Ada stands shivering in the kitchen. The weather is pleasant today, the air balmy. But even so she's shaking with a tiredness so deep that she feels chilled to the bone. All she wishes to do is lie beneath some blankets and close her eyes. But she must get on, because she has matters to conclude with Black Ven.

CHAPTER THIRTY-ONE

Edwin

The news about Edith Winters strikes Edwin as nothing short of a disaster; with such a calamity befallen Miss Winters how will he possibly instigate a conversation about the purchase of the fossils? She will be in mourning and surely in no mind to be negotiating. But after a little while he realises that perhaps the situation will work to his advantage. He surmises that Edith's wage from the mill will have constituted the lion's share of the household income; Miss Winters will surely be anxious about making ends meet. His offer to purchase the fossils (now returned into his possession by the artist) will, he is certain, be too good for her to refuse. What is more, he presumes she'll be in no fit state to continue her search of the cliff for the remaining bones. It feels as if God is smiling down upon him and approving of his plans, so he decides to make the most of divine providence and have his labourers begin digging in the cliff at the earliest opportunity.

He looks down at the beautiful – *perfect* – etching of the two rear paddles, and imagines how fine it will look printed alongside his article in the transactions of the Geological Society. He intends to post both the etching and the article to Bedford Street first thing tomorrow.

His heart quickens as he imagines the rest of the creature. How much of this beast does he need to find for it to have the impact he craves? He understands how rare it is to chance upon a complete specimen. What he has right here in front of him is already a wonderful find. But there is more to come, he's certain of it.

CHAPTER THIRTY-TWO

*I*t is gloomy in the cottage with the shutters closed, and Ada brings more candles to surround the bed where her mother lies, filling the sconces and the candelabra. She boils the kettle and sets the tea things ready, fastens a black ribbon to her bonnet.

Her fellow mourners will soon be here to help take her mother away. She keeps imagining it. How they will traipse her across the beach and through the town to chapel.

To think she'll be gone from the cottage is hard to fathom, and it still seems that her mother might somehow return. That Ada ought to be doing more to somehow facilitate this.

She also frets over Edith's terror of small spaces; her mother always panicked if her limbs were caught even momentarily in a twist of clothing when she was getting dressed. When Ada was small, larking about with Edith in bed in the early morning, she quickly learned how careful to be. Her mother would brook no horseplay that constrained her beneath the covers. And Ada dwells constantly on what Edith knew when Black Ven fell upon her.

It's a physical pain in her chest when she thinks how her mother must once again be put into the ground and covered with soil. Is there really no alternative? Could she not be taken out to sea and buried like a sailor in battle – not even wrapped in a sailcloth, just weighted down a little? She knows it cannot be, and her mind drifts to other possibilities: setting fire to the house and burning them all to the ground – Edith, herself and all that remains of her father. It ought to seem ghastly, but it doesn't. She sees in it only the allayment of her worries. It would be so simple, and the sea would deal with anything left behind: charcoal and ash, fragments of bone. She watches herself in her mind's eye, setting small fires in all the corners of the house. After considering what tinder and fuel she might cobble together for so many fires all at once, and after taking a breath and telling herself she really *could* do it, she places her palm against the wall of the parlour, contemplating its destruction. Is she truly thinking of such ruination? Ada is not afraid of being dead, but she *is* afraid of dying. And as she conjures the details of this particular kind of death, the dream of a fire is all of a sudden only that. It fades as quickly as it flared.

All morning she has a sensation of dreaming. Her thoughts are obscure, fragmented, deranged. Time can no longer be relied upon. Every minute lingers like an illness and the sea is playing silly beggars, stuck mid-tide as if caught in a net. But then like a whispered spell, in the twitch of an eye, the morning is gone.

Mrs Lester came yesterday evening from the mill.

'From a few folk at the Ol' Factory,' she'd said, thrusting into Ada's hands the wages owed to Edith and the gift of a woollen shroud. It had given Ada something to do, and she'd spent the evening sewing Edith into it – all of her but her face.

She goes now to the bedroom with her darning needle.

'I'm sorry, Mother,' she whispers.

And then she closes the fabric with careful, even stitches. The smell of lavender, rosemary and mint permeates through the wool. She runs her fingertips over the fabric, knowing Edith will have likely washed the fleeces that were spun to make this yarn. Her labour and all it cost her is woven through this very garment. Is it a blessing she was ignorant as she pulled twig and leaf from the oily fleeces, as she washed them clean? What cruel trick had her toiling so recently for the sake of her own shroud?

Ada hears footsteps enter the kitchen and move through the house below her.

Annie comes up first. 'They've borrowed a coffin,' she says.

There's the sound of scraping and knocking as the men try to bring it up the stairs, and Ada goes to watch their struggle. The coffin is a great thing, big enough for a large man, and sweat is beading on Pastor Durrant's brow.

'Stay down there with it,' Ada says to him. 'We'll bring her to the parlour.'

'You'll do no such thing,' he insists.

Ada turns back to Annie. She's dressed from head to foot in black crape, her face plain, her hair pinned simply.

'Lift her with me,' Ada says.

Annie looks doubtful. 'The men should . . . '

'She's light as a bird, Annie. Help me carry my own mother. The men will lift her all the way to chapel. Let me at least do this.'

Annie says nothing, but goes straight to the foot of the bed and takes hold of the shroud. Her expression is strangely blank

144

and her mouth has turned down at the edges. Ada knows that she's asked for too much and left Annie no choice. If her mother were here she'd be throwing Ada angry glances. And she'd tell her afterwards, *Ye overstepped, girl*. But is it really overstepping to want to lift her own mother from her bed? To want to hold her briefly before she's taken?

Edith is nothing to lift, but still it's an awkward thing for Ada and Annie to manage – the sagging and slipping of the shroud, the shift of the body within it. Ada cannot help the smile that spreads across her face, or the laughter that rushes through her: a storm conjured from nowhere. Annie looks as if she chews on something bitter, and the sight of her disapproval makes Ada laugh all the more. They are halfway down the stairs, and the men have come to witness the madness. Ada tries to say *forgive me,* but cannot get the words out. Josiah and Pastor Durrant make several attempts to relieve the women of their burden, but they only serve to get in the way and make the task more difficult. Once they're all convened at the bottom of the stairs, and Edith has been laid carefully onto the parlour floor, Ada presses her hand to her mouth to stem her laughter. No one speaks to her. Instead, the men lift Edith into the coffin and slip the lid into place. At the sight of this, Ada grows quiet. Annie wraps a black shawl about Ada's shoulders and presses a fan into her hand.

'It will be quite all right,' she tells Ada, looking at her earnestly.

They take Edith feet first from the house. Outside, there's a young man from chapel waiting with Isaac, and the four men lift the coffin onto their shoulders. There, waiting on the sand a small distance away, is a handful of fishermen; they wear their boots and waistcoats and neckerchiefs today. They nod to Ada as she looks towards them and she notices four bottles of rum on the doorstep: her smuggler friends offering their condolences in the best way they know how.

They move slowly along the beach, ascend the narrow steps at Gun Cliff, and pass through Long Entry. They pass the Guildhall, and turn right up Combe Street. They lean in to the steep hill, the men careful of every step. They pass the Packhorse Inn, the drapers and the milliners. Their numbers do not swell, except for a few curious children with nothing better to do with their afternoon. The grocer is good enough to come and stand outside his shop to watch Edith pass (wondering when he'll now be paid what he's due). And a couple of lads outside the Kings Arms pause their conversation just long enough for the coffin to be hefted by. They were discussing the carnival due to take place at the end of the month, and once the wretched procession has disappeared from view the lads resume reminiscing. Are the tar burnings not the most fun that the town ever has? They've heard it's to be *seven* barrels this year that will be tarred and torched and sent hurtling aflame down the cobbles of Combe Street – the rolling, bouncing infernos lighting up the darkness of the night. How the town will roar! Babbers and their grammers, workmen and boatmen, smugglers and naval officers. Everyone comes out for the spectacle. There are the naysayers with their thatched homes at the foot of the hill, but even they are drawn into the street once the antics begin – if only to protect all that's dear to them with their broomsticks and buckets of water.

CHAPTER THIRTY-THREE

*L*eaden with grief, each morning Ada lifts three floor-boards in the parlour and brings the sea dragon's bones from beneath them. She cleans them one by one, while attending to memories of her mother.

Did she suffer?

She lets the morning drift into the afternoon this way, washing her chosen fossil in a bucket of water, picking at it with her knife, rubbing it with dry sand.

How long before her mother is nothing but bones?

Ada has humeri, clavicles, femurs and coracoids. Cervical, dorsal and lumbar vertebrae. The creature had four paddles of almost uniform size, all of them wing-like, and the shape of its spine suggests it moved through the water quite differently to the fish-like ichthyosaur.

Its neck is long as a giraffe, graceful as a swan.

Did the fall break her neck?

Ada presses her fingers to her throat, to the familiar stone that lodges there. It feels ever larger by the day and she tries to swallow it, but it refuses to move.

She doesn't have the creature's skull, and is yet to ascertain what else might be missing. There's also the matter of the rear paddles no longer in her possession.

Grief has stripped her of her skin, so all feels new. Every day is exhausting, but also, she cannot deny, at times exhilarating. Often she cannot leave her cave of grief: blackness forever and all undone. But then she ventures out and the sun has never been so bright and the world has never been so colourful. Angels, not birds, are singing. And a cup of water is life itself – cold as stars and just as dazzling.

The skull calls to her, more than food and sleep. It is most pressing, this missing piece. On inclement days when she's sure the beach will be deserted she ventures out as soon as it's light to search with her shovel, methodically, where the landfall occurred. And every time she does, she can see that someone else has been doing the same. She wonders if it's Edwin Moyle, and it angers her to think it might be – that he's been here without coming to see her and hasn't returned the paddle bones as promised. But there's some relief at the notion he resides in Lyme still. That at least he hasn't stolen away completely. She ought to keep an eye on Black Ven, to watch for him, but the cliff isn't visible from her cottage and she cannot face the thought of venturing onto the beach during the busy part of the day.

When inside, she keeps her door bolted at all hours, even when Annie Fountain and Pastor Durrant come knocking. If it's Annie, she knocks once, sometimes twice, then leaves Ada something on the doorstep – a loaf of bread, a pot of rabbit stew, a freshly baked cake (Ada has never eaten so well). Pastor Durrant is more persistent, calling out to Ada and imploring her to answer the door. He doesn't bring her food like Annie does, and this adds to the sense that he wants something from her. He's not coming to the cottage with something to give, but has in mind something he wishes to take. At times she can hear the frustration in his voice, and a feeling of shame creeps through her. She is disappointing him, just as she disappointed Edith. Why do people always want something from her that she cannot give?

CHAPTER THIRTY-FOUR

*O*ne evening, when Ada goes into the kitchen, she finds a letter has been slipped beneath her door, addressed to *Miss Winters* and sealed with black wax. She opens it, staring down at it numbly. There's no address included but, somehow, before she glances to the signature, she knows whose hand this is.

Dear Miss Winters,

Although we have been acquainted but a short time, I feel compelled to express my condolences before we see each other again. It is a terrible calamity that has befallen you, and you have my deep and heartfelt sympathy.

Rest assured, I have our fossils in safe keeping.

Perhaps we will see each other upon the beach before too long? I have been spending some considerable time at Black Ven, but am yet to see any sign of you.

Yours sincerely,
Dr Edwin Moyle

CHAPTER THIRTY-FIVE

*S*ome days, Ada is barely aware of the knocking at her door, so intent is she on picking clean her bones. She drifts into the past, imagining the world in which these creatures lived: a world of giant ferns and lizards. Unmoored by her grief, this other place feels momentarily close. So close she might reach out and touch it. She's never experienced this so vividly before – an incorporeality, as if she, like her mother, has slipped through to another place. It is especially real, this feeling, in the middle of the night, and she has taken to leaving the cottage and going down to the water. Removing her clothes, she swims in the darkness, sinking beneath the surface, imagining sea dragons and ichthyosaurs out in the deep. The salty waves lap at her face as she peers for disturbances across the undulating surface. She lifts and falls with the swell, looking up at the stars, bereft for the absent moon.

Eventually, Annie stops calling on her.

One grey day, Pastor Durrant spends some considerable time trying to persuade her to open the door. She calls out to confirm she's alive and well but wishes for solitude. He persists and pleads, resorting to telling her that Edith wouldn't want Ada to shut herself away. Ada is prickling with anger by the time he leaves, and when he returns not half an hour later, knocking all over again, she flies to the kitchen, grabs the rolling pin and hammers on the door from the inside.

'For pity's sake, leave me alone! Leave me be, I tell you!'

And she hammers again, thumping ferociously at the sturdy oak. She growls with fury, letting it flow from her. Slumping against the door, she cries quietly, careful to hide all sound of her weeping lest it be misconstrued as a request for comfort.

After a few minutes she pushes herself away from the door, and places the rolling pin on the kitchen table. Furiously, she wipes her cheeks dry with her hands. She goes through into the parlour and peers from the small, murky window to watch Pastor Durrant retreating across the beach. Except, after all, it is not Pastor Durrant. It is Isaac.

CHAPTER THIRTY-SIX

*T*hey call it an Indian summer. It rained until the best part of September was drenched, but now the sun shines. Ice-cream is served in gold-rimmed bowls, and lemonade enjoyed in frosted glasses. Lobsters are caught and boiled and dressed, all on the same morning; a perfect light lunch for a hot day. Ladies of a sensitive disposition avoid Town Beach in the afternoons because a contingent of men have taken to cooling themselves in the water completely naked. The visitors are dwindling, but the sunshine will ensure that the season continues to the end of October, and at the assembly rooms in the evenings the men leave their jackets off and the ladies are grateful for this season's preferred full-dress: flowing muslin in the Grecian style.

In Ada's dreams, Mrs Hooke has been transformed into a giant beetle: hard-shelled, cumbersome and twitching. Stood on her hind legs she towers over Ada, and eats away furiously at the cottage as punishment for the overdue rent. Ada tries to reason with her, but Mrs Hooke consumes the outer walls as swiftly as a caterpillar eating a cabbage leaf. Ada wakes into a vague relief that is replaced quickly by despair. Her landlady hasn't paid her usual Saturday-evening visits since Edith died, but she slips her bills beneath the door each week, lest there be any mistake about the length and breadth of her generosity. Ada owes for three weeks now, and she doesn't have it.

She is lifting herself miserably from her mattress when she remembers the locket. She hasn't given it a single thought in all these weeks and she casts about in her mind for what she did with it. She hid it well, fearful of being required to explain it to Edith if she'd come across it.

Ada slips from her bed and goes downstairs to the parlour, fetching her stool and standing on it to open the highest door of the cabinet. She reaches behind the jars and tins, feeling with her fingertips, pulling out an old pocket that requires mending. She peeks inside at the decorated gold – such a treasure to have forgotten. Tipping it into her palm, she runs her thumb across the filigreed surface, snicks her nail across the catch. She opens it to check that the lock of hair has survived the seawater. She finds it shiny, sand-coloured, and imagines a lost child or husband, mother or sibling. It'll be precious, and she cannot push away the weight of this knowledge as she wrestles with herself over what to do with the thing. The pressing need for coins in her purse means it's tempting to sell it. She could ask her smuggler friends. But the lock of hair is unsettling her, and she would feel badly if she sold it. She tells herself the young woman will likely reward her for her trouble if she returns it, so decides that's what she should try to do. Anyway, it's not just about the money, or the sentimentality provoked by the lock of hair. She can't shake the feeling that she shares some connection with this woman now, despite her flamboyant turban and

154

feathers, her glossy auburn ringlets that fell so neat and pert about her rounded face. They live in different worlds, but have been brought together by what occurred, and it seems to Ada they should share at least a few words on the matter.

She's hungry now Annie Fountain has ceased her doorstep gifts. She's not been to Fisherman Caddy's cottage to exchange her rum for fish since before Edith died, so she rallies herself to the task. She gets as far as putting the bottles into a basket, covering them with a shawl, and pulling on her hat. But in the end, feeling small against the thought of the fisherman's ebullience, she postpones the visit for another day. She takes a penny from the drawer instead, and goes to the Clarkes' cottage in Cockmoile Square for a pint of pea soup. She waits in line at the window, the women in front of her declaring they've never known it so hot in October. Her stomach growls at the smell wafting from the cottage: split peas and swine bones. Mrs Clarke fills Ada's bowl, hesitating as Ada holds out her coin.

'Keep it,' Mrs Clarke says grimly, no warmth in her eyes. Ada puts the penny on the windowsill anyway and takes her hunk of bread from the basket.

'Mrs Clarke, I don't suppose you know of a lady visitor with auburn ringlets?'

Mrs Clarke snorts. She is ladling soup into a customer's mug.

'Ye think I 'ave many visitors come for pea soup?'

'Copper coloured . . . '

Mrs Clarke is calling forward her next customer, holding out a hand for payment. Ada turns and walks away, curious eyes upon her, hot on the back of her head.

She wanders to Broad Ledge where the beach is quiet. From there, she looks along to Black Ven, for signs of anyone digging. Then she lowers herself onto a flat, barnacled rock. She eats greedily, heartily, filling her belly. She needed this meal but, unsettling dream lingering on, she can't shake the notion that she's eating her own cottage. She slips her hand within her petticoats to her pocket, grasps the locket to calm her nerves.

It'll be all right.

Is this the worry her mother lived with? It's like a creature has made a nest in her ribcage, fidgeting there every other moment.

Eating the dregs of her soup, Ada glances down the beach and sees Isaac in the distance, walking along from Charmouth – his pantaloons rolled up to his knees, his feet bare. She has an urge to slip into the cottage before he notices her, and also an urge to go to him. She pulls in both directions, but in the end stays sitting on the rock.

He's walking in the shoreline and she can feel the water as clearly as if the waves were lapping at her own feet. When he gets level with her she expects him to glance up the beach towards her cottage and notice her sitting there in front of it. But he doesn't, and her disappointment surprises her. She gave him so little thought after the funeral, and felt only vaguely sorry when she saw who it was she'd chased away with the hammering of her rolling pin. But now she *does* feel sorry – troubled by something indefinable.

She eats her last mouthful of soup, and heaves herself to her feet. Walking home, she leaves her bowl on her doorstep while she rinses her hands in the pail, wipes her face with a splash of water. She's just about to go through into the kitchen when the creature in her ribcage wakens. What if she never speaks with him again? It seems odd that this troubles her. Standing in the doorway, stroking the hank of rope with its knot at the end, she tries to imagine what she'd say to him. There is nothing, though, that doesn't make her crumple inwardly, so she decides to leave it. *He doesn't matter*, she tells herself.

Then she finds herself fetching him a fossil.

Lifting her skirts a little, she makes off at a fast stride down the beach until she can see him ahead. She slows, embarrassed at the thought of her hollering and hammering when she chased him away the other day. She must have seemed as deranged as the sack of bones she keeps beneath the floorboards. Did it seem to him that she'd come apart? She supposes it did, and she hesitates. But she pushes her doubts aside, running to catch up with him.

'I brought you something,' she says, coming alongside him, holding out the palm-sized nodule. It is smooth and grey, with a crack running around its circumference. Her breath is laboured and she does her best to calm herself.

'Ada.'

She tries not to stare at his lip: this part of him so unusual that her gaze is drawn constantly towards it. The scar between his nose and mouth is thickened and raised, and it tugs at his face when he speaks.

'Here,' she says, gesturing for him to take the rock.

He lifts it from her palm without touching her, and she takes a step backwards. He turns it over, inspecting its plainness. It looks utterly unremarkable. He looks at her, questioningly. Curls of hair shift about his face in the breeze, soft and flighty.

She gestures for him to give it back to her, and he does as he's told. She crouches, positioning the nodule against a rock and taps it with her hammer. On the third blow the nodule splits apart, revealing a crystallised ammonite within. She passes the two pieces to him and he looks at them with awe, laughing with the joy of it.

'Remarkable,' he says. 'Truly remarkable.'

After a moment he holds them out to her, but she shakes her head.

'They're for you,' she tells him.

Please don't offer me money, she thinks. He looks as if he might be considering it, but then he glances at her and smiles.

'Thank you. They're beautiful.'

'So you've come from Charmouth?' she says.

'It's where I'm lodging, it's quieter there. The quaintest inn on the river.'

Ada knows the place; she delivers the smugglers' lace there often enough. Perhaps he's not as wealthy as she presumed.

'I didn't know it was you the other day,' she says.

He shrugs his knapsack into a more comfortable position on his back.

'You're at liberty to say and do as you please. How can we live, if not honestly? Does knowledge not begin in the body? In what we *feel* . . . ?'

He seems to think better of saying more, and turns for a moment to glance at the calm of the water, all ripple and shadow. Wisps of white cloud hang airily above them, waves kissing at their feet. It's one of those days that holds its breath, and for a moment Ada holds hers, wiping the dampness from her top lip.

'Are you finding any solace?' he asks.

'The skeleton I uncovered has been a distraction. I don't have it all yet, but even incomplete it's . . . it's very exciting.'

Is it *solace?* she wonders.

'Exploring the mysteries of the world, what better for a broken heart?'

He holds her gaze, and somehow she knows that they each

think the same thing: that her endeavour is riven with conflict, tainted by the bargain she made: *Take it all, but give me this.* Tears fill her eyes – she cannot help them.

'It had been raining, Ada. It was a tragedy – not your fault at all.'

She turns away to look at the sea, the horizon, anywhere but his face.

He clasps his hands together.

'Every day, my heart aches for you,' he says.

She pulls her shawl more tightly about her shoulders, turning back to him.

'We did try our best, didn't we?'

'We did everything we could.'

She wants to believe him, and tries to feel the weight of his words.

'Let us sit a while,' he says.

They move away from the lapping waves and sit on a rock each. They rummage in the muddy shingle, passing gritty finds to one another. They speak about seaweed, and tide-times, the autumn late to arrive. They speak about grief, because he asks, and keeps asking, and tells her about his own dead mother and how she used to bring him and his sister and brother to Lyme every summer for her birthday. That she would have been fifty this year on the first day of November, had she lived.

'On All Saints' Day,' he says.

'You said she died on All Saints' Day.'

He nods, sadly.

Eventually they talk about smaller things, and what they are doing with the afternoon. She asks him where he was heading.

'I wasn't sure,' he says.

'You should go to the wishing tree if you haven't been.'

'I know nothing of it.'

'It's in the woods by the river near the Waterside Factory. People go there when desperate – paying for a wish by hammering a coin into the bark.'

Isaac seems to contemplate this for a moment.

'How will I find it?'

'Follow the path by the river and it is thirty yards before the factory, just a little way into the woods. It's a great tall oak, with two trunks entwined. You won't miss it.'

'You could take me there?'

It has been an hour of something unexpected, and she feels lighter because of it. But she knows how quickly that can fall away; how easy it is to say something that causes the conversation to falter, something that brings the clouds rolling in, dark and heavy.

'I can't.'

He scowls playfully.

'I have things to do,' she says.

'What things?'

'A skull to find.'

She rubs at the filigreed gold in her pocket again, like a secret charm.

'Let me persuade you,' he says.

She shakes her head and he looks away from her. Pushing himself to his feet, he shuffles his knapsack onto his back.

'Very well. I shall make do without you.'

She watches him for a while as he walks away, and the desolation that settles beside her feels as real as a living person. She has to look away from its darkness, forcing herself to think about the skull and how exactly she should look for it next. She thinks about the locket, too, and how she cannot search for its owner today because she's used up all her words (she has more of Edith in her than she sometimes cares to admit). She'll look for the head of the sea beast, she decides, because the cliff doesn't require her to make conversation.

But all she does is sit until the day slips away.

Eventually, shivering in the cold of the evening, she sees a fire being lit down the beach and a small crowd gathering. It'll be the Marshes and the Greens – families that have fished together for more than a hundred years. She watches them settling, their bonds and fights and losses sitting like ghosts between them as they draw close to the blaze, a bottle of rum passed from one weathered hand to another.

Something rankles in her, but she isn't sure what. Perhaps the knowledge that she's wasted the whole afternoon doing nothing. What has she learned? What has she gained? Is she any closer to earning her rent? She feels a stab of regret that she didn't go with Isaac to the woodland and the wishing tree.

In the distance, the fishermen start up singing. Everything has darkened to black silhouettes, and feeling invisible she creeps close to their circle. She watches them jibe and tussle as they sing their tales of men lost and women won. Ditties ribald and raw. Their singing billows smoky in the night. Their laughter, too. Their voices are rough as sand, smooth as honey, and they wrap around her, heavy as a blanket. Closing her eyes, she lets them hold her.

CHAPTER THIRTY-SEVEN

*A*da closes the door quietly behind her, burdened by some notion that she's intruding, despite knowing the Fountains will be pleased to see her; they are never anything but welcoming. Still, she is here to apologise for her lack of gratitude for Annie's gifts, and Ada feels nauseous at the thought of the conversation ahead – that it cannot be navigated without some mention of Edith, and Ada is plagued by the notion that no one must touch the memory of Edith but Ada herself.

She takes a breath and steadies herself, relieved that Josiah is busy with a gentleman at the counter. Together they run their fingers across samples of fabric, murmuring soft words back and forth. Josiah glances up, visibly startling at the sight of Ada. He drops the samples upon the countertop, removes his eye-glasses, bustles a quick apology to the gentleman, and hurries towards her. His round cheeks are rosy-pink, his thick and curly hair standing up in grey tufts. He takes her hands in his and kisses one, then the other.

He looks at her kindly, sympathetically. She has always

known that Josiah and Annie pity her. It is well meaning, and mixed with other things: a shared interest in learning, a mutual love of John Winters and respect for everything he believed. But beneath it all there is also pity. *Don't* do *that*, Ada wants to say. She wishes only to be treated like an equal.

She forces a smile.

'Annie will be so relieved,' he says. 'You should go straight up.'

'May I first . . . ?'

She nods vaguely at the shelves, and he gestures with a flick of his hand that of course she may. The gentleman – like a robin, she thinks, his red waistcoat flashing beneath the brown of his frock coat – turns to look her over. Ada is dressed in her best clothes, but still she feels his disdain. He likely wonders what a poor woman such as she is doing in Josiah Fountain's shop. She looks away from him, and he turns back to his binding cloth.

She peruses the shelves, pressing her palm to her father's work every few paces. She pulls a copy of *Melmoth the Wanderer* from the shelf, turns it over in her hand, considering how she would have it bound if she were buying it. What colour would she choose for a lost soul wandering the earth?

At a table by the bay window there are a multitude of magazines laid out: *Bell's Life in London*; *The Gallery of Fashion*; *Amusement and Instruction*; *The Harmonicon*; *The Children's Companion*; *Journal of the Royal Society of Medicine*. She reaches out for the latter, but then sees the transactions of the Geological Society slipped beneath it and extracts that instead, opening it at the contents page. Instantly, as if the letters have jumped at her eyes, she sees Edwin Moyle's name. She has to read the title of his article multiple times before she can fully absorb it. He has written about their find. And she is suddenly at sea. The idea of her name in this journal is like a cresting wave – irresistible. But she knows it will not be. Her breathing quickens and she drowns in the swell of a single thought: *Where are my fossils?*

Edith was right.

Without turning the pages and reading the article she understands that Edwin Moyle has tricked her, and stolen the paddle bones away. She closes her eyes, with her finger pressed against the title of his article. She cannot bring herself to flick through to the correct page. Her disappointment and anger, like thunder and lightning, fight for supremacy.

Somewhere far behind her – it may as well be in another shop down the street – there are the small sounds of Josiah's customer leaving. The polite farewells. The dull shunt of the door closing. There is the quiet clack of Josiah's footsteps, and the bustle of his tidying at the counter.

Ada forces herself to turn one page at a time until she reaches page twenty-seven. The picture that accompanies the article is beautiful. The bones protrude from the page, inviting her to reach out and feel their rough bumps, their peaks and plateaus. It is a short article and she reads it in one nauseous swallow. Of course he didn't mention her. He spoke smugly of *his* find, of Lyme and Black Ven. He described a marine reptile that will have coexisted with the ichthyosaurs. He indulged in some comparative anatomy, pointing out the thickened centrum of the vertebrae, the elongated digits – so different to the piscine characteristics of the ichthyosaur's paddle.

Josiah is there at her elbow, and Ada finds that she cannot speak. She can hardly move at all. It is all she can do to angle the paper in his direction and point to the article. Josiah shuffles it towards himself, pushes his eye-glasses onto his nose.

'Ah! A Lyme find!'

'*My* find, Josiah. This Dr Moyle has tricked me and presented these fossils as his own. He takes credit for my discovery.'

'These are *yours?*'

She nods, thinking of the skeleton and the missing skull – how unsettling it is that this creature has been stolen apart.

'You sold him these fossils?' he asks.

'I let him borrow them! He was supposed to return them to me.'

'Do you have an address for this Dr Moyle?'

Ada's cheeks flush hot.

'You must write to him!' says Josiah. 'Tell him he's acted impudently and demand he makes amends. I'll help you with your letter. We can scribe it this very minute, if it would please you.'

Josiah strides back to his counter, and Ada watches him reach to the shelf beneath for his writing materials. He inspects his bottles of ink, gives one a little shake.

'We don't need to waste the paper. I believe he's in Lyme, still,' says Ada. 'He told me he was staying until December.'

'But you don't know his whereabouts?'

She shakes her head.

Josiah rubs his scalp with his fingertips, as if stimulating his thoughts.

'No matter, we can think about that later. A letter is still the way to proceed, and it most certainly will not be a waste of paper.'

She goes to Josiah, and slaps her hand upon the counter top.

'I will not write to him if I can look him in the eye and speak directly.'

He regards her cautiously.

'I ... I think sometimes a letter is better; it allows one a certain composure.'

'I don't feel the need for composure.'

'But what we wish to say is better heard by the recipient when it's there in black and white, without sentiment clouding matters. We must avoid the risk of misunderstandings.'

'He's stolen something from me and presented it as his own. What facet of that, what *fact*, could be misunderstood?'

'It is only that . . .'

Josiah casts about for the right words, and Ada watches him, patiently.

'It is only what?' she says finally.

'Let me advocate for you, Ada. Let me write this letter on your behalf, and let me investigate his whereabouts – it won't be so difficult.'

'I can speak for myself.'

'Ada! I know you can. But *should* you? You don't speak this man's language. It's as simple as that.'

'I'd make myself understood perfectly,' says Ada quietly.

'I don't doubt it, but the situation requires a little subtlety.'

Ada looks Josiah straight in the eye and reads there a little of what he thinks of her. Not for the first time she feels as if she doesn't belong in this world. There is nowhere that she fits. She is an oddity to all, and she is sick of it.

CHAPTER THIRTY-EIGHT

*A*da fills her hawking basket with a small selection of prize fossils. She nestles her largest crocodilian snout into a piece of clean linen so it looks precious and enticing – just the thing a wealthy *flâneur* may wish to purchase for his curiosity cabinet. Delivery of it to Dr Moyle will be her reason for stepping into places where she most definitely won't be welcome.

Beneath wheeling gulls, she walks towards town. She can't tell if it's the stench of rotting fish that churns her stomach or whether it's her nerves. In between rehearsing the conversation she's about to have, she grinds her teeth until her jaw aches.

Cockmoile Square bustles with carriages, carts and drays. Barrels are being delivered to the Three Cups, and a crowd is gathered out the front of the customs house. Reaching into her pocket, she clutches the gold necklace in her fingers briefly – inspired by its cold, delicate finery. There is tuppence in her pocket also, and later, if she's recovered her appetite, she'll reward her endeavours with a muffin from the boy on the corner, or a mug of pea soup.

Ada enters the assembly rooms, sensing her trespass as soon as she brings her muddy boots onto the polished floor. She sheds sand with every step and the boards creak loudly beneath her feet, as if alarmed by the audacity of her intrusion. The blue walls are stencilled with tangled vines, and the light from the chandelier reflects back and forth in the tall mirrors that face each other across the room. Men of distinction look down at her from the walls: dead, but still superior.

The murmur of conversation and the clatter of breakfast things draws her gaze through into the tearoom. There is the smell of kippers and eggs, of rich, pungent coffee. She turns towards the main room which looks out across the sea, and as she steps into it she finds three maids sweeping, and a barkeep polishing glasses behind his bar.

A man is suddenly there in front of her, his broad frame blocking her progress. He's ushering her backwards and away before she even has a chance to speak.

'Out!' he tells her.

'I've an arrangement to meet Dr Moyle,' she protests. 'He asked me to deliver this to him. He said he'd see me out the front, but he isn't there.'

'Well, he isn't here either.'

The man has hold of Ada's elbow, and he steers her out of the room and across the reception hall. She tries to show him the fossil, as if it might impress him and make him think for a moment. But he isn't interested in looking at what she has in her basket. He wants her gone, and nothing could be plainer. She asks whether he knows where she might find Dr Moyle, conceding she has obviously mixed up their arrangement, but insisting he was most keen to purchase this specimen for an article he's writing for a geological journal. She gabbles

168

keenly, all the time trying to slow down the momentum of her departure.

'We are fellow fossilists!' she says desperately. As if this sliver of truth will make all the difference. But it doesn't, and she's out upon the street with the door being pulled closed behind her.

Gathering herself, brushing off the insult, she proceeds to the Three Cups, and then to the Dorchester Inn. It's the same story at every destination: po-faced staff, no better than she, looking down their noses at her. They tell her that they cannot help. They couldn't possibly divulge where Dr Moyle is lodging, and they certainly haven't seen a young woman matching the description Ada offers. *Will she now please leave?*

Ada is making her way up to the Packhorse Inn on Combe Street, when her arm is grabbed, roughly enough to make her stumble a little across the cobbles. A pain slices through her shoulder and she turns to find herself in the grasp of Mrs Hooke: landlady, beetle, encroacher of dreams.

'Mrs Hooke,' she stammers.

Forceful fingers are digging into her arm and she tries to pull away, but her landlady keeps hold of her. A diversity of worries flood her in an instant. Ada has been calculating lately how little she could eat and how long she could manage with no fuel at all. How deep would the winter need to be before she couldn't bear it? Could she make it to January? Or February – that cruellest of months with its icy coat and spindrift hair? She has wondered whether Annie and Josiah would put up with her in their shop; whether she could be of some use to them? Or whether she could warm herself in the chapel? How often could she visit Pastor Durrant under the pretence of poring over books with him in his parlour by the fire? But she can think of nothing now except the sensation of Mrs Hooke's iron grip. Her landlady inspects every inch of Ada's face, searching for something there. Her mangey stole hangs limp between them, and Ada smells its musty scent. She forcibly drags her arm away, rubbing at it.

'Well, this is a happy coincidence.'

'Is it?' says Ada coldly, stepping away.

'I was planning to drop by, but you've saved me the bother.'

Ada swallows.

'You owe me rent, and it's time you paid.'

Mrs Hooke's accent is drowned beneath short vowels and careful aitches. They share this in common – their struggle to better themselves for the sake of business (Edith used to complain about Ada's changeable accent, accusing her of chicanery).

'It's four weeks that you'll owe on Saturday.'

'I—'

'I suspected as much,' she says, looking down into Ada's basket. She reaches for the crocodilian snout.

'That's not for sale.'

'What are you doing with it then?'

'Delivering it to a Dr Edwin Moyle. He's purchasing it from me. I'm supposed to take it to his lodgings, only I've forgotten now where he said he was staying. I don't suppose you've come across him? A tall gentleman, greying at the edges. He's a doctor from London.'

Mrs Hooke's eyes narrow.

'I also need to find a young woman with copper ringlets. It's just I have something for her also. All for the rent, if the truth be told.'

'They're a couple?'

'Oh no, not a couple.'

170

For a moment it seems as if they're conversing on an equal footing. But then Mrs Hooke heaves a great sigh.

'Ada,' she says, 'I'm giving you your notice. We both know you don't have two pennies to rub together. It were bad enough when there were two of you. Don't try and pretend you can manage this situation on your own.'

'But it's my home.'

'It were your mother's home.'

'And the lease was for three named lives; it's supposed to come to me.'

'My patience has worn thin, Ada.'

'But if I can pay you, then I can stay?'

'My objection is that this will always be our struggle, and how tedious that will be.'

Ada's breath is ragged, panic purling through her.

'But if it wasn't? If I could pay you a whole year's rent in advance, then you would let me stay?'

Mrs Hooke laughs, leaning for a moment on her stick.

'If I *could*, though?' says Ada desperately.

'Well . . . what can I say to that? If you pay me a whole year's rent upfront then how could I possibly object to you staying?'

She laughs again, and continues to laugh as Ada takes her leave and makes her way back down the hill, smarting, cheeks aflame.

CHAPTER THIRTY-NINE

Edwin

*R*eturning to his lodgings after his whist club at the assembly rooms, Edwin pauses beneath the glow of the street lamp to regard the house from the outside. There's no sign of anyone at all; every window its own pattern of darkness. The family who were staying in the upstairs rooms left yesterday, and Edwin's housekeeper must have finished for the evening a little earlier than usual.

As he enters the house he feels a chilled rush of air against his cheek, and it makes him feel, for a brief moment, that he's not alone. If he believed in ghosts then he might find himself hesitating, but he pushes the door closed behind him without a second thought, presuming only that a window must have been left open in one of the rooms.

Illuminated in the small pool of light that falls through the glazing of the door, he removes his coat and hangs it upon the stand. He inspects the three keys in his hand, selecting the correct one. His footsteps are his only company as he makes his way down the darkening hall. Fumbling his key into the lock, he realises the cold breeze is coming from within his own apartments; he feels it trickling across the back of his hand as he turns the key. He calculates, certainty slipping, and when the door swings open he knows instantly, despite the impenetrable gloom, that something is terribly amiss.

At the sideboard he lights the lamp and the ransacked room comes slowly into focus. He goes firstly to his trunk and discovers with utter dismay that the lock has been forced and the paddle bones stolen.

He drops his head into his hands.

For many long minutes all he can do is contemplate the loss.

His most important possession has been taken from him and he feels bereft. Then furious. Then grateful for small mercies: the etching and letter he has already posted to the Geological Society.

A quick look around tells him that the thief knew what they wanted. This was no chance burglary; all his valuables are where he left them. He thinks briefly of Mr and Mrs Fountain who came yesterday with their polite letter, checking on the whereabouts of the paddle bones and Edwin's intentions with regards to returning them. And he thinks of the artist, with whom he spoke about the fossils excitedly and at great length, expressing in no uncertain terms quite how special they are.

Surely he isn't the thieving type?

And then there is Miss Winters herself. But she wouldn't jeopardise her own ambitions by behaving like a common thief. *Would she?*

He fills his pipe and goes to the window, inspecting it for

signs of a forced entry. Finding no damage at all, he struggles to make sense of what has happened, and to fathom a plan of what he should do. He peers hopelessly into the darkness outside, as if he might find the answers there. He can see nothing of the unlit garden, but he imagines the intruder creeping through it; how they came and how they went. His thoughts swirl sickeningly, and he slams the casement shut with a growl of fury.

CHAPTER FORTY

*A*da strides up Combe Street, weary against the hill, passing the chapel and remembering, with a rush of remorse, how badly she treated Pastor Durrant. How badly she has treated them all – this tiny number of people in the town who do not yet hold her in disdain. Her father always insisted that she mustn't take from others if she doesn't have something to give in return. A few years ago when she sold Annie and Josiah her father's books, she asked them to keep half their payment back so she might feel comfortable reading the journals in the shop and consulting their subscription library and making use of their letter-writing services occasionally. It's impossible to know whether they consider this money now spent; they have kept no ledger as far as she knows. She understands that her father gave the Fountains his friendship and affection – something which Ada has benefited from all these years. But surely that will wear thin, like Mrs Hooke's patience? How can she possibly quantify such a thing? She doesn't like to think about it; whether the value of her father's friendship with Josiah and Annie has now dwindled to nothing. She remembers her rejection of Annie; her refusal to answer the door. What was she thinking?

You weren't thinking, were you, Ada?

Edith has taken to commenting on things in the black shadows of Ada's mind; crueller than she ever was in life.

Ada crosses Gosling Bridge and passes the Angel Inn, cutting between the houses on Mill Green and walking across the meadow towards the river. She navigates the trees, her basket chaffing against her arm. Her fury flickers, heating her from within. It is like lightning, this feeling. The kind that crackles in the clouds on a summer night, ancient as rain.

At the wishing tree she falls to her knees and runs her fingertips across the hundreds of coins that have been hammered into the bark. Like a coat of armour. She has never paid for a wish before; has never felt the need to ask for one. She runs her hand across the silver, wondering at its value. A fortune. And here for the taking if she'd be willing to also take home the ailment, the approaching death or the financial ruin that was bartered away. Nobody steals from the wishing tree. Even those who mock the lore don't risk helping themselves to silver from its tired bark.

Ada reaches into her pocket and pulls out the tuppence she'd hoped to spend on something for her supper. She takes her hammer from her basket.

Does she truly need what she thinks she needs? *Does* she need to stay in the cottage? But she's hardly posed the question before the answer rears up: *I cannot leave it!* Her home is where her father is. And it was her father who made her feel she belonged in this world. Who showed her that what could be seen and touched and created could be relied upon. The tree, the timber, the craftsman's hand. 'Do not lose yerself in superstition and tall tales. There be so much wonder in the world. Ye only have to open yer eyes to see it.' He'd remind her that the wonder and magic of the universe is right there in front of her – not hidden in mystical realms.

Ada holds her coin to the oak, thinking only of the sea dragon's skull. As she conjures the creature complete, returned to itself, it comes alive in her mind, and she comes alive with it: alive and whole, as if she belongs. The article she intends to write forms in inky curlicues in her imagination; the thought of copperplates metallic upon her tongue.

'But I need the skull.'

Her mouth waters for this resurrection. And at the same time she feels a fraud, because she doesn't truly believe in the wishing tree.

'Bartering like a fool,' she whispers.

Choosing a fable over a mug of hot soup.

Holdin' wi' the hare and runnin' wi' the hounds?

Gramfer used to say that of her when she prevaricated; that she was no better than those who say their prayers just in case. Is it true? Who does she think she is, aligning herself with the best minds of the geological world, while standing here at the wishing tree of Lyme?

What do you believe? She hears her father's voice as if he were right beside her.

'I believe in what's here!'

It's the answer he'd want.

And she *does* believe in what is here; she believes in the sea dragon and all it has unsettled.

'*I* found it. And *I* will write about it.'

It's her father she's speaking to, as if he needs convincing.

Her words will be published.

Her knowledge will be welcomed.

She will, in time, have colleagues who understand why she spends her time at the rock with her hands in the clay. Who appreciate the practicality of wearing a pair of breeches and a smock-frock and do not judge her for it.

She fingers her coin, undecided. And then she places the hammer back in the basket, pushing herself to her feet. She slips the tuppence back into her pocket and allows herself to think of the hot meal she'll eat instead. She doesn't need to make a wish. She mustn't look to a world beyond her own. There *is* no world beyond her own, she reminds herself. No fairies, no sirens, no sea buccas. No wild wolf woman of Lyme. There is the past, and there is now. There is mystery and wonder. There are questions – endless questions.

On the way home, all is swallowed by darkness. Corvids call from the trees, rough and bawdy. Wet leaves mulch beneath her feet as she walks. Her breath fogs in front of her face, skin tingling with the chill, and the sea air breathes upon her, moist and salty.

The water murmurs, saying nothing.

At her door, Ada notices the parcel only when she trips across it, stepping into the kitchen. She has to grope for it in the darkness, pat at it with her palms. There are no embers in the grate to light a candle. There are no candles.

At the table, she feels at the folds of linen, her breath uneasy with anticipation. She knows what this ought to be, but she hardly dare hope for it. Tentatively, as if unfolding some unknown horror, she peels back the fabric. She runs her fingertips over the muddled cluster of fossilised bones, smiling with relief. The paddles have returned to her.

CHAPTER FORTY-ONE

*A*da returns to chapel on Sunday, where she's met with curiosity, and the steady gaze of too many eyes. She's conscious of being alone, here in this place where before now she was always with Edith. Her loss settles in the pit of her belly, and all she can do is feel her way to the pew that had always been theirs. She steps inside it and closes the door behind her. She sits, relieved to be enclosed in the small, dark chamber of polished wood, the rest of the congregation now obscured from view. Perhaps they stare at the outcrop of her hat, but if they do she doesn't feel it.

Tall windows at the far end of the chapel let the sunshine stream in. Let *God* in, Pastor Durrant likes to say. The ornate lectern looms in the splendour of that light – its great height demanding that the minister climb nine steps in order to preach to his flock. His parishioners must crane their necks if they wish to meet his eye. The lattices of window glass – gold panes of dazzling autumn sun – make Pastor Durrant a spectral silhouette. His words, though, are sure and steady, solid as the Portland stone that built this chapel. His doubt is undetectable; his duty indomitable; he works hard at this. Each night, before retiring, the floorboards unforgiving beneath his knees, he prays for certainty. His whispered supplications are winged creatures in the night, heaven-bound, joining the thousand others that slip beneath doors and tumble from chimneys, fluttering together in the air like jack-o'-lanterns.

Despite loathing the nosy scrutiny, there is some consolation for Ada in the reassuring pattern of murmured prayers, the togetherness that requires no conversation or physical proximity, just a hymn book balanced on her palms, the smell of leather and fusty paper (reminding her of Fountain's Muse, and the circulating library – places where her father remains).

When the service is over, she stays where she is, waiting for the small congregation to leave. Nobody tries to speak to her and she's glad; all her composure will be needed to look Pastor Durrant in the eye and apologise for how she behaved. She must speak of his generosity, she reminds herself. She must use the words *sorry* and *forgive me*. She must remember her manners and swallow her temper, which every day bubbles inside her like a hot spring. Her hands are shaking, and she balls them into fists, burying them beneath her shawl. Perhaps he won't forgive her? She tries to imagine whether it would matter. Whether it would feel like another loss, or whether it might be a relief of sorts. There's a simplicity to being alone, after all. It's less tiring, less perplexing, less vexing.

Ada sits in the silence of the empty chapel.

When Pastor Durrant comes, he opens the door to the pew and sits beside her, placing his hands upon his knees. He smells strangely comforting: milky and sweet.

'Here we are, then,' he says, after a deep, deliberate breath. His countenance seems the same as ever – solemn, but hale and hearty with it. Although, then he says, 'My feelings have been quite disordered these last few weeks, just as yours must have been. How *do* you do?'

After a pause, she tells him, 'I am Lyme in November: rooms shut up and beach deserted.'

He laces his fingers together, ponders a moment.

'I would wager your library remains replete with books?'

She laughs at that, looking sideways at him. He smiles in return, cheeks flushing.

'I wanted to say that I'm sorry.'

He lifts his hands to dismiss her apology.

'I shouldn't have shut you out,' she says. 'It's just ... '

'There's no need,' he insists. 'I quite understand. We are friends, after all, are we not?'

She finds herself unable to answer. *Are we friends?* she wants to ask. She knows if she stays here long enough he'll ask something of her and she'll have to disappoint him. His request will seem reasonable to him, and when she refuses he'll think her difficult. If she were to ask for what she wants then *he* will disappoint *her*.

Is this friendship? So much expectation. So much disappointment.

She sits mutely, remembering what Isaac said to her: *How can we live, if not honestly?* But her words have caught inside her. Would it be easier if they were sitting at her kitchen table with some rocks spread out in front of them? That is, after all, how they have worked best together. But it seems an eternity since they sat across from one another and spoke about oolite limestones and lias clays. Or about the bivalves, gastropods and corals found in the strata of seemingly identical sandstone. It has been so long since they picked over a fossil together, or spoke of some outcrop down the coast, some escarpment inland.

The whole of the world seems to have changed since they last conversed in this way.

I cannot offer you anything beyond that, she wants to say. *Can we please return to our last Sundays of the month? Tea leaves in a twist of paper?*

I could look forward to that, she thinks. *I can give you the last Sunday of every month; is that enough for a friendship?*

'Can I speak plainly, Ada? Without offending you?'

'Of course.' She looks down at her hands, waiting for whatever offence he must now speak plainly about.

'The time has come to be realistic. Your mind is sharp, but you're blinkered to the ways of the world. You'll make yourself ill, not to mention destitute, if you insist on your current path.'

He pauses, looking round at her, and she feels the intensity of his gaze on her cheek.

'You're going to suggest the answer to my troubles is marriage,' she says.

A sharp silence sits between them, cold as a blade.

'Why don't we go through to my parlour?' he says, his tone clipped, no better than the silence.

'I don't want tea. I want you to understand what I'm doing and why it matters,' she says. 'I have the complete skeleton of a new species in my possession. I only need the skull, and then I can sell it to the British Museum.'

He gives a half-shrug.

'It's an exciting find, Ada, I don't deny it, but it won't solve your problems. It's not a solution.'

'Are you truly my friend? Because if you are, then you'd make greater effort to listen to what I'm telling you. This creature is my future. It's everything I want, and it *is* a solution.'

'It's not as simple as that. This is just what I'm speaking of.

182

You make these plans with such confidence, but you have no grounds to be confident. Even if you find this skull and sell the beast, it won't provide for you for any significant length of time. You're only postponing the inevitable.'

He's speaking again in his usual tone – slowly and calmly, as if delivering a sermon.

'It would fetch one hundred pounds,' Ada says. 'Perhaps even one hundred and fifty.'

'Poppycock!'

'Why are you permitted to speak with such confidence, when I am not? Small ichthyosaur skeletons sell for sixty or seventy pounds. This is an entirely new species. And it's a *monster*!'

'Let's imagine you fetch one hundred pounds for your skeleton. How long will that last?'

'It would've taken my mother three years to earn that.'

'And you would spend it in two, if you were frugal; the cost of everything is still soaring.'

'That is time enough!'

'Those years would soon pass, and what then? A find such as this is once in a lifetime. And that's presuming you do find the missing skull. It could be anywhere, Ada. Are you going to search the whole cliff? It's insanity.' He turns towards her. 'But I *do* understand your passion and have a vision for how we can help each other.'

'I cannot help you,' she says, shaking her head.

'You've not heard me out.'

'I know what you're going to say.'

He sighs gently, a wisp of air, like a draught beneath a door.

'I'm leaving the ministry.'

Her breath catches in her chest and she looks at him askance. 'But it's your vocation; your one true path.'

'It is my vocation to listen to the word of God, and that's what I'm doing. I may not consider animal extinction and evolution as heresy, but the vast majority of divines still do. I can't continue ministering whilst being so out of step with my spiritual colleagues and parishioners. I've never felt closer to God than I do today, but my time as minister of this chapel is at an end.'

Ada's mouth hangs open. It's too much sudden alteration from a man who has been hitherto as predictable as the tides. She feels a shiver of excitement at the notion of giving up such a significant part of oneself. Who is he, if not their minister?

'It's very brave,' she says.

'I've wondered, in fact, whether it's cowardly, but this chapel will soon be empty if I continue here. I'm called in a new direction, and I believe it's the same road that you wish to take.'

He looks at her expectantly.

'I . . .'

'You see yourself as a fossilist – a geologist. Well, I see the same for myself. I intend to join the likes of Buckland and Young in search of answers that reconcile the physical laws of natural history with the word of God; to pursue a kind of scriptural geology.'

'You'll be leaving Lyme?'

'Not necessarily, but perhaps. These are details yet to be decided. In the first instance, I wish to persuade you that we should embark on this journey together.'

Ada scrutinises him, his pale skin flushed pink and his eyes bright with possibility. He looks at her directly, and she has to force herself to hold his gaze.

'You mean as man and wife?' she says defiantly.

'We are more or less both outcasts,' he says. 'I fair slightly better than you, I grant you that. But not much more. My reputation, as a consequence of publishing my article in the *Dorset County Chronicle*, has been damaged beyond repair. I'm not a wealthy man, but I have a small annuity from my brother's estate. They're an eccentric lot, if the truth be told, and they'll not care who I marry. I'll be an old man before I know it, and I don't wish to be an old man alone. We have so much in common, you and I. And I'm fond of you, despite everything.'

The wooden walls of the pew are closing in, the space smaller and smaller by the moment. Her mother was right, of course, and Ada had been fooling herself because it suited her. But Ada had also been right: *it is not like that between us*. And it isn't. No matter what he proposes, she doesn't see a future where she is *wife*. She simply doesn't have it within her. An acorn will never grow into a beech – will never *wish* to be a beech.

'I don't want to,' she says.

He sighs. 'I would have thought it was an offer you'd be grateful for.'

'I know why you'd think that, but there are things you don't know that make your suggestion impossible. If you understood them, you wouldn't want me.'

She thinks of these things. How they are like stains that won't be shifted, no matter the scrubbing. It must be growing colder, for she's trembling now.

'I don't believe it,' he says. 'I consider myself well acquainted with your deficiencies, and not one of them is insurmountable. Putting them aside, you have much to recommend you.' He turns to face her more directly. 'You're like an ammonite not yet revealed to the world, yet to be cleaned and polished. I'm not fooled by your unwashed hair and patched garments. Isn't

185

that a thing we share in common – our capacity to see beyond the surface?'

Ada swallows down his insults.

'I cannot leave my cottage.'

This is the easiest of her reasons to speak of; it's the place to start.

'It seems that way,' says Pastor Durrant, 'but you would find it isn't true. When it comes to it, there would be some sadness, but that is all. I could take care of everything. You wouldn't have to go through the trial yourself; I'd spare you all the pain of it.'

He reaches out, rests a palm atop her clasped hands, and she's grateful for the woven wool between her skin and his.

'I can't be married because I don't wish to do what you'll expect me to do. I don't want children.'

He slips his hand away and places it on his knee.

'I suppose I've always known that you . . . '

She waits for him to finish, curious about what he thinks he has always known. But his inchoate sentence hangs there in the chilled air between them.

Her anger simmers, fuelling her. She had thought that per-haps if Edwin Moyle returned her pilfered fossils her spring of fury might ebb away, but it hasn't. There are, it seems, still things to be angry about. Her defiance comes flooding out, and she finds that she doesn't care what impact her words have – she only wishes to say them – finally – aloud – and to have someone else hear them.

'The thought of a child growing inside me makes me sick, and perhaps that makes *me* sick – to be a woman, and to feel this way. I don't know what it makes me, and I don't really care. I only know that this part of me won't ever change.'

These sentiments are met with silence.

Eventually she says, 'I remember going with my father to the famous surgeon of Dorchester. Father was making cabinets for his specimens. He had organs pickled in jars. Hearts and brains, kidneys and livers, wombs and testicles. He had a foetus, too: curled up inside a membrane. It struck me how clearly it resembled what I'd imagined. It had *always* horrified me – a body within another body. But after that visit to the surgeon's rooms, it became the kind of horror that kept me awake at night.'

Pastor Durrant turns to look at her with such an expression that it occurs to Ada that perhaps her honesty has had the desired effect: he sees in her now a deficiency too deep, a crevasse that cannot be bridged. A singular regret rushes through her, surprising and painful. Has she been a fool? *Again*, has she been a fool? Is he offering her a solution that might, in the fullness of time, prove acceptable? She remembers the rent that needs paying, the threat of being without a home at all. *He is a good man.* Her mother's appeals come pouring over her. *Ye need a husband, and Pastor Durrant is a better match than I have ever dared hope for.*

She cannot feel it now, but she knows the essence of him to be steady and resolute. His is a warming presence (sometimes too warm: sickly warm; heavy as a tub of hot water). The solidity of him is not unlike the solidity of her father, and the similarity is not lost on her; they spark memories of each other at times, as if her mind confuses their spirits. It's perplexing that such a thing should happen, because the two men (who hardly met) are not really similar at all. But something about their souls is similar, however unlikely that is and however much John Winters would have scoffed at the notion of his soul. It makes her want to take back her speech of the last few moments. To think again, more carefully. But instead, against all sense and logic, she digs on, down into the clay of their relationship.

'I do not care for your scriptural geology. I do not wish to proceed with an inquiry that has, at its outset, decided the outcome. I wish to always be guided by what I find: by the evidence presented to me. This doesn't matter so much if we proceed as colleagues. But as man and wife? When God is your calling? We have avoided too much discussion of it, but you know I have my doubts. My faith is weak. Why are you so intent on a partnership, when you know there'll be discord between us? And in great quantity.'

Pastor Durrant remains mute. He holds his hands in his lap, looking down at them.

'You're full of fear, Ada. But the word of God is a comfort, if you open your heart to it.'

'I've opened my heart to a past almost infinite, and to an earth so changed and yet seemingly immovable. I open my heart to the dead things that were once living things. And I open my heart to questions, in the hope of answers.'

'God is there in every layer of every inquiry. And it's his spirit that warms us when the world is cold and dark.'

'You see God everywhere, because you always have. You weren't given an alternative. You say that you look beneath the surface, but you don't. You look at everything around you as evidence that God exists. But the wonder of the world is not evidence of God. It makes no sense to suggest such a thing.'

'I feel him in my heart, because I'm willing to.'

'Because you *wish* to!'

'But here you are in chapel?'

Ada wants to laugh. Is he so naïve?

'There are plenty of good reasons to come to chapel,' she says. 'And most of them have nothing to do with God. My father came every week, with no faith at all.'

Pastor Durrant turns away from her.

'And I do not love you,' she says.

'Ha!' He throws up his hands. 'Ada, I do not love you either!'

The spell is broken and she begins to laugh. She cannot help herself, even though she sees his face is stony, chiselled with hurt. She brings her cold, trembling hand to her mouth to stem the choking sobs. *We do not love each other!* She doesn't know why it seems so funny, but it feels good for that spring of anger to have turned in on itself for a moment. To feel something else.

'I'm sorry,' she says, trying her best to swallow her laughter.

He stands, and opens the door to the pew.

'Despite all your efforts to reject the notion, I stand by my suggestion that the two of us might travel a path into the future together, albeit with compromises – *on both sides*, I assure you. I'll not humiliate myself by asking you again. But take the time you need to consider the matter properly.'

And then he is striding away, his footfall heavy on the stone floor of the chapel.

CHAPTER FORTY-TWO

Edwin

With Sunday afternoon stretching ahead of him, composing letters to Christina and his father serves as a welcome distraction to the outrage of the stolen fossils. He must contort himself in his missives – eluding and eliding – and by the end of an hour's writing, he feels himself ill-used by all.

As a reward and comfort, he takes a pip of laudanum, then another, and belligerently a third; to hell with the consequences.

His agitation soon meanders with the patterns on the wallpaper. His umbrage is the twisting vine and his disgruntlement is sumptuous fruit – ripe and weeping, hanging heavy. But not grapes at all, now he looks closely. With the curiosity of a child he sees that these dangling fruits are, in fact, testicles, naked and scrotum-less. The housekeeper (he hadn't realised she'd be doing her rounds, but here she is) laughs at that. She winks, flashes a fossil femur at him from within her skirts.

You, he thinks. *You took them, didn't you?*

Then the Fountains are there in the wallpaper too, sopping wet and wringing their clothes into puddles on his floor. He has been through all this, turning the possibilities over and over, settling on the most likely answer: the Fountains and the housekeeper together.

Josiah Fountain has the face of a rabbit, snuffling and inquisitive. But it wouldn't have been *Mr* Rabbit who orchestrated the purloining. Mr Rabbit is something of a ditherer, good-humoured and well-mannered. He'd have been content to deliver his note and leave it at a quiet word. *A gentle reminder who the bones belong to*, as he put it. *Mr* Rabbit trusted Edwin when he said he was, *of course*, returning the fossils to Miss Winters. But *Mrs* Rabbit is another creature entirely. Beneath her lace and ribbons she's nothing but thumping feet and sleight of hand. Mrs Rabbit, he is sure of it, conspired with the housekeeper to ransack his things while he was at his whist club.

He flies at the sopping shape of her, grapples her by the throat.

He could report her to the constable, doesn't she realise? She squirms in his hands, no longer a gushing fountain, but an actual rabbit – smooth fur and hot belly, and her hind legs punching at him best they can.

He laughs at her feistiness. To kiss? Or not to kiss? She might soften if he kisses that furry mouth. But he doesn't trust her not to bite him. *No kiss for you*, he tells her, holding her at arm's length as she writhes and twists.

With no surprise at all, he finds his spare hand has transformed into a cleaver, and so he holds her down and chops off her feet. Then he throws her across the room and she limps away, back into the wallpaper – every hop a bloody mess.

CHAPTER FORTY-THREE

*A*da goes to the Fountains' bow-windowed shop, and tells Josiah that the paddle bones have been returned to her.

'Does that have anything to do with you and Annie?' she asks.

'Annie and I found Dr Moyle's lodgings and delivered our letter to him. He was quite pleasant when we spoke.'

'He's a pretender, Josiah. He had me believing we'd be colleagues of sorts. It never occurred to me he'd be so duplicitous.'

She remembers then, though, how she sought his assurances that the fossils would come back to her; so perhaps she doubted him all along.

'I grant you, it doesn't explain his decision to cut you out of the article, but I believed him when he said he had every intention of returning the fossils.'

Ada doesn't wish to argue.

'He'd been poorly with a chesty cough,' says Josiah. 'And then heard the terrible news about your mother. He was waiting for the right time, that's all. I'm sure he admires your abilities and sees your talent as a geologist. You *are* worthy of their society, even if they won't have you officially.'

Ada folds her arms, thinks bitter thoughts.

'I should thank Annie,' she says. 'I've not seen her since Mother's funeral.'

'Get yourself upstairs, then.'

'Is she cross with me?'

'Get away with you!'

Ada ascends the rickety steps and in the darkness of the hallway knocks quietly at the room the Fountains use as their parlour. At the sight of Ada, Annie brings her hand to her heart.

'What have you been thinking all these weeks?' Her voice is quiet, but rinsed through with emotion that trembles deep in her throat.

Ada doesn't know what to say and finds herself reaching out and touching her fingertips to Annie's shawl. Annie pulls Ada into a fierce embrace and then releases her, holding her for a moment at arm's length.

'You funny onion,' says Annie, shaking her head. 'Make yourself comfortable while I go down and make a pot of tea.'

Annie returns with tea and slabs of cake, thick and buttered. Josiah follows on behind her, balancing cups and saucers.

'I've locked up and come to join you.'

He puts everything down on the little table and throws some coal onto the fire.

'So we might be cosy,' he says.

They settle into the soft chairs, and Annie pours their drinks.

They speak of Edith, briefly, falling into silence as they sip their tea and nibble their cake.

'I'm in debt to you now,' says Ada. 'For the funeral.'

'You owe us nothing,' says Annie.

'But you must think about finding work,' says Josiah. 'There's no question about that. We were happy to pay for the funeral . . .'

Ada explains how she intends to speak to Mr Muir about her mother's scouring job and whether she might have it. The Fountains nod approvingly, and murmur words that make it clear to Ada she must find a way to support herself, and swiftly. The cost of the funeral can be forgotten about – they say this again, as if it needs spelling out. The implication, Ada realises, is that they've been generous enough. And all of a sudden the topic is a hot coal that's rolled from the fire, each of them staring at it in silence and none of them wishing to pick it up. So Ada says, 'I have news!'

She tells them about the creature she has taken from the cliffs. She doesn't confess to collecting some of the fossils in the wake of Edith's death or that it was the landfall itself that exposed them. She explains that with the paddles returned, she has an almost complete specimen.

'I plan to commission a drawing,' she says. 'And then I'll write two letters. Firstly, to the Geological Society informing them of what I've found. Secondly, to the British Museum offering them the opportunity to purchase it.'

'This is *fantastic* news,' says Josiah, his face alight.

'It doesn't matter that the skull is missing,' she says. 'It would be better to have it, of course . . .'

'You are quite the talent, Ada,' says Josiah. 'Your father always said so – how astute you are.'

'But you must be more circumspect,' says Annie. 'You cannot trust these men. I remember clear as anything what

William Smith told us when we met up with him in Oxford a few years ago. This was before he received any recognition for his wonderful map. He said the geologists he'd had dealings with were, almost without exception, pilferers of information, seeing it as their right to regard all unpublished observations as lawful plunder.'

'They treated him atrociously,' says Josiah, nodding grimly, 'whilst all the while benefiting from his tireless graft and meticulous observations. How many mines do you imagine he descended to complete his map? How many canals did he help to build? How many miles did he trudge on foot in all weather? He got his hands dirty to create that map!'

'But he wasn't *one of them*,' says Annie. 'And you'll never be one of them either, Ada. He says they thought him provincial and uneducated, no matter his masterpiece of craftsmanship. His geological map was the first of its kind, and by all accounts invaluable. It hangs now in the Geological Society rooms, but for more years than you've been alive he was offered only paltriness and condescension. We've had the whole story since. I had no idea what the poor man suffered – plagiarised, exploited, disregarded and ignored for decades. It's a wonder he's so happy in his old age.'

'I have just downstairs told Ada that she *is* one of them,' says Josiah. 'Even if they *won't* have her.'

'Well, you shouldn't delude her. She's a geologist, I give you that. But she'll never be part of their little circle. It's a dinner club, you know. William told me. Fifteen shillings each! It didn't matter how clever William was with his theodolite and plain table and chain, he was always just an unlettered Yorkshireman in their eyes. And you, Ada – you live in a humble cottage on the beach, the daughter of a tradesman, and you're a woman!'

I've already thought of this,' Ada says. 'I'll write my letters under a false name. A man's name.'

'But what if this Edwin Moyle is suspicious, and tries to lay some claim to your find?' says Annie.

'Then he will make himself look like a jealous, grasping fool. He currently knows very little about this creature, and the complete skeleton will be presented to the geological world as an entirely new specimen. My correspondence will say that it was taken out of the cliff much further down the coast.'

The fire spits in the silence that follows. Annie is swallowing her mouthful of cake, licking her fingers, staring into space as she contemplates what Ada's proposing.

'Well,' says Josiah, then. 'It's not such a bad idea. I've a good friend in Dorchester that I could confide in. We could use his address, so the whole thing is completely unconnected with Lyme.'

Pleased with themselves, they spend an enjoyable half an hour ruminating on Ada's pseudonym, in the end seizing on *Adam Gray* (her mother's maiden name).

They also discuss whether Ada should write in person to the society and accuse Edwin Moyle of taking credit for a find that wasn't his to take credit for.

'Sensible to steer clear of accusations,' says Josiah. 'Surely the truth will out?'

'Ever the optimist,' mutters Annie.

Ada senses she has something more to say on this matter. But when pressed, she grudgingly agrees with Josiah.

'Best not to make trouble,' she says quietly. 'The fossils are back with you now, that's all that matters.'

They decide that Ada will compose her correspondence and return in the following few days, at which point Annie will scribe the letters for her. She has an exceptionally neat hand, and the finest ink and paper. Adam Gray is certainly a man of quality and would use only the very best. His worth must bleed from the page.

CHAPTER FORTY-FOUR

When Ada calls at Isaac's lodgings she finds that he's out for a walk. She leaves a message for him, requesting that he comes to call on her as soon as he can: *Will you bring your drawing things?*

After hurrying home, Ada drags the sacks of bones from beneath the floorboards. Carefully, with pride and excitement, she lays the fossils out. Reaching from the far end of the parlour, right into the kitchen, the long-necked sea dragon languishes. Headless, but magnificent. Cleaned up and polished: sternum, vertebrae, bones of the pelvis. Four paddles: each one as long as Ada's arm, the fine finger-like bones drifting across the floorboards as if reaching for something. There are four vertebrae between the last dorsal vertebra and the carotidal, with exceedingly fine ribs attached.

No sooner are the creature's bones restored in their rightful order, than Isaac is rapping at the door. She beckons him in, stepping back.

'As I live and breathe ...' he whispers. 'Is this my commission?'

'You'll have to forgive me . . . '

'It will be my pleasure.'

'Once it has sold . . . '

'I don't need to be paid. You have no idea . . . to draw a creature such as this. To be the first to do so . . . even just to lay eyes on it.'

He crouches to touch it, reverent as a lover. He peels away his coat, kicks off his boots, rolls up his sleeves.

'You're a wonder,' he says, looking to Ada at such a moment that she doesn't know whether he speaks of her or the dragon. He runs his hands through his hair and she fancies that she smells the woods upon him: soil and leaf. She smells the aroma of his body too, and the wool-grease from his coat, the leather of his boots.

'It's a secret,' she says. 'You must promise not to mention it to anyone at all.'

He looks at her curiously and she tells him of all that's happened. Her ammonite drawings that were not returned, her rejection by the society, Edwin Moyle and his article. Isaac stands at the tail of the creature, his arms folded across his chest.

'You should keep it,' he says, looking at the walls of the parlour, at the feather art of heaving waves. 'You should find a way to mount it upon the wall, and charge visitors a shilling each to come and look at it.'

'I want to sell it to the British Museum.'

'But then it'll be gone from here, which would surely break your heart?'

'My heart is already broken.'

His eyes drift from her, back to the floor and the assembled bones.

'Anyway, I wouldn't like people traipsing through my home. I . . . '

But she shakes the thought away. It's too cumbersome to put into words, how she feels around folk; the intrusion she experiences when in the company of others.

'Why does it need to be a secret?'

'I'll sell it under a pseudonym, Adam Gray. I'm not sure what I intend, only that it seems possible to progress in that world if they believe me to be a man, and a man of some standing. Josiah and Annie are going to help me.'

'So perhaps Adam Gray is a reclusive? A man of letters and articles. Not a man who appreciates debating over dinner.'

'Precisely.'

'You want to have some fun with them.'

'It's not so much that.'

She thinks about it for a moment, organising thoughts that are new to her and not yet fully formed.

'They don't want me in their society because I'm a woman. If I conduct myself cleverly then they *will* want me. I want them to *want me* at their society dinner table.'

'You wouldn't want to *be* at their society dinners. You wouldn't enjoy them – they'd be different to how you imagine and you'll find them insufferable. It doesn't matter what you discover, or what you have to contribute. They'll find ways to diminish you because you've pulled the wool over their eyes. They'll not be pleasantly surprised to discover the truth. You'll have humiliated them.'

Ada shakes her head, dismissing his predictions.

'You don't need to bother with them,' he says. 'You don't need their approval, and you don't need this recognition that you think you need. Who *are* these men? They don't matter.'

'Except they do matter; they're building a world of knowledge I wish to be part of.'

'But to be a part of that world you will have to pretend to be something that you're not.'

'The world is full of artifice, Isaac. Being a woman has demanded so much pretence from me; being *Adam* will not feel so difficult.'

He looks at her for a long time without speaking.

'I'm going to write a letter,' she says, 'and send them your drawing. I'm going to offer to write an article about my find. I know they'll want me to, and they'll also want to see the skeleton. They *do* matter, Isaac. I just need to prove myself to them, before they know who I am.'

He looks unconvinced, but he says, 'Very well. If you think so.'

As he admires the angles, curves and rhythms of the skeleton, the beat and song of this creature, from the shelf she brings a small jar. She crouches beside him as he unfurls his rolls of paper, weighting the sheets with rocks that he takes from the table (he doesn't ask permission, and she doesn't mind). She shows him the contents of the jar – a dark powder.

'Sepia ink,' she tells him. 'From a fossil I found on this very beach.'

'I don't understand.'

'It's from a fossilised cuttlefish; a belemnosepia. I found the anterior sheath and ink bag perfectly preserved, and inside the ink bag I found this powder. I ground it and discovered it to be perfectly usable. I've been waiting for something worthy of its use.'

'How old are these fossils that you love so much? *Old*, yes, I know, but *how* old?'

Ada inhales, lets the question wash over her. 'Well, there's much debate about that, but certainly older than is easy to imagine. Millions of years.'

'Millions . . .' he says, contemplating it, gazing down at the jar of powdered ink.

'The world all that time ago was so different to now,' she tells him.

'Different how?'

'In the beginning there was no plant life at all – only rocks. Then came ferns and mosses. Then conifers and reptiles. Vast forests covered the planet and everywhere was so much hotter – so everything grew much larger. Giant tree ferns reached forty feet in height. There were reptiles of enormous magnitude; vertebrae ten inches wide have been discovered from gigantic lizards called Iguanodon. A metatarsal has been found that measures fourteen inches in circumference. Do you know what a metatarsal is?'

Isaac shakes his head.

'It's a small bone in your foot, and yours would measure less than an inch in circumference. Can you imagine *fourteen inches*? For a *metatarsal*!' She splays her fingers to approximate such a size.

Isaac watches her intently, and she's suddenly brim-full with all that she wishes to share with him.

'And just think! We only know it from digging in the ground. A man called William Smith – an uneducated man, a drainage engineer – has mapped the whole of England, describing the stratification of the rocks: layers upon layers that have been formed over millions of years. These layers show that there wasn't one moment when life was created, as the Bible suggests, but that living creatures gradually came into being. That first there were simple invertebrates and that they gradually became more complex. So much life inhabited the earth for such a great stretch of time, long before man.'

'First there were cuttlefish?'

Ada smiles. 'First there were cuttlefish.'

'I don't dare use it,' he says, looking at the powder.

'Better you than I,' she laughs.

'I think not!'

'I think so!'

She takes the jar to the kitchen table and adds a few drops of water, stirring it with a netting needle, bringing the ink back to life.

He crawls around his paper on the floor like a child. He measures the bones, and the spaces in between. He draws first with his pencil, and Ada watches the creature materialise upon the page – a diminutive version of itself. He asks about the neck, how long and slender and tapered it is.

'If you look at it this way, might it not be the creature's tail?'

Ada smiles. 'It's curious, isn't it? Like a serpent, threaded through a turtle. But I'm certain.'

She fetches her notebooks and shows him the hundreds of skeletons she has copied from books and journals over the years. The ichthyosaur skeletons she has found and sold. She speaks of anatomy – of invertebrates and vertebrates, of amphibians and lizards and mammals. He interrupts her three times, to scribble lines of poetry in his pocketbook.

'You are good for my poetry,' he says.

Isaac insists they stop to eat luncheon, pulling apples and cheese from his knapsack. Ada heats some soup, and between mouthfuls she tells him about her gramfer, who, for a man who barely ate, had plenty of words for his meals: dewbit and nuncheon, cruncheon and namnet.

'He loved words and tales and riddles.'

'He sounds fascinating.'

'*Touched*, they used to say. *Away with the fairies.* He must have been blind towards the end, his eyes all clouded over. He said he could see as well as any of us, but he never moved much from his stool so maybe he didn't. He'd chunter on all day, one story running into the next.'

'Tales of the wolf witch?'

'He never told the same one twice, at least not in the same way. He'd gabble on as if she were an old friend. He saw her looking in at the window or out there on the beach.'

'Tell me his favourite.'

'I don't think he had favourites.'

'Tell me *your* favourite then.'

Ada pauses, opening the cubbyholes of her mind, and tumbling out comes that ancient woman with wings and wolf furs. Silver coins stitched in the lining of her threadbare, fur-lined coat. Beetles in her fists and songs in her lungs. Before Ada realises it, she's deep inside the rhyme and rhythm of one story more than any other, and so that's the story that Isaac gets.

'You know,' he says when she finishes, 'these tales could only come from a life lived close to the earth and far from vanity. All goodness and art withers in the face of artifice, and *this* is what divides common folk from the genteel. Everything sublime, obscure and boundless is to be found in the simple things. In nature and the wilderness.'

'Is that what we are, you and I? Common and genteel?'

'Low born? Nobly born? A man of quality? A woman of trade?' He says all this while looking at her directly. He has sat down at the kitchen table, and begins tracing his fingertips over the unvarnished wood. 'I mean no offence.'

Ada sighs. 'I know.'

'After my mother died, my father sent me away to live with one of my mother's cousins. Good people who work the land for a living. I was taken from a world of servants and leisure and put on a working farm. They've been good to me, and I live there still. I owe them so much that I took their family name. I keep the books, and deal with matters of development, of drainage and fertilisation. I lend a hand when it's busy, too. I don't mind getting the soil beneath my nails; it has taught me much.'

'What exactly has it taught you?'

'What I have just explained. That the world's true riches are not to be found in the hands of the better sorts.'

Ada shakes her head. 'It's easy for you to say.'

'But it's true; you don't know how these people live.'

'And you don't know how *we* live. A little dirt beneath your nails once or twice a year doesn't mean you know what it is to labour.'

'I *have* laboured!'

'And how many days have you gone hungry? How often have you been looked down upon, as if you're no better than a rat scavenging scraps?'

Isaac holds her gaze for a moment and then looks away.

'I'm sorry,' says Ada, realising that of course he's been looked down upon.

'You are right, though,' he says.

'It doesn't matter. Tell me about your brother and sister; did they get sent away to the farm too?'

'It was only me that my father couldn't stand to look at.'

He touches a finger to his lip, and Ada feels a stab of shame.

'When I was born it was completely separated, all the way to my nose. He never grew accustomed to it like my mother did. If anything, she seemed to love me more because of it, which my brother hated. The men in my family were glad to see the back of me.'

'I'm so sorry.'

'When my mother died, my father disinherited me, left his title to my brother instead. So we are orphans both, you and I.'

Ada nibbles a piece of cheese.

'How often did you come to Lyme?'

'We came each year, always lodging at the Three Cups. My father only came the once, and it was the year there was a flayed horse strung up in the harbour.'

'That happens sometimes,' says Ada. 'For bait.'

'It was there all week, the fishermen hacking off great chunks. Father could see it from his bedroom window and it *thoroughly ruined the view*!'

Ada smiles.

'What about your sister?'

'She was ten years younger than me. I used to write to her, but she never wrote back. My father didn't spare the rod and was a clever manipulator, so goodness knows what she'll have been told. You wouldn't like my father, Ada. No one with a kind heart likes my father.'

'Did your mother not have a kind heart?'

'My mother liked him least of all!'

Isaac scrapes the bowl with his spoon, then uses his finger as if he'd never been taught any table manners at all, licking smears of juicy fat from his skin. Ada lifts her bowl to her face and uses her tongue. She catches his eye and he bellows with laughter, his face a beautiful contortion of twists and dimples.

CHAPTER FORTY-FIVE

*D*r Moyle takes her completely by surprise, there on the doorstep in shades of blue, his cravat nestled beneath his well-shaven chin. He is full of apologies, telling her that he'd had no intention of keeping the fossils for so long.

'I didn't wish to intrude on your grief,' he says. 'That's all it was.'

He presses his hand to his breast, as if he speaks from the heart.

Do not talk of my grief, Ada thinks.

'You announced our find,' she says. 'You made no mention of me at all.'

'I can explain!'

'You can offer excuses, you mean?'

'Would it be all right to step inside, do you think?'

She regards him stolidly. Part of her wishes to refuse him, but genuine curiosity gets the better of her. She turns and walks away, straight into the parlour, hearing the snick of the door latch behind her.

'The range isn't lit so I can't offer you tea.'

'It's quite all right.'

She gestures to Edith's chair and he sits, casting his gaze about the room.

'I see you've had your men digging all week at Black Ven,' she says.

'They are yet to find anything. I thought we might discuss it, actually – the possibility of resuming our work together.'

She shakes her head, flummoxed.

'I'm sorry you felt the need to involve your friends in contacting me,' he says.

'I tried to find you myself, but you'd taken leave from the Angel Inn.'

His gaze flickers from the floorboards to Ada's face, and back again. It surprises her, but he looks genuinely remorseful. Embarrassed, even.

'I regret it now, not being more diligent in my communicating with you. I was busy entertaining my wife and father and found myself making a few decisions which, once made, ran away with me somewhat. But all that is nothing more than excuses, and I should have come to see you in person, especially after what happened to your mother.'

Do not speak to me of her.

'What you should have done is mention me in your article. Instead, you cut me out completely!'

'I suspected you were feeling this way,' he says. 'The letter Mr and Mrs Fountain brought to me contained within it the suggestion that you feel yourself ill-used, and I'm keen to make amends so you might think of me more favourably again.'

'I shall not sacrifice myself to politeness by telling you I do *not* feel ill-used. Because of course I do! Would you not? How dare you present my fossils to the society, claiming them as your own?'

'It was a starting piece – something to whet the appetite. What happens from now can be a joint venture and I promise you, from the bottom of my heart, that I'll credit you in the future. In fact, I'll communicate to my friends at the society immediately about your involvement. It can all be put right!'

Ada watches him, waiting for what he might say next. She's aware that her hand is the stronger; the tables have turned. He knows nothing of the creature beneath the floorboards. He's ignorant of the fact she's already found what he's looking for. That his men are out there searching in vain. But then she thinks of the skull she is yet to find. They are all now looking for this missing piece, whether Dr Moyle realises it or not. And what if he finds it before she does? She doesn't wish to make this whole thing a competition. At least, not openly.

He is fidgeting in his chair (it has never been a comfortable seat). Then he pushes himself to standing, looking about the room. He sidles to the cabinet, seeking permission to open the drawers.

'Are you looking for the paddle bones?' she asks.

'Are they here?'

There is an edge of uncertainty in his voice.

'I have them in safe keeping,' she says.

'Oh, *good*! Good! That's marvellous to hear.'

His relief is obvious, and it confuses her.

'Things must be difficult for you,' he says, 'with your mother now gone.'

Ada lifts herself from her chair and retreats to the doorway that leads to the kitchen. She turns to face him, leans against the doorframe and folds her arms.

'I'm managing,' she says.

'I'm wondering whether I might employ your services, if

you'd be willing. It wouldn't offend you, would it? I could pay you a weekly wage to help with searching the cliffs for the rest of the creature. And I'm more than willing to pay you for the bones we already have – for half of them, say. We could see them as jointly owned then, and progress together from now on in a search for the rest of it. I'm exceedingly anxious to smooth things over and get us back on an even keel.'

Ada feels the nudge of possibility, of opportunity, the prospect of coin in her purse. She is made queasy each morning when she wakes and remembers Mrs Hooke threatening to evict her. Sometimes she struggles to sleep because of her hunger. And yet she is still to visit Mr Muir about a job at the mill. Each day she intends to go, but then something holds her back – her anxieties fighting one against the other. She needs regular money to pay her rent, but she cannot battle through her fear of that building; how it would wreck her to step inside it day after day. She has been justifying it to herself by dreaming of the sea dragon, of the British Museum, of Adam Gray emerging onto the geological scene, making a name for himself and earning her some coin in the process. She needs a year's rent as soon as possible, not a weekly wage.

'I don't want to sell you a share of the paddle,' she says, meeting his gaze.

'Ada . . . ' He rubs the side of his face with his palm, looking for his words. 'I'll pay you handsomely. I'm quite sure you could do with it.'

'You make it sound like a kindness.'

'I wish to prove myself to you, to make amends.'

'By buying me off? I'd rather my name in the society journal!'

'I'll be frank. Your landlady introduced herself at the whist club, and proceeded to confide that you'd been looking for me with some fossils to sell. She told me you're in arrears, in danger of losing your home.'

Ada flares, blushes, heat suffusing her.

'I don't need your charity.'

'Great Caesar's ghost, I'm offering you my patronage! I'm offering you . . . a partnership!'

'And again, you make it sound like a kindness. But a partnership of what? What are *you* bringing to this partnership? What we have between us are the paddle bones of a new species, which were found by me and belong to me. And by the sounds of it, you believe it is *I* who stand the better chance of finding the rest of the creature. So why exactly do you think you have any right to be standing in my home offering me a partnership of something that is wholly mine?'

He takes a step towards her and she steels herself against his proximity. She smells the combination of perfume and tobacco again: his aroma that had been strangely enticing when he introduced himself on the beach. *Like something from the bakery at Christmas*, is what she'd thought. It's not what she thinks today, though; today it turns her stomach.

'And I believed that we *had* something of a partnership,' she says. 'But you betrayed it.'

He raises his palms, in a gesture of conciliation.

'You are quite right, of course.'

His tone does not match the placating nature of his words. He sounds tired and irritated. He reaches into his pocket and brings out a netted purse.

'Let me pay you up front for a month of working with me on the beach. What about four guineas?'

It's more than three times what she'd earn at the mill in a month, and she feels herself waver.

211

'I have it right here,' he says.

It's so tempting to take his money, but it would make her a cheat because she knows that what he searches for is no longer there. And although *he* cheated *her*, she still cannot justify it. She doesn't want to carry with her the unease of constant lies and pretence. He's muddied this whole thing thus far, and she doesn't wish for it to be muddied further.

'Think about it, Ada. You say I bring nothing to this partnership, but that's not true. We've seen exactly what I bring: access to the Geological Society and space in the pages of their transactions. I *know* these men; we are friends and colleagues. They'll take note of me if I approach them about a new find.'

'They'll take note of anyone who finds a complete skeleton of a new species.'

'They may, if you're lucky, make a note of your name. And then again, they may not. Their interest will be in the find itself, and you'll be nothing more than a fortunate curio-hunter. You wouldn't be invited to our meetings or be able to write your own article. Somebody else would write about it. But I can find a way for you to be introduced. *We* can present *our* find. *We* would write *our* article. Under my wing, you'll get some of what you want. Which is better than nothing.'

'I'll think about it,' she says.

He has taken coins from his purse and he fidgets with them, jostling them in his palm as if the heavy sound of them might tempt her. He looks back to the cabinet and the specimens on display. He goes to it, and she watches him, noticing what he shows most interest in. These are the fossils that are precious to her; those items which, when Edith was still alive, she refused to part with. But everything has changed, and they have ceased to matter. Keeping her home is all that matters now.

'Two guineas and you can have them both,' she says. 'It's a fair price.'

Despite the fact it's *not* a fair price, he doesn't hesitate. He holds out the money to her and she quickly picks the coins from his palm.

'I'll think about your suggestion,' she says, and walks through into the kitchen.

She opens the door, flooding the cottage with the shrill cries of the guillemots, and the slow dance of a chilled breeze.

'You'll get caught by the tide if you don't go now,' she tells him.

He hurries away with the skull of a juvenile ichthyosaur, and a large rock covered with scores of tiny pyritised ammonites.

And that night she settles down to sleep with gold beneath her pillow.

CHAPTER FORTY-SIX

*A*da falls asleep composing her letter to the Geological Society of London. Then she dreams of a vast land mass that she knows, in the fug of early sleep, to be the beginning of everything. Not the Garden of Eden, but arid, windswept plains and salt flats. A land scorched and bare, subsumed eventually by roaring oceans that cascade and flood, then lap benignly, warm and fertile. She wakes in the early hours, bewildered by a sensation of this other place, exhausted by the thrill of it. She tries to return to sleep, to rest, but to no avail. She has no candles, and must wait for daylight.

Once there is light enough to complete the task, she writes a draft of her letter in her notebook, picking over every word: *A new species of marine reptile that likely coexisted with the ichthyosaurs. William Conybeare has suspected such a creature may have existed because of some unusual vertebrae found in a collection of ichthyosaur bones in William Bullock's Museum of Natural Curiosities, in the Bristol Philosophical Institute. This new creature is similar to the ichthyosaur by way of its multiarticulate paddles, but the paddles are also distinct from one another: this beast's paddles are long, wing-shaped,*

highly elongated – we might posit that it flew through the water, as
birds fly through the air. The humerus and femur are much the same
size, so the difference between the length of the anterior and posterior
extremities observed in the ichthyosaur does not exist in this creature: all
four paddles in this case are approximately the same length. At the point
of the clavicular furcula there is a complex apparatus of bones, and this
reptile's sternum suggests it moved through the water quite differently to
the ichthyosaur. The specific details of the vertebrae suggest the same. In
addition, the coracoid bones have a somewhat greater length from their
anterior to posterior tip than might be expected. The creature has strong,
closely spaced ribs that extend to the sides as well as belly ribs that rein-
force the undercarriage, forming a stiff, bony cage for the body. The ribs
articulate throughout, on a single head. Most worthy of note is that the
body is small compared to the neck, making it quite unlike any other sea
creature; this specimen has thirty-five vertebrae in the neck alone. Cuvier's
anatomical work has laid to rest any thought of unearthing the remains
of the mythical creatures that exist in the pages of literature, but still
we might be forgiven for thinking of this new species as a Sea Dragon.

Ada writes it out several times, editing and polishing, reading it aloud. Eventually, she is content with her efforts. And as
if they had arranged it such, Isaac knocks at the door just as she
places her pencil on the table for the final time and turns her
thoughts to whether there is a crust of bread left in the house
that might appease her growling stomach.

He has barely entered the kitchen before he opens his knapsack and pulls out his ink drawing and a pencil duplicate. She
runs her fingertip across the careful dark-brown lines.

'The ink is so beautiful,' she says. 'And your drawing
is perfect.'

She imagines this impressive, professional illustration alongside her careful letter. Surely it will have the desired impact?

'And look!'

He unrolls a third piece of paper, upon which he has painted a depiction of an ancient ocean teeming with life: the sea dragon resurrected, lithe and graceful among fish and squid, turtles and ichthyosaurs. He has imagined the head of her ancient creature to be half crocodile, half ichthyosaur. It is a fair approximation, she thinks, looking at its saucer-like eye, its gnashing teeth. Until they know better, it will suffice. This other-world he has created feels real as anything, as if he straddled those thousands of years and saw a place with his own eyes that they cannot possibly be sure about. That cannot be known or proven. *Of course* it cannot. But as she looks at his picture, she's aware, nonetheless, of its significance and validity. And of its *wonder.* How bewildering it is that she dreamed of such a similar place. That their imaginations took them there separately. She muses on this for a moment, something shifting in her own mind, a realigning of belief and perception. An alteration that she cannot yet name.

'It's for you,' he says, oblivious to the shunting of her world.

Her throat thickens, tears stinging her eyes, although she doesn't know why.

'I can pay you . . . ' she says, thinking of the two guineas still beneath her pillow.

'I don't want your money, Ada. We're friends; it's a gift.'

She glances at him, embarrassed, confused. Reaching out, she takes the painting and gazes down at it.

'I'm sorry,' she says. 'I'm a little strange at the moment.'

He laughs gently, lowering himself onto the stool by the range. After she's taken in every detail of the painting, she goes through and puts Isaac's gift in the parlour. When she returns to the kitchen he's watching her, and she notices something different in his face. He looks pensive, as he did on the day of her mother's funeral.

'What is it?'

'Only that someone told me something about your father, and I wanted you to know.'

'People say all sorts,' she says, breathless at this news, although she shouldn't be surprised; the town folk still love to tell the tale of his death.

He nods, scrutinising her, hungry for the story. *Something has whetted your appetite*, she thinks. *And now you're like everybody else.*

'Were you asking people about me?'

'*No*. The innkeeper spoke of him, when he gave me your note the other day.'

'Don't tell me. I don't want to know what he said.'

She waits, letting the silence pool between them like something spilt. When Isaac says nothing more, she reaches for her notebook to flick through the pages, reading her letter again. She feels an urge to send him away. But his generosity sits four-square in her chest; she can't ignore it, however much she wishes to.

'I have an arrangement with Annie and Josiah,' she says, not looking up at him. 'We're writing Adam Gray's letters this morning.'

She swallows the rising emotion that is partly sadness about what people say about her father still, and partly disappointment in herself: how quickly she is altered, how squally she is within.

'I'll walk that way with you,' he says.

She shakes her head.

'*Ada*,' he implores.

'Oh, very well.'

She gathers her notebook and, sheepishly, Isaac's drawing of the sea dragon.

She drinks from the pail outside, because she's all of a sudden desperately thirsty and has nothing else to drink. *I have nothing to offer you*, she thinks. *You have come to my house with something for me and I have offered you nothing in return.*

She feels all at sea as they walk along the beach together, hardly talking. She takes him down Long Entry, past the butter market and the Guildhall. And there she stops, on Bridge Street, with the River Lim flowing beneath their feet.

'My father organised a protest about the price of bread.'

She speaks softly as she explains that he and a handful of others had formed themselves into a Friendly Society and sworn illegal oaths.

'Other Dorset men had been arraigned and convicted of the same crime just weeks before, and were on their way to Australia for a short life of hard labour.'

She tells him how John Winters and his friends marched through the twisting streets of Lyme gathering supporters, passing the Guildhall where they shouted the loudest, finishing at Cockmoile Square where the lacemakers sit out in good weather with cushions in their laps. There, he stood atop two barrels and raved about how the wars with France – the blockade of European ports and the food shortages and soaring prices that followed – had lined the pockets of the wealthy. *The common labourer has not seen his wages rise in a good long time,* he told them. *Workers have been whittled into paupers reliant on parish charity. Our babbers be cold in their beds while them there landowners live in luxury!* And just as the crowd sent up a roar of agreement, John Winters was struck by a bolt of lightning as if God was outraged by the words he spoke. There was the smell of burning flesh, folk said. The taste of singed hair at the back of their throats.

It feels moth-eaten, her knowledge and memory of his demise. As if she'll turn to it one day and it'll be nothing but dust and scraps in her hands.

'What a fearless man your father was,' Isaac says. 'You were fortunate to have him.'

They begin walking again, in the direction of Silver Street.

'Is it the story you heard?' she asks him.

'There are different ways to tell the same story.'

'My mother never forgave him,' says Ada. 'As if she believed what they said – that he'd brought it upon himself. That it truly was God's wrath that killed him. "Why did he do it?" she kept asking me. "Why?"'

'Because he saw injustice every which way and was angry about it.'

His words are careful stitches, pulling the memory of her father back together again.

Ada stops walking and turns to look at him. The urge to reach out and grab his coat is overwhelming, to somehow fight and tussle her gratitude into him. But she pushes away this instinct that seems decidedly animal – the play and wrestle of a wolf with her young. She has to blink away the strange thought of biting his neck.

As they walk in silence again, she realises it's the first time she's spoken of her father's death so directly. The first time she has recounted *her* version; similar to her mother's version, but without the lacquer of anger and blame. The first time she's heard mention of the gossip around his death without falling into a black mood. The first time she's been reminded of the injustice of it all and not been taken captive by it, tossed about like a ship in a storm. And she's not sure what it all means.

But that she's strange at the moment.

Thinking of justice and tales juggled into different versions, looking for some distraction from the strange impulse she feels to playfight and bite, and thinking of making him happy – of offering him something he wants – she turns to him with a story about the wild wolf woman of Lyme. A tale of seven sisters who sneaked away from their marital beds every full moon to dance together across the Dorset moors. She tells him how these women danced beneath the harvest moon and the hunter's moon, the wolf moon and the snow moon, the barley and the hare and the hay. How their husbands found them out and had a witch turn them into a circle of standing stones as punishment. And how the wolf woman released them from that witch's spell by turning them into wolves.

Isaac takes her hand and tucks it through his arm.

She feels the faint warmth of the October sun on her face even though the day is biting, and she continues to feel it even after she has stepped into the gloom of the little alleyway that leads to Fountain's Muse.

Annie and Josiah notice the alteration as soon as they lay eyes upon her.

Something is afoot, they think.

Annie is soon busy writing the two letters on behalf of Adam Gray, while Josiah shows Isaac the shop – pointing out the best of John Winters' craftsmanship, conspiratorially pressing a book of poetry into his hands (a gift), and showing him the view from the parlour window.

'How big is this creature,' Annie asks, gazing down at the drawing, before folding it into the letter.

'Seventeen feet, without its head,' says Ada.

Annie tries to imagine it as she melts the wax, readies the seal.

'Incredible,' she says, conjuring the monster in her mind. 'Just incredible.'

CHAPTER FORTY-SEVEN

With two guineas in her pocket, Ada goes to Mrs Hooke to pay her rent. Her landlady's large townhouse with roses curling over the doorway sits squat and sure of itself on Coombe Street. Carts and drays trundle past it; to and from the shops and inns.

The housemaid answers the door – a mousy girl, too small for her uniform, with teary eyes and chapped lips. Ada explains who she is, that she only needs a moment of Mrs Hooke's time; that she has come to pay her rent. She waits while the maid disappears into the gloom. She hears the sound of a door closing, then the quiet tread of the girl's hurried steps.

'You can come in,' she says, opening the door wide. It's the first time Ada has been in her landlady's home and she feels herself dither, reluctant all of a sudden. The dark red hallway stretches ahead of her – a tunnel of burgundy gloom like an animal's innards – and she has the sense of being swallowed whole as she follows the maid through the house to Mrs Hooke's wood-panelled parlour.

A coal fire is raging in the grate, but Mrs Hooke still has her furs wrapped about her. She's sitting on a kingfisher-blue sofa, the bright pink cushions tucked all around as if she needs propping up. Dogs sprawl across her feet, and she puffs on a pipe.

'Unexpected,' she says, by way of a greeting.

'I've come with my rent,' says Ada, reaching in to her pocket.

Mrs Hooke does not invite her to sit.

'Two guineas,' says Ada. 'I've calculated it'll cover eight and a half weeks. I owe for five. And in the next few weeks I'll have a much larger sum, to cover my rent for . . . well, I'm not certain precisely.'

She feels flustered then, losing steam as she tries to reckon up the impossible. In truth, she'll not have a large sum in the immediate future; sales of fossils to museums take many months to negotiate. But she has bought herself some time, and that is all that matters.

'Where did you get it, this money?'

Ada wants to tell her it's none of her business. But that's not how things work. They both know how it works. Mrs Hooke *has*, and Ada *has not*. And that simple fact determines the choreography of their dance.

'I sold two specimens to Dr Moyle. He came to see me after you kindly spoke to him in the assembly rooms.'

Ada takes some pleasure from owning this information. But she treads carefully, knowing it'd be shrewd to flatter her landlady by permitting her to believe that she herself orchestrated this fruitful transaction. It would surely make it harder for her to turn Ada away (for she's fearful of this – that talk of her eviction might have solidified in Mrs Hooke's mind since they last spoke).

'So, thank you,' she says, pressing upon Mrs Hooke this version of the story: *You have helped to make this happen.*

223

Ada recalls with some regret her bold promise of an entire year's rent, and also Mrs Hooke's hearty laughter. The memory still stings.

You have no idea who I am, Ada wants to say.

The haughty, bruised part of her that wishes to be someone other than a collector of curios living in privation upon the beach puffs her chest and grapples with how exactly to conduct herself. Mrs Hooke eyes her, takes a tug on her pipe, coughs a phlegmy cough. Then she holds out her hand to Ada, who navigates the backgammon table, careful of the snapping dogs. She keeps Mrs Hooke at arm's length, full stretch, and drops the coins into the older lady's shaking hand.

Perhaps it's no surprise that Mrs Hooke is prepared to accept her coin, the threatened eviction for now postponed. Her husband may be a wealthy industrialist, but Mrs Hooke is a keen and regular gambler; no doubt she needs her pocket money.

At just that moment the door opens and a man enters the parlour. Ada straightens, and looks to her landlady, half expecting to be swiftly dismissed.

'My son, Frederick,' Mrs Hooke says, smiling warmly at him.

Ada has never seen such an expression on Mrs Hooke's face before and is quite perturbed by it. She has to drag her gaze away to nod briefly at the young man. He is tall, striking, familiar, and she tries to place him. She finds herself staring, and *he* is staring at her in return – a blank, open expression upon his face. But then that openness closes, like a curtain being drawn, and they recognise one another at the very same moment. And as if to confirm it to both of them, he touches the skin above his eyebrow, where a purple-red scar is visible.

'It's *you*,' she says.

Immediately, she regrets having spoken the words

aloud – unable now to hide from the truth of what sits between them. Namely, his impropriety and aggression, the fear and danger of that moment on the beach, the way he pursued her and the notion of what he'd intended had he caught her.

He seems to be calculating, plundering his thoughts for how to proceed. Then he laughs, so sure of himself that it turns Ada's stomach.

'What *is* it?' Mrs Hooke demands.

'This little witch threw the stone that did this!'

'She never did!'

He doesn't look at his mother, but regards Ada, pressing a finger to his scar.

'Now, here she is in my house,' he says.

Mrs Hooke pushes herself to standing, wobbling there at the edge of Ada's vision. 'I don't believe it,' she says.

Ada looks to her landlady, desperately.

'He was attacking a young lady, forcing himself on her. I swear it!'

Mrs Hooke looks taken aback by this news. She's leaning on her cane, worrying at her stole with bejewelled fingers.

'*Frederick?*'

He goes to his mother and places his hands on her shoulders, smiling down at her.

'Mother! For goodness' sake. It was the night of the falling stars. Perhaps we kissed, but that was all.'

She searches his face, then gives a quick nod. He glances over his shoulder at Ada, a look of distaste on his face.

'Drunk as a whore this one, looking for trouble. Was it even me you were aiming at? Creeping about on the beach taking your frustration out on amorous lovers.' He turns back to his mother. 'Not *lovers*, that was a turn of phrase.'

225

Mrs Hooke pushes Frederick away and steps towards Ada. 'How *dare* you?'

Ada shakes her head, swallows hard.

'He's lying to you,' she says, the words thick and mealy in her mouth.

'My son doesn't lie to me. We've always had an understanding.'

Ada feels their hostility pressing against her and all she wants is to get away from it. She makes to leave, but Frederick comes for her, grabs an arm. She flings him off with every bit of strength she can muster, and finds herself rushing through the bowels of the house. She fumbles with the latch and key. There's the scuffle of footfall behind her, and then Frederick is there, pressing his palm against the door, leaning his weight against it.

The air is warm with his breath.

'Get away from me!' she tells him.

He laughs, steps back from the door. She manages to open it, but as she stumbles out onto the street Frederick grabs a fistful of her clothing. They stagger together, as if country dancing at the end of the night – worse for wear. He pulls her close, his face in hers.

'Get lonely in that cottage of yours?' he whispers.

She writhes to be free of him, but he holds her tight.

'Let go of me!' she cries.

The world has shrunk to his knuckles hard against her collarbone, her neckerchief taut and throttling against her throat. She can see nothing but his dark stubble, the spittle on his lip, his chipped front tooth. But all the same, she's aware that in the road a crowd is gathering – customers who've trickled from the shops to watch the spectacle.

'You'll get your comeuppance,' she says, through ragged breath.

He scoffs at her threat: a deep, rasping chuckle. And although her mouth is dry as blotting sand, she spits in his face. The crowd gasps, someone claps. And then there is Mrs Hooke, out with everyone else upon the cobbles, shrieking her outrage and threatening Ada with eviction all over again.

Frederick leans in.

'I'll see you,' he whispers.

She kicks him, and he lets her go so suddenly she sprawls backwards across the ground.

'You'll be sorry for this, Ada Winters,' shouts Mrs Hooke.

'It's your son who'll be sorry!'

And then she's on her feet, striding away with everything hurting. Under scrutiny. Blood swarming in her ears. Knowing that now she will be – all over again – the topic of Lyme gossip. And understanding that she has, through her foolishness, damaged the thing she most wanted to protect: her home. So then she is sobbing, sidling into an alleyway at the bottom of Coombe Street so she won't be seen, covering her mouth with her hand to smother her cries.

CHAPTER FORTY-EIGHT

*A*da lies awake long into the night.

No sooner is she asleep than she is hauled from her slumber by a roar and a rumbling. The bed-trembling *sense* of it enters her tentative dreams, but subsides before she reaches full consciousness – before she can hear with proper listening ears, *feel* with her wits about her.

The air she breathes is unsettled, and she thinks she tastes dust.

But as she lays there in her bed, staring at the pitch black (thick, tangible), she can hear nothing – can *feel* nothing.

Did she imagine it?

She remembers the events of yesterday afternoon: remembers Frederick. She contemplates whether she might be in danger. Whether he has come for her as he promised, entering her home by force. Was it *that* she heard? But something tells her that it wasn't. What she heard was elemental. Bigger than Frederick. Bigger than any man.

CHAPTER FORTY-NINE

*T*he landslip is felt throughout much of Lyme, although most sleep through it.

Some turn beneath their covers, sigh, grunt, sleep again.

Others light candles and prowl from room to room, alert and afraid.

And the anxious lay awake for the rest of the night, thinking of God and beasts, the devil and their own sins, wondering, *What on earth made that sound?* And more pertinently, *Did anyone else hear it?*

As the crow flies, Ada is closest to the tumult. Although she doesn't hear them, the bones beneath the floorboards in the parlour rattle one against the other. A stone's throw down the beach, the skull that would make a beast of those bones moves with the roaring earth. But beyond the outrage of the landscape rearranging itself, it is a moonless, starless night and the sea is still as a millpond.

What everyone says the following day, when they speak of it in the tavern and the coffee shop, with the fishmonger and the baker, is that after the roar it was eerily quiet.

'It were silent,' they say, 'like the whole of Lyme were 'olding its breath.'

But Lyme is never silent. Even when the shipbuilders take their mallets and saws and heckling throats home for the night. Even when the tide is out and the wind has dropped there is always something to be heard: sounds on the cusp of silence. The monks that came a thousand years ago, or Monmouth's soldiers fresh from the water, marching up the beach to fight the king. The cries of the men hung, drawn and quartered for insurgency on this very sand. Muttered prayers. Canticles of praise. The whispering of stories told for the umpteenth time – wild tales of wolf women eating children for their supper.

Nowhere is ever silent, Lyme least of all.

Marl fills the sea dragon's mouth, and softens its teeth. Slimy clay blinds its eyes. But when the sun rises, and the townsfolk come in their multitudes to look at the largest landslip in living memory, the tip of its snout protrudes: a single tooth tasting the cold air, pointed and sharp.

People teem.

And Ada sleeps, exhausted and oblivious.

CHAPTER FIFTY

Edwin

*H*is housekeeper breaks the news of the landslip when she brings him his breakfast, and he can hardly eat his eggs for the urgency that assails him. After swallowing a few mouthfuls of toast, washed down with a cup of tea, he changes into his working clothes and gathers his tools.

It troubles him as he strides down the street that the whole of Lyme seems to be doing similarly – heading to the beach in a hurry.

Once he's there upon the pebbles, the crowds thicken.

'Damn you,' he mutters, as he pushes his way through, striding past Church Cliffs in the direction of Black Ven and Charmouth.

As he gets closer to the spectacle, he realises the place he has been searching with his men has been obliterated. The landslip is vast, the alteration strangely terrifying.

'A hundred metres at least,' he mutters, looking at the length and breadth of what has moved and fallen.

Everything is ruined. It is all he can think: *What a* damned *mess it is.*

Unable now to get his precise bearings, he couldn't say how far along it had been where the paddles were discovered, or how far along he and his men had been working. He had been methodical, but now his method is lost.

He tries to orientate himself, walking along the edge of the slip, assessing distances, looking back towards the town, and to the cottage that belongs to Miss Winters.

Perhaps about here, he thinks. But everything is guesswork.

People are thronging all around, and he wishes to chase them away.

This is important, he wants to tell them.

In the end, realising his men will have a better grasp of how the land lies than he does, he returns to the town and calls on his labourers.

'It seems that God has lent you a hand,' he says, his jovial tone belying his fears.

'Come! Come!' he rallies. 'We have work to do!'

CHAPTER FIFTY-ONE

*F*or the second time she's woken by a sound that brings her lurching from her sleep. *Something is wrong.* Immediately she knows she has slept long into the day, and feels disorientated because of it. And strangely afraid. The room swims, and she realises how hungry she is, weakened from lack of sustenance.

Startling at a hammering on the kitchen door, she hurries out of bed and into her clothes, easing on her mother's slipped shoes. She peers from the window and sees what she thinks is Isaac's knapsack. *Not Frederick, then,* she thinks. She plucks her shawl from where it's draped across her linen press, wraps it about her shoulders and takes the stairs quickly, two at a time.

'Thank God,' he says, as soon as she opens the door, looking her up and down. 'So all is well?'

Given all that occurred yesterday she's not sure where to start.

'Have you not been out?' he asks.

She shakes her head, realising all of a rush that there *has* been some calamity; her dreamful interlude in the middle of the night was not after all her nerves on tenterhooks.

'What is it?' she says, thinking of Frederick, of Mrs Hooke, of privateers causing havoc on the water. Of other trouble that she cannot yet name.

'There's been a landslip.'

'A landslip?'

'A huge one.'

It all settles into place, and she feels stupid for not having realised. If she hadn't been so distressed from yesterday afternoon, she'd have known what the sound was when she heard it in the early hours. She'd have thought of Edith in the darkness, and felt anew the abyss of her grief. She feels that grief now, but there's no time to contemplate it with Isaac here and the day half gone.

'The skull,' she says, her heart lifting and dipping in the space of a breath. 'Is it busy out there?'

'It is.'

She's torn by matters equal in urgency.

'I need to earn some coin,' she says, making a decision. 'Wait here.'

She hurries through into the parlour and exchanges her slipped shoes for her boots. She pulls on her father's overcoat, takes up her rush hawking basket and fills it with her finest fossils. Days like this are a gift – the townsfolk reminded of the wonders of the world, the visitors thrilled to have witnessed something extraordinary. They'll all part with their pennies and shillings today.

As soon as they're out of the cottage and walking towards Charmouth, Ada can see what's occurred in the distance: a mass of land slipped across the beach, stretching itself towards the sea, rolling out a long black tongue into the water.

They walk in silence towards this newly emerged scarp

of clay and limestone. Boulders have tumbled, seemingly from nowhere.

'I had to climb over it,' says Isaac. 'Our villages are separated now by a hill.'

'It'll be lost,' she says, thinking of the skull.

'You will look, though?'

She nods and turns away. It's hopeless, but she doesn't want to believe it.

The beach is scattered with people, most of whom put some distance between themselves and the newly shapen land as if it might lash out at them. Ada imagines it, shivering. *Do not trust Black Ven.*

'I'm so sorry,' says Isaac.

His voice is quiet enough that she barely hears him, the shingle grinding wetly beneath their boots. She grapples with what he's referring to, thinking of Frederick Hooke. He cannot know about that, though, surely? She wishes that he *did* know, and feels a sudden, surprising longing to tell him about it. She turns to look at him, the tale rising up in her, confident he'd have something comforting to say on the matter.

'I'm just so sorry that she's gone,' he says.

Ada screws her eyes shut, remembering all over again the terror of that moment, the feel of the soil beneath her hands: how cold it was, how heavy. She grapples with an alternative thought – her mother now resting, clean in her woollen shroud. This is what she must think about (it has become her habit, to haul out this image). Her suffering was brief, she tells herself. *It's over.* She has to make herself believe it, to repeat the words and push away anything contrary.

'I'm sorry too,' says Ada, turning to look at the sea. It may have been tranquil when she woke in the middle of the night, but the wind has picked up now and fights with coats and shawls and bonnets all along the beach.

'I should go . . . '

She gestures with her basket and he nods.

Then she hesitates, uncertain, troubled by the conversation that's left undone and by a rumbling urge to share her thoughts about it.

'Something happened,' she says.

'What is it?'

'Can we speak soon?'

This simple request brings with it some sense of trepidation, and immediately she wishes to take it back, afraid she's about to make a fool of herself. She flounders, as if out of her depth in the water; feeling how she used to feel when her father was teaching her to swim: stretching for solid ground and never finding it, gripped by the fear of choking.

'Of course,' he says. 'I'll call by.'

Then she walks away, prickling with embarrassment, towards a group of women gazing with wonder at the altered cliff. After she has approached them and they're busy looking through her basket, she turns to watch Isaac walking away in the direction of Charmouth, skirting the furthest edge of the landslip, kicking at the waves.

She spends a fruitful hour selling fossils to the visitors who speak excitedly of how glad they are to have stayed for the end of Lyme's holiday season. How they nearly didn't. *It's cold now, after all*, they tell her.

All the while, she keeps a lookout for Pastor Durrant and for Dr Moyle; these men who want answers from her and who hope she'll fall in line with their way of thinking. Glancing up and down the beach every few moments she's convinced she'll see them. But when it's time for afternoon tea and the visitor numbers dwindle, she concludes that they were more than likely here much earlier, impatient to see what the slip had uncovered. She looks for Frederick Hooke, too, her stomach unsettled at the memory of his promise. And despite her best efforts to pull herself together, she cannot help but imagine the shadow of him lurking in the dark folds of the cliffs.

Once her pocket is full of coins, she allows herself to wander up into the landslip itself, casting her gaze across the fresh earth. Her boots become heavy with soggy clay and she stumbles at times over the ridges and furrows. She descends again to the level of the beach, scanning the ground, bending at every curve and pattern. She picks up an ammonite, adding it to her basket. So much has shifted and she regards Black Ven anew, reasoning with herself that the cliff has not fallen from the top, but moved forwards – a great mass of it pushed towards the sea. The front section is still the front section. And so she knows that the skull is most likely to be here at the furthest tip of the slip where it licks at the salty water. In this area to the west. She walks in the squelching mud, the shingle crunching underfoot.

Here, she thinks.

She surveys the ground, letting her eyes run across the undulations and jagged rocks. The water laps hungrily at her boots and she bends to what looks like the tip of a belemnite, feeling some resistance as she pulls at it. She realises it's more likely a tooth, and she presses her fingers either side of it, feeling below the surface. She pauses her investigation to deposit her basket a few metres up the beach, away from the encroaching sea. Returning with her trowel, she digs at the earth around the tooth, exposing a section of fossilised jaw. Her heart lurches in disbelief, then lifts, soaring, full of hope.

At that very moment she's startled by the barking laughter of a gentleman nearby. Frederick Hooke leaps to the forefront of her mind, even though she's never heard him laugh and has no reason to suppose it's him. Heart racing, she steals a look in the man's direction and sees with relief that it's an older gentleman with grey hair, laughing happily alongside a young woman with bright auburn ringlets. Ada stands straight, shoulders back, staring openly (*rudely*, her mother would say).

It is you.

Without doubt, it's the woman from Gun Cliff.

As the man and young woman begin to make their way back in the direction of Lyme, Ada decides to follow them. Hurriedly, she digs around the mud-caked skull, lifts it out of the marl and rinses it. She smiles as it reveals itself, excitement trembling through her as she sees what it is she holds in her hands. *This* is what she's been searching for. She runs a fingertip across the creature's teeth and small crocodile-like nostrils. The skull is broad and short with a wide, flat snout and pointed tip. It's enthrallingly perfect, like nothing she's ever seen, and she can hardly believe it.

'I've been looking for you,' she whispers.

CHAPTER FIFTY-TWO

*A*da wakes in the morning with her mind churning. She fetches the sea dragon's bones from beneath the floorboards, pulls out the cervical vertebrae and spaces them across the parlour floor. Given the great size of the beast, it seems odd its head could have been so small, and yet as she positions the skull in place she realises how strangely perfect it is; on such a slender neck of course its head was tiny.

She wolfs her bread and cheese staring at the thing, while also thinking about the couple on the beach yesterday evening, and the villa on Silver Street that she followed them to. The idea that this woman might be of some assistance to Ada reasserts itself. Surely, between the two of them, something can be negotiated with Mrs Hooke?

I helped you, she thinks. *Will you help me in return?*

She wraps the skull and neck bones tenderly in a piece of cloth and places them beneath the floorboards with the rest of the creature. Her anxiety about Frederick and Mrs Hooke, and about everything she must achieve today, cannot stop the rush of pleasure and pride she feels. *See, Father?*

By the time she leaves the house an hour later, she's in her Sunday best. Her hair is brushed and secured beneath a bonnet (more presentable than her hat). Her hands and nails have been scrubbed pink, so they tingle on the edge of sore.

Tom Green is working with his nets a little way off down the beach, and he gives a quick nod in Ada's direction. 'Ye been makin' trouble for yerself again, Miss Ada?' he shouts.

Perplexed, she responds with a joke – 'Forever making trouble' – because that is how they have always conversed: glancing blows, more than words.

In her pocket she has money and the locket, and all the way to Silver Street she practises how exactly she'll ask at the door for the woman in question. What she'll say when faced with her. She will speak of the locket first, of course. And from there Ada is certain she can rely on being offered some refreshment: a quick chat in the parlour by way of thanks. Her heart is galloping at the idea of the exchange, and she tries to gather her thoughts and her intended words. But no sooner has she wrestled them into some kind of order than they scatter all over again. She reassures herself, muttering beneath her breath.

It's a relief to eventually arrive and lift the heavy knocker: a grimacing lion.

A maid answers the door and looks stolidly at Ada, giving the impression of almost-but-not-quite rolling her eyes.

'Can I help you?' she asks flatly.

'If it's not too much trouble, I'd very much appreciate a brief conversation with the young lady staying here.'

There is a pause as the maid considers this.

'She has ringlets,' says Ada quietly.

'I don't need a description. I take it you're not acquainted?'

Ada shakes her head.

'What do you want with her, then?'

'Nothing but a short conversation.'

'She's out.'

'I have something of hers I believe she lost.'

'You can leave that with me,' says the maid.

'I'm sorry, but I can't.'

'Well, what is it, this *something*? So I can tell her, at least.'

Ada pauses.

'I'm not wishing to be difficult, but it's private. And I'd be most grateful if you could speak to her discreetly when you mention me calling. I think she might appreciate it. My name—'

'I know your name.'

Ada studies the maid's face.

'I used to go to chapel,' the young woman says. 'We did our letters together at Sunday school.'

Ada remembers, maybe, vaguely. And then the door is closing.

Disappointed, she makes her way down the hill. Perhaps she anticipated too much from this encounter, but when it comes to Mrs Hooke she doesn't know in what other direction to look.

She crosses the road to the bakery, the smell so welcoming.

'*Out!*' she is told, though, as soon as she puts a foot inside.

'Jacob!' warns the baker's wife.

But he ignores her, comes around the front of his counter, waving his fist at Ada.

'Out my fuckin' shop! Don't want the bloody trouble of ye!'

Ada scurries back out onto the street, heart pounding, unsure what to make of it. In the grocer's she is served, but without a word spoken, the grocer throwing her change onto the counter top.

'Mr Thompson?' she says, hoping that he'll glance at her and the spell will be broken. But he turns his back and busies himself with emptying a crate of cabbages. It makes no sense. Even when things were at their worst Mr Thompson was always civil with Edith, even if he wasn't terribly friendly. Ada drifts away, clutching her loaf of bread and hunk of cheese.

Nearing Cockmoile Square, she sees Josiah coming out of the tobacconist and she calls his name. She's certain that his face drops at the sight of her, but he waits for her and she goes to him. Straightaway, there's something awkward between them that she doesn't understand. She wants to ask him what it is, but instead she finds herself telling him about the skull. She can hardly muster the enthusiasm it deserves. It seems that he, too, is working hard to conjure some positive reaction, and the conversation seems to die between them as soon as she stops speaking.

'Anyway, seems I've managed to upset people again,' she says.

'You won't wish to hear it, Ada, but I do feel you sometimes bring it on yourself.'

Shame washes over her.

'I'm not so daft to think you're responsible for what's happened to him, but surely you can see how it looks?'

Ada clutches her bread and cheese to her chest, staring at Josiah.

'I don't know what you're talking about.'

'I'm talking about Frederick Hooke.'

'What *about* Frederick Hooke?'

'You threatened him in front of all of Coombe Street, and now he's half dead.'

242

The loaf falls from Ada's grasp into the gutter, from where she retrieves it. She stares dumbfounded at Josiah, whose face has sadness and sorrow writ all across it. He's not a man accustomed to these feelings, and his features seem to twitch with the discomfort of being arranged such.

'That had nothing to do with me! How could it?'

'That's not really my point.'

'What happened to him?'

'He was attacked last night by ... by ... a dog, perhaps, on his way home from the assembly rooms.'

'*Perhaps?*'

'People are saying all sorts, you know how it is. Mastiff! Wolf! Bear!'

'*Bear?*'

'I've literally just heard an account of one witness claiming they saw a woman who looked very much like you, late last night, with that dancing bear from Dorchester on a chain.'

For a moment Josiah looks on the edge of amusement.

Ada slumps, imagining the rumour mill – how fast and furious it will be turning.

'When you say *half dead?*'

'I mean half dead. His hand was almost severed; the surgeon had to amputate it this morning. His face has been mauled beyond recognition.'

He pulls out his handkerchief and sneezes three times, blowing his nose. And Ada sees then how tired he looks.

'Are you ill?' she asks.

'This sore throat that everyone has, I think I'm coming down with it. Annie, too. Best to keep your distance for a bit.'

'You're not cross with me, are you?'

Josiah sighs. 'I'm tired of worrying about you, and thinking that perhaps I should stop. Your father once said that you'd go your own way, and I'm seeing that he was right – he knew you best, after all. You could change, though, Ada, if you really wanted to. You could be better liked. It's not necessary to meet the world with so much belligerence. To be quite so angry all the time. It's uncomfortable for people, and does nothing to serve you. You were so ready to tell Dr Moyle what you thought of him. To start a fight with the man. But a polite letter, and a nudge in the right direction, was all that was required. You got your bones back, didn't you? All without a scuffle!'

Ada stares at him, unable to speak.

'Would it really kill you to fall in line a little? To get a position at the mill? Would it really undo you? Of course it wouldn't. You attract these rumours because you single yourself out. You don't need to make grubbing about in the mud your sole occupation. Plenty of women look for fossils on a Sunday afternoon, it's quite fashionable.' He says all this in a kindly tone, avuncular and instructive. 'And geology is a fine interest to cultivate. But you must consider what your mother was always suggesting – a proper paying job or a husband.'

Her cheeks are burning hotter with every passing sentence.

'I get the impression that at times you fancy yourself hard done by, Ada?'

All she can do is shake her head, his words like wasps, swarming around her. She turns and walks away, clutching her lunch that she has no stomach for.

CHAPTER FIFTY-THREE

Edwin

*E*dwin is ambivalent about this little nugget of information that has come his way. To believe it, or to dismiss it as aggravation from an interfering woman?

In any case, it was unfortunate he should bump into Annie Fountain coming out of the tailor's shop on one of those mornings that follows a terrible night's sleep and renders him ill-disposed for conversation and quick-thinking. He didn't have his wits about him and was quite wrong-footed, flushing bright red (he still cringes to think of it) when she told him how pleased she was to learn that the fossils had made their way back to Miss Winters. Her tone made the whole thing entirely plain: she considered *him* the guilty party. He could think of nothing cutting enough to communicate he knew perfectly well it was she who orchestrated the removal of the fossils from his lodgings. She looked him straight in the eye as if utterly unclouded about the whole affair. The bare-faced cheek!

His thoughts have been disordered in the extreme since their encounter. Not only because of her impudence, but because of what she then let slip: that Miss Winters has found some other part of the creature. She intimated it, rather than stating it explicitly. What *was* it she said? He turns the memory, investigating it from every side, but struggles to pin it down. Something about him losing the race ... Or that the race is lost already.

He finds himself undecided about his next step. He'd rather hoped he would hear from Miss Winters after his offer of patronage and partnership. And then he thought he might see her on the morning of the landslip. Seeing no sign of her there lent weight to Annie Fountain's side-swipe; after all, if Miss Winters were still in search of the skeleton, surely she'd have been all over that landslip at first light. He and his men were there soon after breakfast, and they dug all morning to find nothing of significance.

It infuriates him, because he *is* involved in the discovery of this creature, whether Miss Winters likes it or not. Whether she cares to admit it or not. She herself involved him. Did she not come begging on the beach for assistance, and did he not simply oblige? Was she not asking to be noticed, and has he not already begun the task of making it so? He struggles to understand why she's being so foolish, when what she professed to most want is now within her grasp.

CHAPTER FIFTY-FOUR

*F*ish heads and rabbit innards are left on Ada's doorstep overnight. They're a gruesome slop, eyeing her, stinking, and they slip from her hands as she scoops them into a pail. She's familiar with the soft bruise-blue of rabbit guts and the filmy stare of a dead fish, but today she retches repeatedly at the sight of them. She throws them into the sea, rinses everything, pours water over the step and scrubs at it with a brush.

Her fingers are numb with cold by the time she's finished and the breeze has an icy chill to it. The autumn, so late to arrive, is now being chased away by an early winter.

After cleaning up, sitting at her kitchen table she eats fingerfuls of dry bread, trying not to think about who paid her this visit and whether they might be back. Most likely one of the lads, she tells herself: nothing but fun and games to them.

Her insides are the tumbling waves.

It'll die down, she promises herself. *Don't think on it.*

All the same, she stays in the house with the door locked for the rest of the day. She makes sketches of the bones missing from her sea beast: six digits from the left paddle, three lost teeth and four missing ribs. She then passes the hours whit-tling silver driftwood facsimiles with her penknife. She makes a paste from ink and soil and tea leaves, rubs it into the pale wood and leaves it to absorb overnight.

The next day she takes a bottle of rum to Tom Green and he gives her three mackerel in return, promising her more at the start of the week. She builds a fire on the beach and cooks the fish, eating one of them straight away. It leaves her fingers oily and blackened.

She notices how Isaac has settled himself down in her mind; he doesn't visit, flitting in and out, but has brought his own stool and made himself comfortable.

It's been a few days since she saw him last and she feels a quiet longing for him. Wood-smell and sandy hair. The pull and twitch of his lip, so often on the cusp of saying something surprising. It is new to her, this nudge to seek someone out, knowing she'd be all the better for his company. It's not usually other people that she looks towards for companionship or comfort. It's her treas-ures she relies on to lift her, or considering the past through her notebooks, or getting lost in the shingle and the clay.

You are good for my poetry.

It still pleases her when she remembers him saying it; that he doesn't look at her situation as a thing to be remedied or pitied. Even if he doesn't fully understand it. Even if he is yet to be cut by its sharper edges. She sucks mackerel flesh from the bones and thinks how Isaac would surely enjoy doing the same. Squatting by the dying fire, the back of her head is chilled by the cold wind, but her face glows hot from the embers.

When the remaining fish have cooled, she wraps them in a piece of oilcloth and leaves the small parcel on a shelf in the kitchen, from where it fills the house with the smell of smoke.

CHAPTER FIFTY-FIVE

The next day is Sunday, and she finds herself preparing to go to chapel. There's a fire kindling within her, and she rails against the wagging tongues. Why *should* she hide away, cowering by her cottage? Let them tell her what they think if they like, and she'll tell them what *she* thinks. As well as this unapologetic desire to face her accusers (that Josiah Fountain might surely call belligerence), there's something else calling her to attend chapel this morning. There are only three people in Lyme who are her allies, and Pastor Durrant is one of them. She hasn't seen him since his proposal and, although she doesn't want a romantic partnership with him, she does owe him the courtesy of an answer. She wants him in her life, if only for geological discussions at the kitchen table. She knows that she looks to him now, in part, only because the town is turning against her, and shame sidles through her. How easily she dismissed him when it suited. She squirms at the thought of it all. But, he's a forgiving man, she reminds herself.

Ye know where ye be with Pastor Durrant.

She walks through town towards chapel, hackles up, assaulted by images of Frederick's injuries, confounded by the thought that anyone could believe her responsible. She remembers the stories, and laughs out loud at the thought of anyone daft enough to imagine her bringing a bear from Dorchester, or conjuring a wolf from nowhere and setting it upon a man she has quarrelled with, or achieving the same with some borrowed dog.

She laughs again, but it's a hollow laugh – dry as driftwood.

Chapel proves itself a comfort, the small congregation paying her little attention. The prayer book is familiar in her hands, and Pastor Durrant offers her a subtle, reassuring nod at the beginning of the service. She waits for him at the end to finish saying his goodbyes, at which point he turns to her, ushers her through into his living quarters, down the gloomy hallway and into his parlour. There's a fire smouldering in the grate and she sits in the chair closest to it, holding her hands towards the trembling coals as he goes to the kitchen.

'You'll get chilblains,' he says when he returns, and she pulls her hands away, curls them into balls of hot flesh and cold.

On the tray, as well as the tea things, there are generous slices of bread and ham. He pours the tea and passes her a plate that he has heaped with food. Although she's hungry, she cradles it in her lap without eating.

'I don't know if you've heard about Frederick Hooke,' she says.

'I've heard indeed, and it roused in me a dreadful anxiety for you. Before we say another word, I hope you know you have my full confidence.'

'You *say* that.'

'And I mean it.'

'You don't know what I might be about to confess.'

He smiles gently. 'Just tell me everything.'

She thinks, shivers, breathes deeply, and tells him about the night below Gun Cliff. What she saw and the stone she threw.

She puts her fingers to her eyebrow.

'It was actually a piece of coprolite,' she tells him.

'How strangely fitting.'

They manage a small smile each.

'I didn't know him, and it was dark, but when I went to pay my rent a few days ago he was there in Mrs Hooke's house – it was Frederick. We recognised one another, and I . . . I'm not sure exactly, I can't remember . . . I was trying to get out of the house. But he followed and grabbed me – right here!'

And Ada clutches the fabric of her dress above her collarbone.

'He was threatening me, saying I must be lonely living by myself. Saying he was going to come and find me.'

Pastor Durrant's gaze is steady.

'I shouted at him to leave me alone, and said he'd be sorry.'

'This is the part I've heard.'

'I'm sure everyone has heard that part. And then I don't know what happened, only that he was attacked by something – a dog, I presume. Do you think so?'

'I have no idea,' Pastor Durrant says, lifting his bread and taking a bite. He nods at the plate in her lap. 'Eat your food. Heaven knows, you look like you need it.'

She takes a shaky sip of tea, coating her mouth with sweetness before swallowing.

'I'm furious to hear it,' says Pastor Durrant, after they've eaten a few mouthfuls each. He doesn't look furious, though, she thinks. He looks precisely as he always looks: unruffled. And she supposes that is what the world expects of him.

'This place!' he says.

'You sound like someone who's had their fill of Lyme.'

He shrugs.

'Or is it the people you've had your fill of?'

He looks at her for a moment, smiles warmly.

'People are the same everywhere, Ada.'

'But – this place!' She mimics his tone.

'I meant the earth! God's experiment!'

'You despair of it *all?* And there was I, hoping for a little comfort.'

They laugh together.

'But you hope for happier times somewhere new?' says Ada.

He studies her for the briefest moment.

'In the sense that I'll not be ministering in the place I venture to. That I can speak my mind about geological matters and not be castigated for it. And I shall choose a town where the Congregational church is thriving. These things will bring me happiness, of a sort.'

She feels the weight of these last words and knows this is the moment to speak of his proposal, but she can't bring herself to. It's pleasant here in the parlour. And she's in no hurry to leave. Lyme is full of darkness at the moment, and she's out at sea in a cockleshell boat. Pastor Durrant was a beacon of light when she thought of him earlier that morning. She doesn't wish to be married to him, but there's something between them that needs preserving.

She keeps away from the topic they ought to be discussing by telling him about the skull that completes the skeleton. He sits tall in his chair as she tells him exactly where she found the fossil in the landslip. She then shares with him the awful thought that some exchange had taken place – her fear that she'd struck some bargain with Black Ven.

'That's not the case,' he reassures her.

252

'I know,' says Ada, reminding herself of what she's chosen to believe.

They regard one another for a moment.

'You felt yourself neglected,' she says, 'when I allowed the paddle bones to go with Dr Moyle. And I'll confess it was a poor choice on my part. You were right to be aghast. Have you seen the transactions this month?'

Pastor Durrant shakes his head.

She tells him about Moyle's betrayal and thievery. She owns her foolishness, not seeking to soften it in any way.

'I should have come to you with it in the first place. I don't know why I didn't.'

'You must be more careful, Ada.'

'But I'll have my revenge,' she says, taking a mouthful of bread and ham, letting the moment of anticipation unravel between them. She tells him about the letter and the accompanying drawing she sent to the Geological Society – under the pseudonym of Adam Gray.

'I'm telling you in confidence,' she says.

'Only the Fountains and myself?'

'Isaac, too.'

He leans back, adjusts his cravat.

'Perhaps this is another situation where it would serve you to be cautious; you don't know this character, Ada.'

'*This character?* He's not some privateer from foreign lands who's staggered into the tavern! He helped pull my mother from the cliff.'

'He's still a stranger.'

'He's a *friend.*'

She realises what she's said, and how emphatically she said it, feeling the glow of possibility.

'He's showered you with attention, and it'd be prudent to question why,' he says. 'You've been at a low ebb, and you must be careful of your feelings.'

She presses crumbs from the plate onto her fingertip, raising them to her lips, knowing it's probably bad manners and wondering whether Pastor Durrant cares.

'We . . . have things in common,' she says.

'We've both met men like Isaac before, Ada. He's one of a breed. Obsessed with poverty and the everyday – as if these are things to be glorified. Not one of these men would care to ever give up their luxuries. You do know what I'm talking about, don't you?'

She says nothing, unwilling to voice her own thoughts on the matter. As if agreeing with Pastor Durrant would make it truer than it already is.

'They're all heart, to hell with the head,' he says.

'That isn't fair. The heart is moved by beauty and that in turn helps tease out our thoughts. Contemplation of the sublime helps us grapple with the questions of life – with what it means to be human. He cares for heart *and* head; the two are connected. We might welcome this as geologists. Whether in the field or in the study, the facts are not always here at our fingertips. What appears as evidence is at times merely a suggestion, a glance in a certain direction, and we're inevitably left to wonder. We *must* wonder in order to get anywhere near the truth. And we must do it from a place of openness, not from an obsession with certainty.'

'These artists look in every direction for the truth, and anywhere they shed a tear they think they've found it.'

'Imagination is the link between man and the world. Perhaps between man and God, also. Isn't that worth a tear or two? When *was* the last time you cried?'

'The world is wild for men who cry these days, and I refuse to weep for the sake of fashion.'

Ada chuckles, then laughs, and Durrant joins her.

'I only mean,' he says, 'that you're a worthy muse for any man. But be cautious, Ada. You know how it is with these poets and artists – they come and go.'

CHAPTER FIFTY-SIX

*J*ust as it's getting dark and Ada is thinking of lighting the lamp, there's a knock at the door. She hopes it's Isaac, but holds back from answering, because she can't be sure and Frederick Hooke is frequently in her thoughts.

He would call out to her, if it were Isaac. So when there's a second knock, and still no reassuring voice, she finds herself waiting. She thinks of pushing the bolt across as silently as possible. Of creeping in her slipped shoes up to bed.

But the third knock has her rooted to the spot.

'Miss Winters?'

Edwin Moyle's voice is bold and resonant, conveying a sense of urgency and the notion that he'll likely remain at the door until she answers it. He may very well wait there all night if necessary.

Realising who it is provokes relief and disappointment in equal measure. But the relief is enough to have her lifting the latch and inviting him in. She inwardly concedes there is indeed a matter to be discussed and she may as well get it over with.

Deliberately, she doesn't stand on ceremony, and busies

herself with lighting the lamp. Inviting him through into the parlour, she adds some wood to the fire. They stand there for a moment in the orange glow, and when she glances outside she sees that the last colours of the evening have faded away – everything is a misty grey.

He leans his cane against the chair, and rubs his hands together. It is cold; the small fire has kept off the worst of the chill throughout the afternoon, but it hasn't warmed the room.

'I'll speak plainly,' she says, as soon as they are settled in their chairs. 'I can't work with you, because we won't find what you're hoping for. The landslip is of such a scale . . . '

He watches her intently, his face severe and unmoving.

She wants to tell him that, anyway, the fossils and their whereabouts don't matter. She could never work with a colleague that she doesn't trust. He deceived her by keeping the paddle bones and having a drawing made of them and publishing an article that didn't mention her. Why *should* she trust him? But she knows this will only upset him, and she doesn't wish to make an enemy. Despite what Josiah thinks, she's not careless with how she conducts herself. Far from it; there are all manner of opinions she keeps to herself; a multitude of social niceties she observes. And all the while she's perfectly aware that she lives beneath the weight of other people's power. People who *have*. Men, mostly, in silk shirts.

So she'll not tell him to his face that he's behaved abominably, and that she'd never have done what he has done. She'll spare him the brief discomfort of having to listen to her thoughts on the matter. *Brief*, because he'd dismiss those thoughts soon enough – whittling them away until they fit against himself more comfortably. She understands in the very depths of her that her opinions do not matter. *She* doesn't matter. She's no more real to Dr Moyle than the wolf woman of Lyme.

Ada may seem real to him now, but only because she has something that he wants. And as she meets his gaze she knows he's fixed upon it. She can see it in his eyes: his imagining of the skeleton he believed would pave the way to notability.

He looks down at his clasped hands, straightens his fingers, curls them once more, watching them carefully as if looking at them for the very first time. As if marvelling at the wonders of jointed bones and of supple skin, the usefulness and convenience of sturdy nails.

'I believe you might have found the creature already,' he says, glancing up to gauge her reaction.

Immediately she imagines it beneath their feet: disassembled, but waiting all the same. She thinks of it crouched, listening to their conversation.

'I'm tired of having to defend myself,' she says, almost to herself.

'So you don't deny it?'

'You ask me this as if you have a right to be interrogating me. As if you're here with a just complaint, having been wronged in some way. If you'd returned the fossils and included me in your article then we might be sitting in my parlour having an entirely different conversation.'

She shakes her head, and cannot help the bitter laugh.

'I wanted to work with you then, Dr Moyle, but that time has passed.'

He stands and walks to the cabinets on the back wall, opens a drawer and rummages through it. He opens others, rifling through them.

'You have the paddles at least,' he says. 'That much I *do* know. So, where are they?'

'I'm not going to tell you, and I'd like you to leave.'

He stands back and looks at the cabinet anew, as if he might be missing something. As if the curves of wood themselves are deceiving him. He bends to open one of the cupboard doors, then slams it shut. He opens another and she jumps to her feet, anger rising at the sight of him molesting her father's craftsmanship.

'Dr Moyle!'

He begins looking through the drawers again, more carefully this time. She wishes to manhandle him by the collar and escort him from her home. But she can't.

He looks about the room, and then he turns to her.

'You're lying to me, aren't you? Thinking you can pull the wool over my eyes?'

And before she's even managed the first word of her reply, he has made it to the foot of the stairs and disappeared. His heavy footfall is like a giant's heartbeat. And then there is the sound of him above her. It's truly an outrage that he's taken himself into her bedroom, but there's so little up there that she tells herself it doesn't matter. She stands guard over what he's looking for, keeping a slipped shoe steady over the loose nails of the floorboard.

He's gone barely any time at all (enough to root through her linen press), and then he returns back down the stairs. He has failed in his quest, of course, but still he looks strangely triumphant; a smile tinkering there at the corners of his mouth.

When he opens his fist, the gold locket glints on his palm.

'What do we have here, then?'

'Nothing to do with you.'

259

'I imagine it's nothing to do with *you* either.'

'Give it back to me!'

He slips it into his waistcoat pocket, and presses his hand flat against the fabric.

'Where did you get it?' he demands.

'Please return it to me.'

He retrieves it from his pocket as if complying with her request, but he merely studies it.

'S.P.,' he says. '*Certainly* not yours.'

'I found it on the beach, and I know who it belongs to.'

'Then you should have returned it.'

'I've been trying!'

'I'll return it to the rightful owner myself, Miss Winters, because you are a liar.'

She rushes at him, grappling with his closed fist, attempting to prise open his fingers. He stands steady and resolute, hardly wavering.

'I've done nothing wrong!' she says.

Rashly, she leans down and bites his fingers. He cries out and snatches his hand away.

'It's true what they say about you, then – what an animal you are.'

She slaps him, and he slaps her back.

They face one another, each of them trembling.

'Give me the locket,' she says, with as much authority as she can muster.

'If you give me the skeleton.'

She laughs a tremulous laugh.

'The skeleton for this measly locket? Do you think I'm stupid?'

His hand is round her throat before she calculates what's

happening. Somewhere in the distance she hears the sound of the locket clattering onto the floor. He walks her roughly backwards, knocking over the small table of fossils, presses her to the wall. She's drowning in his frock coat and perfume, the cloying sweetness of tobacco. She tries to hit the side of his face with a closed fist as her father always taught her, but it's a glancing blow that hardly makes contact.

He hurls her across the room and she lands against the cabinet, crumpling to the floor in pain. And then he's upon her and the pain has gone – there's only panic.

He's heavy as a landslip; dark and cold as one.

She fights. Moves through heavy clay.

Beaten back, and pinned.

He's faster than she; one step ahead.

He sits on her to pull off his coat and waistcoat, to slip his arms through his suspenders, to unbutton his fall front.

Her screams are muffled by his hand over her mouth.

She struggles to breathe.

The floorboards are cold beneath her when he pulls her drawers away.

And the pain returns: a deep, dark hopelessness made manifest.

Too late, she thinks. *Too late.*

She closes her eyes to the darkness and tries to lose herself in it. Lightning strikes in the place where she used to formulate her thoughts.

She reaches out blindly to the butter-smooth oak of her father's cabinet, and she clings to it. As if it were his hand she holds.

CHAPTER FIFTY-SEVEN

*A*da lays curled on the floor, lightning striking. The moon rises, and the tide comes in. Eventually she sits, then pushes herself to standing. She pulls up her drawers, rearranges her dress and petticoats. Then she goes from the house, down the beach to the shore. She walks, clothed, into the water and continues to walk until she's lifted from her feet by the swell. She moves in the water without swimming, as if she doesn't care about drowning.

She sinks, completely submerged. She drifts. Her hair plumes like seaweed. Her toes touch the rocks and some part of her reacts, pushing upwards – the part of her that wants to live.

She takes great gasping breaths.

Then she sinks.

Rises.

Breathes.

Sinks.

Screams into the water – rage and revulsion flowing from her.

Eventually, she staggers to the shoreline, collapsing onto the shingle, sitting there where the waves are reaching. She lets them love her as they always have. Gently, more than anything else. They don't play with her today. They wash her, kiss at her, soothe her where she stings. And when she lays back, they cradle her and stroke her hair. They hold her as she trembles, and continue to hold her as the hours pass and she becomes so cold that her jaw clenches shut, muscles seizing. This is where she wants to be – no longer feeling.

Then she's talking with the wolf woman, mad as Gramfer. *I'll tell ye the only thing ye need to know*, that wild woman says. But she doesn't tell her anything because her wolf kin are playing and fractious, nipping her for attention. *What do I need to know?* Ada asks, over and over again. *What do I need to know?*

When Tom Green walks along the beach with his three sons and the Marsh boys he sees Ada from a distance. Because it's barely light, he mistakes her for a lost sack of smuggled lace, split across the pebbles. When they're almost upon her, they see her as a dead girl washed up on the beach. *Please not someone we know*, Tom prays. When he recognises Ada, he feels something like relief. Not because he doesn't care for her, but because he does. He's watched her grow from a babber into a queer one, and little by little watched her situation go by the wayside. She's one of those unfortunates who attracts bad luck through no fault of their own, as far as he can see. He's always been careful not to dwell on such folk, scared of his own sorrow and where it'd take him.

Maybe better that she's gone, he thinks. *For her own sake.*

Looking down at her, though, realising she breathes still, he's swift as a cutter – lifting her and barking orders at his boys to fetch the women, to bring coal and broth and bread. Suddenly he's desperate for her to live.

It's not too late, he thinks, then, regret slapping at him like a wave.

Ada wakes in her own bed, in clothes that belong to someone else. Blankets are being changed – the cold taken away, warmed ones replacing them. Wrapped bedpans, hot as baked potatoes, nudge against her feet and ribs. And although it takes her some time to realise it, her hands are being held. There is a woman on either side of the bed; she sees through bleary eyes the plump folds of mobcaps, the puff of gown sleeves. Their fingers press at hers, and she doesn't mind. She presses back, because it's easier than speaking.

On the second day they sit her up and fill her with hot food: soft eggs on toasted bread, porridge with honey. They return her laundered clothes and tell her she can keep what they've put her in. They explain they've mended her torn drawers and petticoats, treated her grazed thighs with an ointment.

They do not say, *We know.*

In the evening, when they bring her downstairs, she sees that her ammonites and belemnites have been neatly arranged back upon the table, and the gold locket has been placed among them. A fire is raging in the grate. And leaning against the kitchen door is Edwin Moyle's walking cane. She shudders when she sees it, innards clenching.

Martha Green brings Ada to the fire and settles her into the chair, tucking a blanket around her. She talks about John and Edith: little stories she remembers from being at school with Ada's mother. She chatters on until the night is gathered about them.

Later, Martha helps Ada into bed, pulls the covers over her, puts a palm to her shoulder. Ada closes her eyes to better feel the firm pressure of this woman's hand. It occurs to her that all is deadened, the whole world a fainter version of what it used to be.

'These things happen,' Martha says.

Ada opens her eyes and meets her gaze.

'Let your sorrow be a seed you sow, a sacred thing for you alone. Your sorrow, your anger, whichever it is.'

Ada tries to take in what she's saying.

'And then one day you might forget it happened,' says Martha, tucking the blankets tightly.

Ada can't imagine forgetting. At the moment it feels as if the ghostly memory of him is all she'll ever remember. The feel of him. The smell of him.

'Shall I take his cane away?' Martha asks.

Ada thinks about it for a long time, staring into this friendly face. Martha is nodding, clearly thinking it would be a good thing, trying to encourage her to make the right choice. But Ada shakes her head.

'No,' she says. 'Leave it here.'

CHAPTER FIFTY-EIGHT

*T*he sight of her is a shock, as if she's come from another time. It was only a few days ago, but it seems like forever since Ada was knocking at *her* door, pinning so much hope on a conversation: the chance to discuss Frederick Hooke and what he'd done to each of them. To discuss *Mrs* Hooke, and Ada's threatened eviction. To return the locket and be gifted something of value in return – not coin, but assistance with her predicament.

Everything has changed since then.

It seems as if it were a year ago that she was making such plans.

It seems like a dream.

The young woman bobs her head, ringlets swinging, and instead of dropping a curtsy as she ought, all Ada can do is stare at her. She is so very out of keeping with the briny air and the tang of decay and the raucous calling of the gulls. Her auburn hair is piled atop her head, dropping down in perfect glossy ringlets. Her green eyes are bright as gemstones, her skin the colour of milk, her lips a striking cupid's bow. She doesn't wear feathers and yards of flowing muslin now; she wears a smart green walking dress, a short spencer coat. But, still, she is like a ripple of clean silk against the seaweed-strewn shore. A flash of amber beside Tom Green junior who untangles his net ten paces away.

'It's you,' says Ada, simply, and the young woman blanches.

'Yes,' she whispers, and Ada hears the taint of emotion in her voice, the tremor of a rushed heartbeat. It's all too familiar – the sensation of netted breath, knotted and complicated.

The woman brings a hand to her throat, her fingers worrying at the velvet collar of her jacket. Then it seems that she gathers herself, pushes her shoulders back.

'I am Miss Phillips.'

She is like a brand-new doll in a shop window: neat stitching soft around brittle porcelain.

'You can call me Sarah.'

Ada grasps for some sense of what this encounter is about to bring. Her mind feels slow and reluctant. It's been only three nights since she was dragged from the water, and today is the first day she's been fending for herself (the Greens and Marshes having yesterday afternoon taken their women home). She has been left with coal for the fire, with bread and beef stew. She is warm and well fed.

She is cold inside and numb.

'I called on you,' says Ada quietly, reminding them both of what they already know. She's trying to anchor herself against the facts, as if they might guide her onwards.

Was it wrong of her – a woman of low birth, without rank or connection – calling unannounced at the home of Miss Phillips? Perhaps it aroused suspicion. Ada scrutinises Sarah's face, wondering whether accusations this very minute are taking shape in her neat angelic mouth. Wasn't her mother always telling her to steer clear of other people's business? But Sarah doesn't seem like a woman about to pounce; she fiddles nervously with the fur on her gloves.

'I hope my calling didn't cause any bother,' says Ada, nonetheless.

Sarah shakes her head. 'It doesn't matter.'

They regard one another in silence. It had been so vital to speak with Sarah before, and there's some part of Ada that senses that still. They shared a shocking moment, and it only seems right to acknowledge it. But it's a moment that has now become something else. It has deepened and darkened, like a storm gathering. She no longer cares to speak of Mrs Hooke, but doesn't know what to speak of instead. Or, more truthfully, she doesn't know *how* to speak of it.

Sarah looks about herself, as if the sea might be creeping up to eavesdrop.

'Might I step inside?'

'Sorry, of course.'

She brings with her the scent of rose water, light and bright against the cottage's musky smell of wool-grease and beeswax, of sweet oil and woodsmoke.

Ada closes the door, and Sarah is straightaway shaking her head.

'I can hardly believe everything that's happened. What a mess it is.'

She looks directly at Ada.

'Yes, a mess.'

'It was all bad enough, but when I heard about Mr Hooke . . . ' Sarah drops her face into her hands, lets out a moan. 'It's just too terrible – *all of it.*'

A little spark burns through Ada's numbness.

'You do not *know* all of it,' she says.

'They said . . .'

'I know what they say.'

Sarah looks at Ada, doubt shifting across her face, eyes calculating.

'I had nothing to do with what happened to Frederick Hooke,' says Ada. 'More's the pity. He's wronged us both, I assure you.'

'So, it wasn't you?'

'That tore off his hand? That savaged his face?'

Sarah plucks at her gloves, staring down at them.

'I heard you threatened him.'

'He assaulted me when he realised who I was. I lost my temper, angry about what he'd done to you and the fact he had no shame at all.'

Ada can hardly fathom it, even now.

'But I don't understand why you came to the house,' says Sarah.

'You dropped your locket.'

Sarah's face clouds, then blooms in happy recognition.

'I *did*! You mean to say you have it?'

'I was returning it,' says Ada, beckoning her into the parlour.

The room is warm, the coals trembling with tiny flames.

'I found it the following day,' she says, going to the drawer, retrieving the filigreed gold. 'I'd have returned it sooner, only . . . I've been dealing with some important matters, and then it took me a while to find you.'

Sarah takes the locket from Ada, turns it over in her palm, snicks the clasp to open it.

'*Thank you.*'

She whispers this last, and doesn't look at Ada as she says

it. So Ada knows this gratitude is meant for God or saint or some deceased relative; she has clearly prayed for the return of this treasure.

'Thank you for taking so much trouble, and for what you did that night. I'm most grateful,' she says, smiling. 'Perhaps we can both now put it out of our minds.'

Ada considers this through a pall of indignation.

'I would love to forget it,' she says. 'But the *town* will not forget, I assure you of that.'

Sarah turns away, stares out of the small, salt-streaked window that looks down the beach towards the water.

'I can see how this leaves you, but what can I do?'

'Have you told anyone what he did?'

Sarah shakes her head.

'Then accuse the man of impropriety. Tell your family, and have them confront him.'

'I can't do that. No one must know.'

'But the town should know who he is. *That* would help me.'

'My aunt and uncle would be distraught.'

'You shouldn't have to worry about that.'

'My father would never forgive me.'

Sarah is back to fiddling with her collar, her eyes glassy with tears. She turns back to the window.

'Did you see the falling stars that evening?' she asks quietly.
'I did.'

'They were spoken of over dinner and Mr Hooke suggested stepping outside to look. My uncle accompanied us, but then retreated to fetch his pipe and must have been detained by someone. Before I knew it, Mr Hooke was leading me further away – "Away from the light," he was saying. "They're a sight to behold."'

'You don't need to explain yourself.'

Sarah turns to look at Ada.

'But I want you to understand that I wasn't seeking his attention.'

'He's an undercreepen scoundrel.'

'I can't believe how foolish I was.'

'You're not to blame.'

Sarah's gaze flits about the room as she weighs the matter, then she shakes her head, closing her eyes in resignation.

'I should never have stepped out with him!'

Her cry of frustration is so sharp and fierce that Ada feels a rush of understanding. She wishes to say it plain – *I know that feeling.* It is betrayal. It is deceit and false accusations. It is Moyle and Hooke and what she feels when Lyme folk remember her father falsely; words darting from their mouths like bats from a cave. It is talk of bears and wolves, and rumours of women's revenge. It's the ugliest thing – careless gossip left to grow like mould on rotting fruit. And as Ada remembers how futile it is to fight that ugliness she softens, seeing something childlike in the anxious flinching of Sarah's face, in the way that she plucks at her gloves. She is, despite the expensive clothing and accoutrements, little more than a child – seventeen perhaps?

'Sarah, it wasn't your fault, but I give you my word that I'll speak of it to no one, if that's what you want.'

'It is just what I want.'

Ada thinks of Edwin Moyle, acknowledging reluctantly that perhaps she feels similarly. Even here with Sarah, she can't imagine describing what took place in this cottage; couldn't right now conjure the necessary words. She has presumed, though, that her silence is not a choice. She couldn't accuse Dr Moyle because she's a nobody and her word counts for nothing

271

compared to his. He's an educated man and a doctor. Respect is his right, and he can take it for granted. Ada can count only on disbelief and disparagement. She has no credibility, no stage from which to speak. Here now, it seems that Sarah perceives herself to be in the same situation, which makes no sense to Ada at all. *You're a lady*, she wants to say. *A person of standing.*

'You *would* be believed, though,' says Ada weakly, wondering if there's any truth in that. Why does she think it? What does she presume to know about this young woman's life?

Tears are running down Sarah's cheeks.

Ada tries to resist the anxiety that blooms so warm and humid in the air between them, but she can't help breathing it in. It merges with her own and she wishes to shake them both out of this weakness and into something more useful.

But it isn't just anxiety that they feel, she realises.

'You're ashamed,' says Ada, troubled to realise it; to recognise it.

'Of course I am,' says Sarah.

Ada sinks down into her chair, rests her head in her hands.

'Why am I ashamed?' she whispers.

She imagines Moyle unscathed by what he's done, and wonders how he'll justify it to himself, understanding that he will.

'I can't stay any longer,' says Sarah. 'I crept out before breakfast, and I need to get back.'

After some awkward and hurried leave-taking she goes from the house, rushing away as quickly as a respectable woman is permitted to rush. Ada watches her, incongruous again upon the sand, as the visitors often are. Looking beyond Sarah, Ada sees the figure of a man who she recognises immediately as Isaac – striding along the shoreline in the direction of the cottage. Her heart springs towards him across the beach, and something lifts within her. It's such a relief to feel less numb, to feel a flicker of hope at the sight of her friend. Despite all she's just been contemplating, she realises that she *will* tell Isaac what's happened, and what Edwin Moyle is guilty of. And it dawns on her that what she said about Isaac to Pastor Durrant is true – *we are friends*. Just the sight of him is as good as the hot porridge and honey the women gave to her.

In a short moment he will pass Sarah going in the opposite direction.

But he doesn't pass her.

The two of them stop to speak. And then, as if watching them through the haze of a dream, uncertain whether she can trust her own eyes, Ada watches them embracing until there is no longer two of them at all. There is just a swirl of coat and arms and hair. And then they are walking away together, back towards the bustle of the town.

CHAPTER FIFTY-NINE

*T*he following afternoon Ada brushes the tangles from her hair, plaits and wraps it about her head, secures it beneath her hat. She pulls on her boots, and around her shoulders wraps the comfort of a large, thick woollen shawl that Martha Green left for her as a gift.

The cane is waiting by the kitchen door, and she regards it, readying herself to pick it up. She's convinced the handle will be warm from his hand still. That her defences will be somehow breached if she touches it. That he'll be back inside her. Suffocating her.

She dithers, gathering her courage.

In the end, she thinks of the craftsman who worked the malacca cane with his sand and emery, with his fish skin and varnish, who charred and etched. She thinks of the silversmith who hammered the handle so smooth that the bearer might forget they were holding it. She thinks of these men, their skill and toil. She thinks of the cane itself, and for how many years it grew in that faraway land. She thinks of the hands that cut it down, the tools they might have used. So, when she finally touches it there's nothing of Edwin Moyle in it at all.

Holding the cane beneath her shawl, she walks into town and positions herself down a small side street between the customs house and the Three Cups, directly opposite the assembly rooms. The muffin boy is pacing the street and every pass he makes Ada gets a whiff of dough, warm and fragrant from the oven. The inn is alive with the incessant clatter of afternoon deliveries: flour and suet, then sacks of potatoes, barrels of ale. She settles her shoulder against the side of the damp building and watches the street. In less than an hour Dr Moyle's whist club will commence in the gaming room.

Her anxiety about Moyle is countered by her feelings towards Isaac and Sarah. How confusing it is to remember their embrace. How strangely saddening. It's difficult, however, to know exactly what is prompting such feelings. A simple consternation that they know one another?

Am I jealous?

I am not!

She tells herself she never thought of Isaac romantically, because she doesn't think about anyone that way. She doesn't wish for a romantic life. Everything she said to Pastor Durrant is true. She doesn't want to be married or to have children. Does not want to *think* about having children. So the absence of romantic love is not the cause of the befuddlement and agitation she feels. It is Isaac's lack of openness that has caused the upset. His giving the impression of wearing his heart on his sleeve and encouraging Ada to do the same.

She can't help but ruminate on all that Pastor Durrant said about him, and wonder whether there's any truth in Durrant's gently disparaging assessment. When Ada considered Isaac and thought, *We are friends*, was she being naïve? Might it be as Pastor Durrant warned – that Isaac has tired of her? That men like Isaac come and go? Was she serving some purpose that's now fulfilled? *You are good for my poetry.*

She doesn't wish for things to have altered, but it seems that they might have. She finds herself looking at Isaac anew, as if through an unfocused telescope, unsure what exactly she's looking at.

He's my friend, she thinks.

But the thought is a will-o'-the-wisp, gone in an instant.

Where has he been this last week?

She remembers the day of the landslip and how she'd asked whether they could talk. How he said he'd call by. She frets that perhaps he's heard the rumours about Frederick Hooke and wolves and bears. About Ada being something of an animal. And she wonders whether he is, beneath it all, a turncoat? He speaks bravely enough of being an outcast, but perhaps he's not as brave as he's given her to believe? Perhaps being brave is something he aspires to because the notion of it is good for his poetry. Perhaps this latest rumour is one rumour too far.

In between all these thoughts, like a sickening stomach that cannot settle, there is the constant rumble of Edwin Moyle. She watches the street for him, the whole of her shivering.

'I'm just a little cold,' she tells herself.

I'm not afraid.

She has no idea how much time has passed, although the church bell is yet to ring for three. And then she sees him. Jaunty on the street, a replacement cane tucked beneath his arm. Forcing herself to walk in his direction, she keeps her gaze upon him, face lifted. When he notices her, he slows, almost imperceptibly, but Ada marks it. She stops in the middle of the road and holds out his cane. He has reached the steps of the assembly rooms and glances up at the doors. She watches him calculate. Then he's striding towards her, and she braces herself. He reaches out, his eyes looking directly into hers, and she brings the cane close to her body, out of his reach, holding his gaze.

'You owe me an apology,' she says.

For the briefest moment he looks wrong-footed.

'I owe you nothing. If anything, you owe *me* an apology.'

His face is flushed, his breathing disordered.

'How can you say that?'

Her words are mauled by a dry mouth and trembling jaw.

'Shaking like a baby bird,' he says, smirking, grasping his cane and tugging it away from her. 'We had a gentleman's agreement, but you went your own way, hiding things from me after I'd made you a favourable offer – which, can I say, you hadn't turned down.'

Ada cannot think of where to begin.

'You then proceed to have my lodgings broken into and ransacked, which was honestly an outrage by anybody's standards.'

Ada shakes her head. 'That's a lie, and you know it.'

'If you wish to change your mind about the skeleton and resume our partnership, then I believe you know where to find me.'

He turns and walks away.

She strides after him.

'Dr Moyle,' she calls out. 'I'll tell people who you are. I'll tell the people you care about!'

He reaches the assembly room steps at the same moment as two other gentlemen. He mutters something and they turn to look at her.

'Apologise for what you've done!' she says.

'I told you, shoo!' And he flicks his hand at her, as if she were nothing more than a stray cat begging for titbits. 'Stop embarrassing yourself and leave me be.'

CHAPTER SIXTY

*H*aving conjured various versions of the letter in her mind, Ada contemplates a visit to Fountain's Muse to at least make use of their quality paper, if not Annie's neat hand (the actual words she understands she must scribe for herself). But she settles in the end on her inferior pen and poor-quality paper, bringing them from the cupboard. She will make do, and be what she is, and not pretend otherwise. Despite the certainty of this thought, still she feels nauseous as she begins to write. Still, her fingers tremble.

Struck down at the weekend by a painful sore throat, Isaac has taken to his bed. Sarah visits daily to nurse him, sending down to the kitchen for broth, bringing tinctures from the herbalist. In-between attending him, they delight in one another's company.

> *Dear Sirs,*

begins Ada,

*I am writing regarding Dr Edwin Moyle, who you will be
well aware lately published an article in your journal, citing
therein his supposed discovery of the paddle bones of a new
aquatic reptile. I am compelled to inform you that Dr Moyle
has behaved dishonestly, masquerading as someone he is not.
These bones were found by myself, a Lyme resident and local
fossilist. They were in Dr Moyle's possession only because he
requested to borrow them.*

Despite the lure of sleep, the muddle of fatigue, the blessed
and distracting gift of Sarah's presence (her stroking hands
and gentle kisses), Isaac requests his writing things, and pens
a note to Ada.

You will hardly guess what I am about to tell you …

*Dr Moyle has since asked me to work with him, assisting in
a search for the rest of the creature. I shall not waste the ink
explaining my reasons for refusing this offer, but suffice to
say Dr Moyle has been left thwarted and frustrated and, I
believe, harbouring a grudge against me.*

*My sister, Sarah, has been lodging in Lyme for the season,
awaiting the anniversary of our mother's death on the Ist November.
We met one another quite by chance and, as I'm sure you can
imagine, my heart is brimming with the wonder of this encounter!
I shall save the details until I see you in person. I would have
come sooner, but have been struck low with a bad throat and fever.*

*It pains me to write this, as I am certain it will fall on deaf
ears, and collectively you shall wish to think the best of Dr*

Moyle and to doubt my credibility, but I should like it known that whilst challenging Dr Moyle, and attempting to remove him from my property, he attacked me in the most vile and disgusting manner. He raped me, Sirs.

If you are so inclined, you might visit one afternoon when Sarah is here. She has been staying for nuncheon, and returning to her lodgings afterwards, when our aunt, my mother's sister, collects her around 2.30 p.m. I feel sure that this will remain her habit for the next few days, and I would love for you to meet her. Do come!

Having no father or husband to speak on my behalf and seek justice for this crime, I should like you at least to know that you have a cruel and dishonourable pretender in your midst.

After Ada has addressed her letter and failed to find her little nub of sealing wax, she realises she'll need to visit Annie and Josiah after all. When she steps outside the cottage she notices how quiet and still the beach is. But then she's struck by something else, something stark enough to stop her in her tracks. Her gaze is drawn to the clay-green sea, dull and brooding. To the ghostly silhouette of Portland on the horizon. To the strange haze in the distance that might only be a trick of the light. It's as if she *sees* the heaviness before she feels it; but she *does* feel it. As if the dying autumn is sombre as her heart. *A storm is coming*, she thinks.

It is the innkeeper's son that Isaac entrusts to deliver the note to Ada. He gives him a three-pence piece and asks the child to repeat his instructions.

'There be only one cottage over yonder,' the boy says impatiently.

'Very well. You'll be back before it's dark if you go now.'

It feels to Ada that a veil covers her, and through it nothing looks right. All is haunted and other-worldly. Or *she* is these things; it's hard to tell. Josiah and Annie don't seem to notice anything different, but how can they not when she's entirely changed? Isaac would have seen through this veil of hers, she thinks. He'd have found some way to lift it from her face and look at her directly.

Josiah clearly contemplates what he said to her when they met last, out in the street, because he stutters through his greeting a little, looking askance at her as she speaks to Annie. But his insults have faded in Ada's mind – too much else has happened since they spoke for her to care what Josiah thinks about the details of her life.

She procures the wax and seals her letter.

'I can post it for you,' Josiah says, gesturing to a small pile waiting to be dealt with.

She's conscious of arousing his curiosity if he sees where her letter is bound.

'I'll post it myself,' she says.

'Oh, be away with you.' And he snatches it from her hand. 'Let me help.'

He's feeling guilty, she thinks, and she doesn't fight him. But she also doesn't wait for him to ask her any questions. With only a muttered *thank you*, she makes her excuses and leaves.

The innkeeper's son, as he makes his way down to the beach, is waylaid by his friend Beatrice. She lives across the river in the

282

largest house in Charmouth, and is the only girl who looms in his imagination when he finds himself with five minutes' peace. He's struck dumb as a fool in her presence, and has no idea how much pleasure she takes from his embarrassment (she watches him intently as she talks about the landslip, the lobsters this year, the stable boy at the King's Head, the storm her grammer swears is on the way, and the chimney fire at Beer that destroyed six cottages all in a row). When he regains his senses, remembering the tide he was racing, he still cannot pull himself away. He can only wait for her to release him, and when she does he runs as fast as he can, convinced of his speed and ability, full of some shining light that tingles in his chest and throat, his fingers and toes.

Josiah stares down at the letter Ada has left with him. He tries to think why she would be writing again to the Geological Society of London. He muses on this for some time, taking a turn about the bindery, fiddling with a knife that needs a sharpen, shaking a bottle of ink. He sighs, troubled by some suspicion that he can't pin down. It goes against his professional integrity, trusted as he is with people's private correspondence, but he returns to her letter, breaks the seal and opens it.

As the boy reaches the landslip in the gloom, he decides not to scrabble over it (muddy breeches would earn him boxed ears). He splashes instead through the shallow waves. He thinks of Beatrice – thoughts he doesn't quite understand – and all of a sudden he loses his footing and falls face first into the water. He jumps up, shocked and spluttering, waiting for the world to settle itself. Remembering the note, he peers at it in the dimpsey light. Even though he cannot read, he can tell that the ink has bled too much for the words to be legible and for a moment all he can do is stare at the mess of them. After a cold, damp moment, heart sinking at his failure, he turns for home. He walks slowly, in no hurry at all, picking tiny pieces from the note, feeding them one at a time to the swallowing sea. He feels guilty about keeping the threepence, but stronger than his guilt is his fear of a second hiding: his drenched clothes will earn him the first.

Josiah's cheeks burn as he reads the letter. He thinks of showing it to Annie but decides against it. He's a tumult of conflicting thoughts. What Ada describes is a shock and it turns his insides. But her accusation turns them just as much. She'll gain nothing from this disclosure but enemies, and he wonders how she doesn't see it. Or why she doesn't care? He takes the letter upstairs to the parlour where a fire is flickering in the grate and, fingers trembling with the betrayal, he lays it upon the coals. Instantly, the flames flare and the letter is gone.

CHAPTER SIXTY-ONE

*I*t used to mark the end of the year, and the land still knows it – eager for the stamping of dancing feet, and the silken white ash that comes after the festivities: whipped up by the wind like thistledown. Born of long custom, bonfires burned all across these parts during Samhain. Flames in the name of Thunor and Woden, Tiw and Frig. Flames burned to welcome the winter, to bring home dead ancestors and ward off evil spirits. If not Samhain, then Nos Kalan Gwar and later Allhallowtide: three days of feasting.

After chapel, on All Saints' Eve, Ada bakes soul cakes for the following day. She rubs butter into flour, adds sugar and milk. She makes crosses over the top of them with currants, and is careful not to let them catch in the oven. The cottage fills with a sweet aroma and memories of Gramfer. It didn't matter how stretched they were, he always insisted on the baking of soul cakes. They would go hungry for the rest of the week so that he could lay out his sweet offerings on All Saints' Day, gathering his ghosts about the range and telling them everything that had come to pass in the twelve months previous. And each year after her gramfer's passing, Ada and Edith kept up his tradition – making the cakes, lighting candles and opening the window in the parlour so ancestral spirits might join them for the evening. She thinks of this gathering tomorrow, this ceremony she'll mark because she may as well than not. The last twelve months have been such a turmoil that Ada feels tired at the thought of trying to convey it all. Not only tired, but awkward and ashamed.

Perhaps, though, it will be a relief – to tell it from the beginning, and to tell it all.

All Saints' Eve falls this year on the last Sunday of the month, and although Ada wasn't expecting him, Pastor Durrant chooses this particular day to resume his old habit of calling on her.

'Dirty weather,' he says, almost falling into the cottage.

The wind slams the door shut behind him and he shrieks in fright, which makes them both laugh. But when their laughter dies away a great ravine seems to open up, reminding Ada of everything he doesn't know and all that will remain unspoken – everything she will be required to navigate, unbeknownst to him. Deflecting her thoughts away from Dr Moyle, she busies herself immediately with pulling up the nails from the loose floorboards, with hauling out the sacks of bones.

He shuffles from foot to foot, a pink glow suffusing his cheeks.

'I've never seen you so agitated,' she says.

'I'm excited indeed!'

She smiles, and hands him a sack.

'They are the cervical vertebrae. Lay them out in the kitchen, head towards the door.'

And she busies herself with a similar task in the parlour. They work in silence, piecing the creature together like a jigsaw.

'These are some replicas I fashioned,' she says, bringing her drawer of facsimiles. They lay these out also, before walking between the two rooms, discussing the sea dragon's anatomy. How it is similar and how it differs from other creatures. Pastor Durrant beams at her and claps his hands together.

'It's incredible!' he says, repeatedly.

She smiles, and lets the feeling wash over her. It *is* incredible. *It is here, and complete.*

As they drink their tea, Ada happens to glance through the window and notices a woman who looks very much like Mrs Hooke, picking her way across the stones towards the cottage.

'Oh good Lord,' she says, going closer to the glass for a better look.

It *is* Mrs Hooke, and without a second thought she runs through into the kitchen and bolts the door.

'There's no need to hide from her,' Pastor Durrant says.

Ada regards him stolidly, thinking about this.

'But Frederick?'

'Should be ashamed! His mother, too! I'll tell her myself if I have to!'

'I'm not strong enough for a fight.'

Durrant shakes his head.

'You don't have to be.'

'She'll want to throttle me.'

'Well, she won't.'

'She *might*.'

'Not with me here.'

Ada is about to take issue with this, but decides instead to humour him. It will do no harm for him to think he can act as her protector.

'She mustn't see the skeleton, though,' says Ada.

Durrant is already placing the cervical vertebrae back into their sack, and Ada hurries to do similarly in the parlour. Any moment she expects the harsh knocking of her landlady's cane against the door, but it doesn't come and the moment grows thin with anticipation. She quickly plucks rib bones one by one into her sack, her heart clamouring, until she notices the room has darkened. Slowly, somehow anticipating the sight, she looks up to see Mrs Hooke peering in through the window, cupped hands shielding her eyes. Ada freezes. Three of the four paddles are still in position, as are most of the creature's ribs. Mrs Hooke's eyes are wide, and then she is gone, scurrying, Ada knows, to the kitchen door. She bounds to meet her, self-consciously barefoot, readying herself for whatever is coming.

The fierce wind rushes into the cottage, whipping at Ada's loose hair, running icily across her feet. Her landlady has no umbrella with her and her hair hangs in sodden clumps about her face.

'Mrs Hooke,' Ada mutters, placing herself in the small gap of the open door, preparing to slam it if need be. Despite the foul weather, Ada can't summon the courage to invite the woman into her house and Mrs Hooke shows no sign of wanting to come in; she seems, if anything, to be keeping her distance a good few paces away.

'It's just the rent,' she says.

'It is?' says Ada feebly. *The rent?*

'Neither of us want any more trouble, do we?'

Ada looks at her, completely at a loss. She waits for Mrs Hooke to burst out laughing, or to come at her with the cane. But as Ada scrutinises her, she sees a haunted look in her landlady's eyes. She sees, in actual fact, what she believes to be fear. She notices a hag stone on a silver chain around Mrs Hooke's neck, and everything rearranges itself.

'We've always been civil, haven't we, Ada?'

Mrs Hooke tries a smile.

Still, all Ada can do is stare.

'We've had our misunderstandings, but it's all water under the bridge now.'

Ada tries to think of something to say.

'You've been careful of your own skin,' says Mrs Hooke. 'And that's fair enough, as I see it. But now I want to be careful of mine, and so I'm here laying things down. It's all square as far as I go.'

'All right,' says Ada. 'All square?'

Mrs Hooke gives a curt nod, jowls trembling.

It starts to rain heavily, but she hardly seems to notice.

'Same rent, paid weekly, if that's all right with you. I'll not come down for it any more. You can bring it to the house.'

Ada nods, shuddering at the thought of having to step inside the Hooke residence again.

'What's that thing you have in there?' Mrs Hooke asks, voice wavering.

'Just some fossils I found.'

'Looks unusual. Special, is it?'

Ada shrugs.

Mrs Hooke clutches the hag stone, silent for a moment before turning away, leaving Ada wet through with astonishment. Pastor Durrant appears at her back, and Ada hears him breathing. Together they watch as Mrs Hooke disappears into the pouring rain and descending fog.

'Can you credit it?' says Ada, as they come inside and close the door.

Pastor Durrant seems to be thinking the matter through.

'It's unfortunate in a way,' he says.

'That she's now afraid of me?'

He nods.

'Yes,' she says, thinking of the way that the town has spun this yarn. There has always been whispering of witches and wolves in Lyme. Things sworn as seen. Old crones with wild hair and too-sharp teeth. Wolfish shadows skittish on the moors.

Ada shrugs again, too weary to think about it in too much detail. All that matters is that the cottage is hers; she doesn't have to leave. But as they sit with their tea, resuming their discussion about the sea creature, Ada begins to realise that the cottage being hers once more is *not* all that matters. What Mrs Hooke has just revealed ought to have brought relief, but it hasn't. Nothing feels settled at all. Nothing feels right.

'It's damper than ever in here,' she says, looking at the mottled walls. She glances at the place on the floor where Dr Moyle raped her, and for a moment she thinks she sees a puddle of water: a dark stain spreading outward.

I cannot live like this.

She cannot bear the feeling of her own powerlessness. She thinks about the letter she sent to the Geological Society. Will they pay it any heed? Will they believe her? Will they care? She doubts it.

What else can I do?

'The place needs keeping warm,' says Pastor Durrant, looking at the empty scuttle.

A silence descends and Ada wonders if he's thinking of his proposal and the answer she owes him. Perhaps he brings to mind his warm parlour, and questions why she wouldn't choose it over this.

'I did think about it,' she says, looking down at the swirl of tea leaves in the bottom of her cup. 'And I'm sorry for being dismissive when you made me your offer. It was generous of you to put our shared interests above everything else.'

Durrant regards her, and Ada meets his gaze briefly before looking away.

'It's foolish of me, probably, to turn you down. I can't explain it, other than I think we'd be miserable. For all the reasons I said. But I value our friendship, and I'll be sad when you're gone from Lyme.'

Our friendship, she thinks. Finally, she sees that's what they have, now he's about to quit the town. It is safe, she realises, to like a person who is going to leave you.

When Pastor Durrant has disappeared into the gloom of the wild beach, Ada stands outside awhile. Far out to sea a darkness is gathering. Black clouds are pressing down and the ocean is rising up to meet them, as if to share some secret. The wind is hurtling off the water to pummel her chest, and she plants her feet among the pebbles so she might lean against the approaching storm. It has been coming for days and now it's finally here she feels strangely bolstered. She prickles with impatience, although unsure for what. Outrage and apology from the Geological Society? For Edwin Moyle to find his decency and acknowledge what he did to her? For Isaac to return, to explain himself and tell her that she matters? All this *waiting*. As if waiting is her due as a woman, and a humble one at that. She tries to imagine what she'd do if she didn't feel the need to wait.

Am I stone, or am I wolf?

And in that moment, thrumming with possibility, an idea begins to form.

CHAPTER SIXTY-TWO

When she wakes on All Saints' Day, it seems that the old belief is true: the portière that separates this realm from the next might now so easily be pulled aside. There's something haunted about the gale that rattles the house, as if it's more than an earthly tempest that shakes the timbers and slings slates from the roof, smashing them upon the pebbles.

It's the first day of November, the turn of the old year, and darkness embraces her as she folds back the blankets and rises from her bed. She thinks of Isaac, of his mother who died on her birthday and would have been fifty today. Fumbling blindly with her tinder box, she lights a candle. Navigating the stairs, her shadow whispers beside her, and in the parlour she listens to the howling in the chimney and the rattling of the casements.

She lights more candles, because it's no day to be frugal with the light.

The full moon burned bright in the sky last night and she hears the high tide not far from the cottage. The sound of the waves breaking so close makes her feel as if something inside her might overflow. She's always liked the spring tides at this time of the year – the jeopardy they bring as the water licks at the bricks of the house.

Respecting the lore to welcome the spirits, Ada opens the parlour window and the wintry air rushes into the cottage. The candles gutter, throwing dark shapes across the damp walls.

She starts a fire with handfuls of twigs, then brings a plate of soul cakes to the small table that sits between her chair and Edith's. Wrapping herself in Martha's shawl, she thinks back over the last twelve months.

She conjures her gramfer: the bony-edged shape of him settling beside her and reaching hungrily for a cake. Her mother is harder to imagine, and she can't ignore the feeling that Edith is the creature in her ribcage that tosses and turns and refuses to settle. Her mother's spirit won't come visiting, because her mother's spirit hasn't left her yet.

Briefly, she hefts the part of her that doesn't believe in spirits; it is weighty, solid and real. And the part of her that does; ethereal itself, light as a feather, impossible to disregard.

In the end she finds that she speaks only to Gramfer, recalling everything from the very beginning of the year. It's easy enough remembering last winter and all that happened in the spring. But when she brings to mind the summer and her discovery of the paddle bones, she stumbles to recount the deal she made with Black Ven. How she promised the cliff everything and it took her at her word, as if her own mother was part of the bargain. She speaks of the betrayal she felt, and how foolish that was. Then she speaks of a new understanding – that her imagination is a link between herself and the world. That her daft, fey thoughts are not wasted thoughts, even as a scientist. That there's a place for intuition as well as for evidence, and

294

that she needn't choose only the latter to be credible. This year, she tells him, I've learned that I can hold with the hare and run with the hounds. You always laughed at me for that, she reminds him. You saw it as a weakness.

'But some questions demand a wild imagination.'

She tells him about the sea dragon.

She tells him about Isaac and his pictures and his poetry. She tells him about Pastor Durrant and his proposal. She tells him everything about Frederick Hooke and how folks' tongues are now wagging.

Some things never change.

She tells him about the locket, and about Sarah Phillips.

She says that she misses the poet – this man she'd opened to.

She speaks of letters sent in good faith, and letters false.

Her voice drifts away to nothing, and she eats soul cakes to give her something to do with her mouth other than talking.

'There is something, yet,' she says eventually.

But she cannot speak of it. She looks within and it seems for all the world as if there's a vast and endless darkness there. She glances at the place on the floor by the cabinet, and her insides clench, muscles tensing. Her body is stiff from holding the memory, of keeping it small. Every part of her aches.

She takes a slow, deep breath and, telling it to the spirits, she speaks her tentative plan aloud. The air shifts around her, kissing her neck, and she notices the sun has risen.

When she reaches for it, she finds that the plate of soul cakes is empty, and she wonders at the depths of her hunger.

CHAPTER SIXTY-THREE

*A*da watches Dr Moyle exit his lodgings and fumble with his umbrella.

The rain is bouncing off the pavements, flowing fast in the gutters.

He sets off down the hill and she follows behind.

After a moment she comes alongside him, walking in the road to keep some distance between them.

He doesn't seem to notice her.

'I've come to make you an offer,' she says.

He stops walking, but she keeps going, unwilling to dance to his tune.

I will not wait.

For a moment she wonders whether he'll follow her or let her go, but then he's there beside her again.

'I've been living with the threat of eviction these past few months,' she says. 'And therefore I've decided to sell the sea dragon to the British Museum. *Or,* because it would be quicker, perhaps to sell it to you.'

'So you *do* have it!'

'Of course I have it.'

'I was right!'

She hears the happiness and relief in his voice and she clenches her teeth, grinds them together.

'I want two hundred pounds for it,' she says.

'That's pretty steep.'

'It's a special price for you.'

He laughs, as if she's joking with him, and she lets him think what he wants to think.

He stops walking again, and she supposes that she's expected to halt also. To look him in the eye perhaps. She cannot be sure, but she imagines him wanting to shake her hand to seal the deal. *The foolish man.* She doesn't stop walking, though. She maintains her brisk pace just the same and after a brief pause she hears him running to catch up.

'Can I come and see it now?' he asks.

'I'm busy now, but you can come this evening. I'll be there at six o'clock, but I have an arrangement afterwards, so don't be late.'

And she continues on, striding away from him.

CHAPTER SIXTY-FOUR

*I*n the afternoon Ada brings the sea dragon one final time from beneath the floorboards. Starting with the tip of its short tail, she lays out its bones one by one. Assembling it is like a ritual: the words of a story she has known for ever. With the attention of a good midwife, she arranges the hundreds of finger-like fossils that make up its four paddles. She places the femora and ilia. Nudges the vertebrae into line.

Laying out the many slender rib bones, then its sternum, she marvels anew at its fantastically long neck – this impossible feature that will be so puzzled over.

Last of all, she takes its broad skull into her hands and gazes at its flat snout. She runs a fingertip over its long, conical teeth. She conjures the jaw clamped around its prey: the brackish taste of salt and blood.

'If I could give you life I would,' she whispers, lifting the skull to her face and blowing into its small nostrils.

Thinking of Edwin Moyle, she says, 'You don't deserve him, so you'll have to forgive me.'

She shudders to think of him crouching over the fossils,

touching them and making them his own. Possession is everything to him, and she can't bear the thought of his entitlement. But, she reminds herself, the creature won't suffer him for long.

By five o'clock the rain is so heavy it's all she can hear. Water trickles down the chimney breast, disappearing between the floorboards as if the house is drinking it. She lights her candles and sits in the shadows to wait for him, heart drumming at the thought of permitting him entry. All of her that is flesh and blood tells her to batten down the hatches and keep him out. But her bones say to let him in; everything that is ancient tells her not to be afraid.

Look at what he did and see it for what it is.

She glances at the floor by the cabinet and her breath comes quick and panicked.

You will not die to remember it.

She goes to the back of the parlour, to the place where it happened, and she sits, crossing her legs and smoothing the fabric of her breeches. Closing her eyes, she presses her palms to the floorboards. A stone's throw away, beyond the cabinet and waterlogged cottage walls, the sea churns and froths like her heart.

Your anger will not be the end of you; let it be a seed you sow.

CHAPTER SIXTY-FIVE

*B*y the time the church bells are ringing for six o'clock the world is etched in black and white. Torn clouds have let the moonlight through and it falls across the parlour floor like a sword. Just as Ada is lost in the allure of that blade of light there is the sound of something at the door – a soft, ragged tapping.

When she unlatches it, the wind snatches the door from her grasp, flinging it wide. The hank of rope is swinging back and forth, knocking and brushing against the doorframe. She clutches at the charm, knowing that on a night such as this her grammer would have been full of trepidation and fretting at the door with incantations on her tongue.

The last knot, that must never be loosened, sits wetly in her palm and without a second thought she digs into it, pulling and twisting to loosen the hemp. Eventually she feels it give, and unthreads the knot. It hangs limply from her fingers and she waits, listening for an answer from the storm itself. *Let it come*, she thinks.

A singular lamp, yellow and swinging, moves in the distance.

Heart galloping, drenched by the rain, she waits for the shape of Dr Moyle to emerge from the darkness.

'Beastly weather!' he exclaims when he draws close, his eyes hidden in dark sockets.

She feels the water dripping from her face, her hair clinging wetly to her cheeks and neck, and when she doesn't respond with chit-chat about the weather it's as if he sees her properly. His manner alters and his gaze slides quickly away from her to the creature on the kitchen floor.

'Great Caesar's ghost,' he whispers.

He puts his lamp at his feet, collapses his umbrella, picks up his lamp again and pushes past her into the cottage.

'I can hardly believe it,' he says.

Falling to his knees he begins mauling the bones, just as she knew he would. As if he cannot bear to leave any of them untouched.

When she pulls it shut, the kitchen door shudders and thumps in its frame, objecting to some nameless thing. While Moyle crawls about on the floor inspecting the skeleton, she goes to the window in the parlour and opens it a little wider, desperate for the fresh sea air and the sound of the waves. Then she sits in her chair and pulls her shawl around her shoulders.

Moyle is scribbling in a notebook, seemingly in no hurry.

The fool, she thinks.

She realises that he's sketching, his tongue clamped between his teeth in concentration. He pauses every so often to move his lamp, bringing the light to the creature's skull, to its neck and complex sternum.

'I cannot *see*,' he mutters, reaching for a candlestick from the kitchen table. He continues with his furtive drawing, as if he knows he's being rooked and that after tonight he'll never see the creature again; that he must record every detail and as quickly as possible. She muses on whether he trusts her, and concludes that even if he doesn't he probably trusts himself to get the better of her.

There is a dull knocking beneath her feet, as if something has woken under the house, and her breath catches at the ghastly, enticing thought. It is no behemoth, but the sea that has come thus far and now gushes and sucks beneath the floorboards. Moyle is oblivious, intent on his pocketbook, and Ada listens to the water draining, to the momentary absence, to the rush and slap of it returning. They pass what must be half an hour in this way, until water is rising up between the floorboards and creeping in at the door. Just as she knew it would.

'Good gracious!' says Moyle, leaping up when he notices it. He looks wildly in Ada's direction.

'It always does this on a spring tide,' she lies.

'We'll be flooded!'

A sudden gush of water from beneath the door knocks over his lamp, extinguishing it.

'Great Caesar's . . . !'

'It's quite all right. I know it seems alarming, but it's just a high spring tide on a stormy day. This is what it means to live upon the beach.'

'We'll not be cut off?'

She goes to the doorway that separates the kitchen from the parlour.

'Oh, you're already cut off,' she tells him. 'Unless you wish to scrabble up the cliff, but I wouldn't recommend it in this weather. In half an hour, though, it'll have changed again. Let us have our discussion in the parlour and perhaps afterwards the sea will oblige and you can take your leave.'

302

He glances anxiously at the water lapping at his boots.

'Come on through,' she says. 'The cottage slopes slightly, it'll stay dryer in here.'

'I can't believe you live like this.'

He looks at her aghast.

'It helps me remember.'

'Remember what?'

'Come on,' she says, beckoning him through from the kitchen.

He mutters something that she doesn't catch, and he fiddles with his coat buttons. He's afraid, and she wants to say how appropriate that is. She wants to say, *How does that feel?* Instead, she says, 'We're nothing, are we – pitted against the elements?'

He returns his gaze to the fossils as if he might resume his study, glances at his notebook, then stuffs it into his pocket.

'This is ridiculous!'

'Sit down awhile. There's nothing else to be done for now.'

He looks at her coldly, then throws up his hands and sits.

'Shouldn't we collect it all together?' he says, gesturing to the fossils. 'Get it safely packed away?'

'The fossils will do just as well where they are until the water's finished with us.'

He sighs tetchily, rubs his hands against his thighs. 'I suppose I may as well say at the very outset that I intend to draw up something for you to sign. Not just a receipt of payment, but an acknowledgement that the search was a joint endeavour.'

'Draw up whatever you like, I don't care. Anyway, there's something more pressing to discuss.'

He waves his hand.

'We do not need to discuss it. I agree to your price.'

'It's not money I'm thinking of, Dr Moyle. It's the terrible way you've behaved that must be spoken of. The violent and repugnant thing you subjected me to in this very room.'

She feels her composure slipping, her mouth suddenly dry.

He leans forward in his chair, elbows on his knees. With his head hanging, for a moment she fancies that it's regret he feels. And it suddenly seems as if what she's been planning for has come so easily – for him to be sorry. To be full of regret. For him to apologise for what he did. To confess what a brute he has been. Can it really be so simple? It wouldn't put everything right, but it *would* unravel some of the complexity of what she feels.

His face, though, is untroubled when he looks up at her.

'Come, Ada, we both understand how the world works. That men and women play quite differently. It suits you to be coy about your feelings now, but I remember how you looked at me in the beginning – how you coaxed and flattered.'

Her anger breaks against her like a wave.

'I imagine you wish to deny it because you fancy yourself ill-used,' he continues. 'Or perhaps you were pretending all along because you wanted something from me. Either way, you played your hand and now you must make your peace with it.'

'You snake! That's a lie and you know it.'

'I must press upon you my sincerity in this matter. You may not wish to own it, but I fervently believe that if you look honestly enough you'll be forced to admit, if only to yourself, that you wished for my attentions. I imagine you fantasised about something more romantic, but I've never been one for blandishments.'

A great thud at the kitchen door makes him jump.

'Good God! I will not sit here for this!' he says, springing from his chair just as water surges into the parlour, wetting the sea dragon's paddles and pelvis. It flows over Ada's boots, seeping through the many holes to her stockinged feet, cold as the contempt she feels.

She wills the storm inside the cottage, glancing around the familiar room now made strange. Moyle wades through the roiling gloom to the kitchen, stumbling over unseen bones, sprawling onto all fours. He jumps up, sodden and furious, reaching for the latch just as a wall of water tears the door open and lays siege to the cottage. He is swallowed completely, and Ada reaches to the cabinet to steady herself. The water is at her knees, her thighs, her waist. This is not a little floodwater, but the sea coming into town – reminding them all that it can. It is vanishing her home, stealing away its stitched and knitted core. As swift as a squall it has transformed the cottage into something new: a damaged boat, listing and lost. It doesn't feel as terrible as she thought it might. How little her things anchor her, in truth. She has clung to them all for so long, to keep her father alive and to create some sense that she belongs somewhere. But they've saved her from nothing.

Moyle is back on his feet in the kitchen. All around him the water breathes, making him small.

She clutches the cabinet, holding on.

'We'll have to swim,' she calls.

Hurriedly she removes her shawl and pushes it into a high cupboard. Scrabbling for her father's puzzle box she pushes that into the folds of the shawl. She pulls her arms from her braces and drags off her breeches. Struggling under the water with her boots, she prises them from her feet. Then she peels away her stockings so she stands only in her drawers and shift.

Glancing into the kitchen, she sees Moyle clambering on to the table, kneeling there as if in prayer. Water hurtles about

305

the parlour like an animal trapped – leaping from one wall to the next. Lunging through the water, Ada reaches for the open casement, grasping the windowsill.

'*Can* you swim?' she shouts.

'You tricked me!' he shrieks.

She does not mean to, but she smiles.

The storm has brought what she hoped it might bring – the alteration of everything.

'You had no intention of relinquishing the skeleton!'

'Sitting there will not do,' she says. 'Not if you wish to live.'

The timbers of the cottage strain and creak, and the last candles extinguish, plunging the house into darkness. The sound of the water in the parlour is eerie – a sucking and swallowing as if they're caught in the throat of a great beast. Looking out of the window, she can see only heaving black water. Whether *she* can swim in this tumult is yet to be seen.

She pulls herself onto the windowsill, pausing there in the narrow space, the sea flooding in around her. It seems entirely possible that soon she will drown, but this thought doesn't fill her with horror, only a vague sadness. *Better to die here than beneath the heavy clay*, she thinks. Better to die in the cold peace of the sea than by the fury of a lightning bolt and the judgement of neighbours.

'Don't you dare leave!' Moyle shouts.

'You need to come too,' she says, feeling that she owes him some meagre assistance at least; she brought him here knowingly after all. The flooding is worse than she had imagined. She had planned to frighten him. To diminish his power. To make him sorry. She hadn't intended to kill them both.

'It's safer inside, you stupid woman!'

'It isn't! The storm's bringing the sea right up into the town.

I've seen it before. We must get to the cliffs – there's a path we can reach.'

Of course there's a part of her that, like Moyle, wants to choose what is left of the cottage. To hold fast to the bricks and timber that right now seem solid. But she knows her strength will drain from her if she waits here for the storm to pass; she'll die clinging to this promise of safety.

'You back-biting scrub! I tell you now, you'll be sorry for this.'

'You can't swim, can you?' she says.

'Of course I can swim.'

She despises him, and suddenly doesn't care whether he can swim or not. It's not *her* doing that he's here. It is greed and arrogance that brought him.

Shivering, muscles stiffening already, she eases herself a little further out of the window.

He leaps from the kitchen table into the water, swimming powerfully towards her.

Convinced for a moment that he's seen sense, that he's coming to escape with her through the casement, she watches him. But then she sees a flash of his expression, and without a second thought throws herself into the arms of the tempest.

All at once she's disorientated, plunged beneath the frothing waves. She chokes, salt burning her throat. The savage wind throws blades at her face and she can't see in which direction to swim. Her feet find solid ground, then lose it again.

Already she's exhausted: flesh like ice, limbs like stone.

She hears Dr Moyle roaring, and catches a glimpse of him there in the window. For a moment she wonders whether he will plunge in after her, but quickly sees that he won't. That is precisely his fury. That she will leave him behind. That she will not wait with him. And he cannot come into the water because he has no faith in her. He doesn't trust her. He cannot trust the sea, either, or his own ability to weather it.

Sucked at by the water, she begins to swim in the direction of the cliffs, her shift heavy as a millstone. She must free herself from it, she realises, to have any chance of making it ashore. With stiff, shaking fingers she loosens the ribbons around her neck and chest. She seizes the billowing fabric as best she can and manages slowly, clumsily, to pull it up and over her head, sinking as she does so. It is quiet underwater, as if the gale has ceased. And she rests momentarily, thinking of the sea dragon after all this time wetted once more by the ocean. She longs for it to come for her – flying through the water like a hawk through the sky.

She lets go of the fabric and it hangs in the darkness like a ghost. Breaking the surface, gulping the air, she looks around for the cottage and thinks she sees it – a black shadow some distance away. Then she looks for the shore, but doesn't know whether what she sees is the outline of Church Cliffs or whether it is only low-hanging cloud. There is the town, she thinks, with relief: the warm glow of amber lights. But then they are gone. She looks behind her, at what she presumes is the open expanse of the sea and sees a light in that direction too, unable to fathom whether the bell she hears is a bell-buoy or the steeple bell.

Beyond her confusion, and beyond the swelling, spitting water, she hears voices calling. She focuses on the sound of them and begins to swim, painfully slowly. She can't tell whether she's making any progress at all, and part of her is sure she's heading in the wrong direction – straight out to sea. She hears the voices again and cleaves to them, swimming in their direction with all the strength she can muster.

As she stares at it, she's convinced the looming shape *is* Church Cliffs and there is movement atop it. She swims towards that bustling movement, her eyes fixed, hoping for rescuers with ropes at the ready. There is only one path up the crumbly rocks to safety, and it's treacherous enough in good weather. She imagines the slimy clay awash with water, and thinks of the graves that tumble from it on nights such as this.

She listens for the calling voices as she swims and, every so often, when the wind inhales and there's a brief reprieve from its roaring, she hears them again. There are several of them, she realises. More than several. And they seem to be singing. But as she draws closer she wonders if her ears deceive her. Whether it isn't singing, after all, but howling. Whether it isn't rescuers with ropes that call to her, but a pack of wolves.

CHAPTER SIXTY-SIX

*A*da arrives at the looming black wall on the swell of a hateful wave, and a new terror assails her. This is surely where she will meet her death – at the face of Church Cliffs.

The stone tosses her to the churning water.

The water throws her to the stone.

She screams into the darkness and the wolves howl back.

And then her frozen fingers astonish her by finding some purchase at the cliff face. Miraculously, with a relieved leap of her exhausted heart, she is anchored to the land. Reaching up to a stone ledge, she finds a deep ridge for clinging to. Feeling at the stone with her bare feet, she presses down and steps up, nauseous with the sudden victory of being out of the water. She rests her naked chest on the cold, muddy stone, waiting for the land to settle itself, for it feels as if it quakes.

She retches, dizzy and weak.

The wind bites and tussles.

Looking upwards, she regards, with some horror, the steep, slippery cliff path. Swallowing bile, flexing her fingers on one hand and then on the other, she begins to climb.

She listens for the snarl and pant of the wolves, but whenever she looks for them now there is only the dark sky beyond the clifftop.

Her progress is so slow that for long moments she forgets where she is and what she's doing. Whether she is going up or down. Whether she is chasing or whether she is being chased.

Then she finds herself on level ground – prostrate on wet grass, jaw throbbing and her left arm burning with pain.

Is it the wolves she hears again? No longer howling, but singing her name? Is it a celebration she hears, and shouldn't she be dancing as folk have always danced on All Saints' Day?

She drifts to some other place where there is no pain, where there is no cold.

And then she is back, lifting her head to make sense of the curvature of a gravestone. The rain has stopped and the moon is bleeding through the clouds. She pushes herself onto her hands and knees and crawls towards the outline of the church. The bell rings in its tower, and she hears her name once more, broken into pieces and stolen away.

Is someone calling to her?

She longs for it to be true; for someone to be looking for her. For *anyone* to be looking. For any*thing*. It doesn't matter where she goes now. Or with whom. The cottage has said farewell, and she could walk from Lyme without a backward glance.

I belong nowhere, she thinks.

And you belong everywhere.

Looking up, she sees the butter-yellow glow of lamps approaching. She hears the same wind-snatched voices, tremulous and desperate. They call to her, she is certain of it, but she cannot reply. She retches again, and drifts, everything fading.

311

And then there are boots, right there in front of her face, caked in mud.

Warm hands are lifting her, wrapping her in blankets.

She sees a man she doesn't know, and then Isaac's horrified face.

'Thank *God*,' he says.

The unknown man bundles her into his arms and carries her, following Isaac who is striding away, swinging a lamp in each of his hands, shouting instructions. She closes her eyes and feels everything swaying, the sucking of a ghost-sea, her insides heaving.

The cold gets colder.

The darkness darker.

There is the clatter of angry voices. The clink of a bridle, the crack of a whip.

Then they're away and there's nothing she can do to stop it: the bump and jostle of the curricle brings up her insides, and she vomits into Isaac's lap.

CHAPTER SIXTY-SEVEN

Edwin

*S*traddling the ridge of the roof as if riding a horse, his legs are lost to the water. Every tile is submerged and Edwin himself, arms wrapped around the chimney, is swallowed by a great swelling wave every few breaths. All the same, his panic is easing a little as the water retreats. He's convinced that the tide is finally going out; would wager his last guinea on it. A short while ago, just after he lost all sensation in his legs, the sea had reached almost to the top of the chimney, but now it laps again at the ridge.

As he clings on, angry at the audacity of the water (for all the world it seems to be goading him), he tries in vain to deny what he knows: the human body is but a collection of organs, swimming in blood; so easily set out of balance; full of weakness and hidden sensitivity. He has seen it more times than he cares to remember – how the body can betray a man in an instant.

It is the cold that troubles him; how insidious it is, creeping through his flesh and into his veins, into his blood and bones. Turning him slowly to stone.

It is only a little chill, he reassures himself.

Black water stretches all around as if a dark ocean has risen up from hell and flooded the earth. He knows the town must still surely lie behind him, but he dare not move an inch to look, even though it would be comforting to see some sign of life – the glow of gas lamps or the flicker of torches. But who, anyway, would be out in this? Who would not have their shutters battened? He has grown so tired of his lodgings of late, but can think right now of nothing more pleasant than the terse familiarity of the housekeeper, the parsimonious meals she prepares for him, the flickering fire in the small grate.

How has it come to this?!

Bitterly, he ruminates on the fossils that languish beneath him in the cottage. How hard he fought to make this trip to Lyme a success.

Why can no one be trusted?

He can only bear to think of Miss Winters if he imagines her dashed against the rocks. He conjures that very scene, and feels a weak relief at the thought of it. Furthermore, he permits himself to believe that the fossils rest safely within the house and that soon the tide will rescue him and all will be well: he will not die here on the roof of a rotten cottage. Despite everything he's been up against these last few weeks, he still churns with the belief he deserves more than life has hitherto granted him. Is *destined* for more. He feels it in his frozen bones – that his moment is yet to come. In the meantime, he won't dwell on how odd he feels; how strangely warm suddenly; how sleepy. He tries to move his fingers, but they fail to answer him. It seems likely that they're not, in actual fact, his hands at all.

He coaxes thoughts of success to the front of his mind; imagines returning home to praise and admiration, and, in time, his great discovery displayed in the British Museum with his name beneath it.

He closes his eyes to better concentrate on keeping upright. He counts to ten, then twenty, then fifty. A peacefulness settles over him, and even the sobbing of the wind abates. When he opens his eyes the tiniest sliver, he sees that the clouds have parted, and the moon has scattered a million diamonds across the water. A good omen, he thinks.

He wills the tide to ebb away, and it seems that perhaps it's doing just that, for he feels a persuasive pulling: a hundred hands now tug at him. The effort of holding on to the chimney is exhausting, and the siren call to sleep – to sleep *now* and *deeply* – is a song he cannot banish. He thinks of Christina, the soft parts of her where he likes to rest his head. Lost in a reverie about his wife, he startles when everything shifts: a quake and rumble beneath him. The chimney dips and slips away, and before he understands what's happening he's falling with the roof, plummeting beneath the surface of the water with stone and slate. And although he strains desperately for something solid that might save him, there is nothing that isn't also heading downwards.

The moon shines brightly upon his descent, illuminating the tumbling bricks of Ada's home – the splintered timbers where the roof had been. As he drifts past it, he tries to grab hold of what's left of the back wall of the parlour, as if he might leap upwards from it and gulp a lungful of air. But he cannot command his limbs at all; he's solid as a fossil.

Back inside what's left of the four walls – a ghost cottage that ripples in the argent light – the cabinet looms in front of him as he settles helplessly on the floor, weighted down not by the collapsed house but by a crushing impotence.

His face is inches from the turned wood of John Winters' creation.

The best cabinetmaker in Dorset, Miss Winters had told him.

He remembers her words, how proudly she'd spoken them, and a dim envy trickles through him. He doesn't know a dovetail from a mortise and tenon, but he knows that what he looks at in the murky water is a thing of beauty.

The current lifts him, then lays him down: a mother's love, all-forgiving.

It dawns on him what's happening, and that there'll be no fighting it. He feels suddenly that he's not alone, fancying that the man, John Winters, is standing over him: looking down his nose, watching and waiting.

Panic comes like a thrashing beast and, when he can resist it no longer, the air rushes from his lungs like a symphony of blown glass.

CHAPTER SIXTY-EIGHT

*A*da sleeps while Lyme counts its losses.

Twenty-three homes have been destroyed by the storm, and more boats than that lost in the harbour. Blocks of stone are scattered across Town Beach. Floorboards and window frames have splintered into firewood and float on the water, tumbling ungainly in the waves, as if even the tide is now broken. And in the dawn light children pick shards of glass from The Walk – jewels on their palms.

As people gather, reporting on the whereabouts of friends and neighbours ousted from their homes, there's talk of only Ada Winters being unaccounted for. Tom Green volunteers to search for her and walks his family, women and all, to the sea-wrecked remains of Ada's cottage on Broad Ledge. They find no wall standing higher than Martha's four feet and ten inches. The furniture has been swept away, and the half-smashed door swings by a single hinge. A great pile of stone crowds what is left of the parlour, like an animal sitting over its prey.

When they find Edwin Moyle's body in the corner of the

room, they lift him out and lay him on the broken door, like a pauper ready for his grave. Once they're certain that Ada isn't there and have given the place one final search for anything of value, they leave its bones to the mercy of the elements.

CHAPTER SIXTY-NINE

*A*fter three days of sleeping, Ada wakes in a strange bed, in a strange room, in a strange house. There are posts and bed-curtains, and between the thick fabric the sunlight falls in warm pools across the embroidered coverlet. She runs her fingers over the handiwork, losing herself in the precise stitching.

She's never spent a night in a bed other than her own.

As she pushes herself to sitting, the room swims a little, but she's surprised to realise she isn't feeling badly. Her left arm is bandaged and her thirst is riotous, but there's no greater damage than that. Looking about herself, she sees a carafe of something on a small table on the other side of the room. She folds back the blankets and eases her legs out of bed. Testing the floor with her toes, she lets her feet fall flat, pushing herself to standing. The housecoat draped across the chair beside the bed seems as if it's meant for her and she slips her arms into the quilted fabric, smelling rose water.

She has a vague memory of Sarah attending her, speaking to her softly and giving her liquid on a sponge. She presumes she's in the villa on Silver Street and goes to the small window, recognising the houses opposite and the meadow beyond.

Remembering her thirst, she goes to the table. It's a currant cordial, with a hint of something medicinal, and Ada gulps three full glasses. She wipes dribble from her chin, and, with a shaking hand, returns the glass to its small tray.

Looking around for a pair of stockings or slipped shoes, she finds none. Pulling the housecoat tightly about her she goes slowly and carefully from the room, finding herself in a long hallway. She takes in the mullioned windows on the opposite wall – a windswept garden bleary through the mottled panes, a low sun in the distance. She sees a staircase at one end of the hallway and a closed door at the other. She prevaricates, with little energy to spare, deciding in the end to head for the stairs.

The stairwell is gloomy, lit halfway down by a gas lamp attached to the wall. Careful on the well-worn rises, she brings her full attention to every step.

An empty kitchen must be crossed if she's to follow the sound of voices. Cracked, uneven slabs are cold beneath her bare feet. A curmudgeonly table as large as her kitchen fills the middle of the room, two chickens ready for plucking sprawl on the block. Pans and skillets hang from the wall and a bowl of milk waits in the sink.

In the room yonder, the chirrup of laughter comes repeatedly.

Wandering through a stranger's house in her bare feet ought to make her feel uncomfortable, but Ada feels nothing of the sort. She feels very little, in truth; just a simple curiosity about what and who she'll find on the other side of the heavy door.

She turns the cold iron handle and pushes. It doesn't budge, but it has no lock, so it can't be that. She tries again, putting her shoulder to it. As it springs open a bright light greets her and for a moment it is all she can see – sunlight and mirrors and sparkling glass. Then she sees an emerald sofa, and the bustle of human form. Isaac and Sarah lounge together: her feet balanced on his knees, her petticoats drifting to the floor.

And then, as if they are one being, they leap to their feet in perfect unison and rush to her. They are gabbling like children, leaving no space at all for her to answer their questions.

'*Oh!*' says Ada, noticing the family resemblance, astonished not to have seen it before. 'Your sister?'

'Isn't it incredible?' says Isaac. 'Did you not receive my note?'

Ada shakes her head, confused, her thoughts slow.

'In any case, I hear the two of you have met,' he says.

Hesitantly, Ada looks to Sarah, who gives a quick shake of her head.

'Just on the beach,' Sarah mutters.

Ada baulks inwardly at the lie, but she's given Sarah her word and has no choice but to honour that.

'I'm so delighted for you,' she says.

She *is* delighted, but knows it doesn't show upon her face quite yet.

'And I'm delighted that you're awake,' Isaac says. 'You've no idea how frantic we've been.'

'You have nothing on your feet,' says Sarah, then, rushing out of the room.

When Ada steps towards Isaac and leans her head against him, he wraps his arms around her. She allows the comfort of him to suffuse her, closing her eyes, breathing him in.

CHAPTER SEVENTY

When Annie and Josiah call by the following day, Isaac insists that they stay for lunch. His aunt and uncle join them, and they eat chicken and potatoes, boiled eggs and lettuce. Isaac's relations are silver-topped as the Fountains – four grey doves, Ada thinks. And no sooner has this thought materialised, than they proceed to confirm it: chortling contentedly and rousing themselves, shaking out their pleasant feathers, pecking messily at their apple tart and cream. Ada eats only a tiny amount of everything she's offered. Afterwards, though, with a thirst she can't satisfy, she swallows glass after glass of blackcurrant cordial.

Later, when it's only the three of them, Annie and Josiah sit either side of Ada and tell her how bereft they've been at the thought of losing her. That she's the closest they have to a child of their own and she mustn't forget it.

'We've visited each day to check on you,' says Annie, tears trembling in her faded blue eyes.

'Have you been along to the cottage?' Ada asks.

Josiah nods, snatching a look at his wife.

'Isaac has told you, I believe,' he says, 'that it's mostly gone.'

'What about my father's furniture?'

Josiah nods. 'That too, I'm afraid to say.'

Ada imagines the place stripped back to its stone; how simple the sea has made it for her.

'Ada,' says Annie, 'was Dr Moyle with you, the night of the storm?'

She meets Annie's tentative gaze.

'Dead or alive?' Ada asks, the words stumbling in her throat.

Annie nods. 'Dead.'

Ada slumps; it's such a tangled knot of emotion.

In the quiet that follows she thinks of the people she has loved. Her grammer whom she hardly remembers, who spoke to the spirits more than to her living family. And Gramfer, whose stories return to her, regular as the tide. She thinks of Edith, who preferred the silence. And John Winters who shouted from the rooftops. She wonders at her own voice, and how to find it. Whether, with enough words, anything can be explained? Whether she need not fret about the *best* words. Or the *right* words. She begins to think that perhaps there are many ways to explain herself; that to speak, and to keep speaking, is the most important thing. That what she intends to say will be heard in the end.

So she begins with a single sentence, and follows on with another. And as Ada tells her story, Josiah and Annie say nothing. They don't interrupt her, or discourage her with their shock and discomfort.

They hold her hands, and they listen.

Ada, though, leaves some things unsaid. She doesn't tell them that a part of her seems to have dropped away. That she left something of herself behind in the sea that night, and feels lighter because of it. She doesn't tell them that some creature had been living in her ribcage. That she thought it might be her mother's spirit. That now it's gone.

Later, when she recounts the same story to Isaac and Sarah, her voice doesn't tremble quite so much. Her shame, she understands, has loosened its grip.

Isaac listens silently, although struggles to steady his breath. And when she's finished speaking, he says, in a wavering voice, 'Never have I been so glad to hear of a man's demise.'

Throughout the whole exchange, Sarah sits quietly, hands clenched, cheeks aflame. And the following morning she tells her brother about the falling stars and Frederick Hooke. About Gun Cliff and a stranger with stones in her pocket.

'A stranger swift as a wolf,' she says.

CHAPTER SEVENTY-ONE

*P*astor Durrant visits the following afternoon and Ada knows immediately upon seeing him that he has some news; his excitement crackles off him like sparks from a hoppy coal.

'What is it?' she demands, as he hovers in the doorway to the drawing room.

'I have something for you,' he says, at the same time pulling Isaac away, out of the room. She hears them scurry down the hallway, and in no time they're back, dragging two sacks each behind them.

'From the rubble in your cottage,' says Durrant.

He proceeds to empty the sea dragon's bones onto the drawing-room floor, one careful sack at a time. He has sorted them logically, Ada realises, as she falls upon the fossils, straightaway piecing them together so she can see what's there and what's missing.

Sarah, Isaac and Pastor Durrant watch the creature emerge.

'I hoped it might come alive and save me from drowning,' she says, as she constructs its elegant neck. She laughs, looking at each of them in turn.

'It would have eaten you,' says Durrant.

And Ada nods, smiling.

'Yes,' she says. 'Of course, it would have eaten me.'

CHAPTER SEVENTY-TWO

*S*ome afternoons Ada and Isaac are left undisturbed for hours at a time and they talk unceasingly. He folds his paint-smudged fingers around hers, kissing her nails, her wrists, her palms – quite idly, in-between rambling on about wild Scottish heaths and the lakes of Cumberland and Westmorland, about Shakespeare and Keats, about poetry and the burden of being human: mortal and flawed. She speaks of Wollstonecraft and *A Vindication of the Rights of Woman*, about fossils she is yet to find and papers she is yet to write.

They squabble about the virtues and oversights of Rousseau and Godwin, and whether the world would suffer more greatly without poets or scientists. After discussing the freedom of childhood, and the chains of their adult lives, they spend an afternoon wearing one another's clothes, and the following morning cut Ada's hair into something short and tousled.

They practise speaking honestly, as if feelings cannot be hurt, and separately both wonder what they are still to learn about the other.

They speak of how marriage would be like the mill – a

tyranny of the soul. Why sexual union might be less rewarding than a desire never realised. And given how Ada feels about such a union and how she feels about the notion of pregnancy, perhaps the sublimity of longing and chastity would be the making of them.

'I believe I'd be more than content desiring you for ever,' he tells her.

He is not easily embarrassed, but his face flushes pink after he confesses this. She smiles at his flustering, and how he finds his equilibrium by quoting another man's poetry to her.

'Heard melodies are sweet, but those unheard are sweeter . . . Fair youth beneath the trees, thou canst not leave . . . Bold lover, never, never canst thou kiss.'

She permits him to read her the whole of 'Ode on a Grecian Urn', and then they speak of ancient Greece, of myths and painted pottery, and whether living beneath the baking sun makes philosophising easier.

CHAPTER SEVENTY-THREE

*O*ne afternoon at the start of December, when the air is white with the thought of snow, and Ada is just beginning to wonder how much longer they can continue in the villa on Silver Street without a plan for the future, Durrant breaks the news to them that he'll soon be taking possession of an empty farmhouse in North Yorkshire that belongs to his family.

'It's stood empty for a few years, after my brother had an altercation with the tenants.'

He's sitting next to Ada on the emerald velvet sofa when he tells them this, pulling at his cravat as if it strangles him. He snatches glances at Ada, although mainly addresses himself to Isaac, who sits on the sofa opposite with Sarah.

'It's near Runswick Bay, where the fossils are almost as fine as they are in Lyme, and I'm inviting you all to join me.'

Silence falls as they collectively measure this information.

'Join you?' says Ada.

'Come live with me.'

Sarah laughs and claps her hands.

'The four of us!'

Isaac reaches over and pulls her towards him, wrapping her in a fierce embrace designed to constrain and frustrate. She wriggles free and takes his hand.

'Don't say anything yet,' Durrant tells them. His cheeks have coloured, and he busies himself with his cup and saucer. 'But I've thought about every detail and believe it would suit us all. There's land to be farmed, enough to sustain our needs. Isaac – you have the skills and have talked at length about the pleasures of a life that keeps one close to the soil.'

Nobody speaks.

'Ada,' Durrant says, turning towards her, 'you've made it plain to us all that you don't wish to be married, but do you really want to be alone? I don't think you do. But your honesty on the subject has provoked in me all manner of feelings, which I've been contemplating at some length. You made me realise that I shouldn't look to be married for the sake of being married, although I must say that of course I see it as an opportunity for companionship with someone I admire. But I've come to see that I, like you, would choose a scholarly life over family life. Having thought about it, I'm certain I'd prefer peace and quiet and the opportunity for study to the clamour of children in the house. I wish to pursue my scriptural geology with men and women of like minds. I'll need to travel, and it wouldn't do to be constrained by the expectations of a spouse.'

'And so, you propose we all live together as friends and colleagues? And you could brook the consternation and speculation of our neighbours?'

'To hell with our neighbours! I'm sick of wagging tongues and all the damage they do.' He pauses, then says, 'All of us have spoken these last weeks of our desire to start afresh in a place that's unfamiliar. Would it not be a solution? Your aunt, Sarah, has cousins in Scarborough that she visits regularly, so I understand. And she supports your desire to get away from your brute of a father.'

Sarah nods earnestly, looking to Isaac.

'It's true,' she says.

'I'm not sure Aunt Catherine will like the idea of Sarah living with a merry band of dissenters,' says Isaac. 'She may have our mother's heart, but she'd likely still put up some opposition.'

'We can persuade her!' says Sarah. 'Our uncle is a painter, after all, and quite an eccentric himself.'

Isaac looks at Ada, leaning forward to rest his elbows on his knees.

'You've spoken about leaving Lyme, but do you mean it?'

She meets his gaze and the whole room drops away; this is the only conversation that matters.

'The cottage is gone; it doesn't matter where I go now.'

'Annie and Josiah?'

'They can visit; they love their little holidays.'

'But you mustn't just go anywhere on a whim. Where do you *want* to be? If you could choose.'

'By the sea, where there are fossils aplenty.'

'So let us be together!' says Durrant. 'I do genuinely believe that we might all go quite happily.'

'We *should*!' says Sarah.

'Sister, you'd be bored out of your mind in a few weeks.'

'How dare you dismiss me! You're always talking of the countryside and how good it is for the spirit. Why should you believe that my spirit's not cut out for it?'

'Why indeed?' says Ada.

Sarah jumps from her sofa and comes to squeeze between Ada and Pastor Durrant.

'Perhaps it's you, brother, who doesn't wish to take a risk and join the three of us.'

Durrant laughs.

'You writers,' Ada says, pulling a face. 'It's all very well to muse on a simple life for the sake of your prose, but to live the reality is an altogether different matter.'

Isaac gazes at the three of them, shaking his head.

'Cast your aspersions all you like, I know very well of what I'm capable. I'm not afraid of labouring for our daily bread. Will you be content making that bread, sister dear?'

'I shall!'

'Then let us go,' says Isaac.

And Sarah leaps again from one sofa to the other, to pepper her brother's face with kisses.

CHAPTER SEVENTY-FOUR

er bedroom is a perfect pitch black, and the sense of nothingness drags Ada's thoughts towards the darkness of Moyle. He may well be dead, but some nights as she tries to sleep it feels for all the world that he crawls upon her skin and lives upon her breath. That still, somehow, he resides within her. She tries to reason with it, to work it into something new. But it returns, fever-hot, like a night hag sitting on her chest.

She rises in desperation from her bed, pushes angry feet into slipped shoes. The air is icy cold, flitting across her. Blind in the dark, she shuffles to the wall with her arms outstretched. From there, she creeps to the door, fumbling for the latch.

She follows the length of the hallway, the shallow rises that lead her down, then up again. She guides herself with drifting fingers, counting carefully the rooms she passes.

When she reaches Isaac's door she feels for the latch, breathes three deep breaths, gathers her courage and opens it. She waits for some signal that he might have heard her, but there's no indication of that. Only the slow, quiet whisper of him sleeping.

Shutting the door behind her she says his name and he stirs, the silk of his counterpane rustling.

'Isaac.'

'*Ada?*'

She moves towards his voice and the comfort of him, towards what she hopes will be an answer of sorts.

'Can I come in?'

It's what she used to ask her parents whenever she crept from her pallet to their bed, and the sudden memory unsettles her. How altered things now are. How time gathers up everything in the end and throws it all away. This too, she thinks. This too will soon be gone.

There's the sound of movement: the pulling back of the bed-covers, the rearranging of things between them. Then Isaac's hand is there on her arm, guiding her towards him. She kicks her slippers beneath his bed and eases herself between the layers of warmth.

'Ada?' he says again.

'I don't know,' she says. 'I was having dark thoughts.'

He pulls her into an embrace, pressing his lips into her hair. He smells somehow of the sea, and they lie there together for so long that Ada wonders if he's fallen back to sleep.

'He's haunting me,' she says.

Isaac's breathing is careful, as if measured out.

'He's *gone*,' he whispers.

'But I feel him . . . inside me.'

Isaac holds her tighter.

'It's just a feeling,' he tells her. 'It's not real.'

'I was thinking that you should do it.'

'Do what?'

'If I had that memory too, the memory of you.'

'You don't want that, Ada.'

'I want to blot out the darkness of him. I want a memory of somebody else – a memory of you.'

She feels him shaking his head.

'You can't blot darkness with more darkness,' he whispers.

'It wouldn't be . . .'

'It *would*. It's not what you want; we've talked about this.'

She starts to cry and he pulls her close, kissing her head. He's crying too, and she wipes his tears away with her thumb, licks at the saltiness. And then they are kissing soft, gentle kisses. Salty, teary kisses that deepen the further in they wade.

They draw back, breathe one another's breath.

'He's gone,' says Isaac. 'I *promise* you.'

She wants to believe him, but isn't sure that she can. Loosening the ribbons of her shift she tugs the fabric apart, dragging it over her head. She reaches for his hand and places it against the curve of her hip, the planes of her stomach, the small outcrop of her breast: the landscape of her.

'I want you to,' she says, pulling at his nightshirt.

He gently pushes her hands away, shuffling to put an inch or two between their bodies.

'Isaac!'

He breathes – she hears how deeply.

'Let us use our imaginations, then,' he says. He cups her face in the darkness, kissing her cheek and chin. *Zygomatic and mandible*, she thinks. He brushes her neck with his lips, and then her collarbone. 'Clavicle,' she whispers, clinging to the word. He kisses her breast and rib, her belly and hip. She imagines herself as a skeleton, wholly exposed, the clean simplicity of every curve of pale bone offered up to him: *ilium, sacrum, pubis, ischium.*

He rests the side of his face upon her belly, laces his fingers with hers.

Carpal, metacarpal, phalanges.

She notices moonlight creeping along the floorboards in the furthest corner of the room, and remembers how she always feels when swimming in the moonlit darkness. How it slakes some thirst, that silver tranquillity. Throwing back the covers, the cold air skits across her skin, and she brings Isaac's hand to her lips so she can taste him again. So she can realise that he smells not only of the sea, but of the forest too. With her other hand she strokes his hair – moss beneath her fingers. One day soon they'll share the same scent; they'll smell of the earth. He will be farming it and she will be searching it. Beyond that, they will lie in it.

His mouth between her legs is a shock of pleasure and she holds her breath, waiting for a landslip of darkness to come for her. To suffocate her.

But it doesn't.

And soon, tears stream one after the other down her cheeks, pooling in her ears and wetting the pillow beneath her.

Her relief is as clear as the moonlight; perhaps she's not as haunted as she thought.

Or perhaps what seemed true today will not be true tomorrow.

Or perhaps it doesn't matter what she feels, because whatever she feels won't be the end of her.

For a brief moment she has no outer edges. No bones within. She cannot tell what is her pleasure, and what is his.

Where his love ends and hers begins.

CHAPTER SEVENTY-FIVE

London

1828

*A*s Ada enters no. 20 Bedford Street, Covent Garden, simultaneously two things occur. It is always the same. Firstly, she lets part of herself slip away so that she can become Adam Gray. *She* becomes *he*. Secondly, Adam allows his gaze to be drawn up the grand staircase to the magnificent, engraved and coloured geological map of England and Wales that looms from the wall. A map like no other: lined, stippled and patched. Its description is engraved in copperplate: *A delineation of The Strata of England and Wales with part of Scotland; exhibiting the collieries and mines, the marshes and fen lands originally overflowed by the sea, and the varieties of soil according to the variations in the sub strata.* Beneath the description is the signature of William Smith, dated 1815. It is the first true geological map of anywhere in the world. Imagined, undertaken, created and presented by a single man: the son of a blacksmith. A self-taught and stubborn visionary, thwarted at every turn by debt and privation.

Today, Adam does as he always does: gives an almost indiscernible nod to this map. To William, who, like Ada, has been deemed unworthy of membership of the Geological Society of London.

Adam's heart pounds as he ascends the stairs, but he keeps his shoulders back, grateful for his five foot nine inches. If his colleagues have ever noticed that his clothes — the very best quality, perfectly fitted — are the same month to month, they never mention it.

He's accustomed to presenting at these meetings, being one of the more prolific fossil hunters, and will talk today of his recent astonishing find: a jumble of bones with a long tail and wings. Correspondence has been flitting between England and France about this discovery; a rare new species: a flying reptile they are calling a pterosaur.

Slowly climbing the stairs ahead of him is the thin elderly man that Adam first met on the beach in Lyme. He remembers that day, four years ago — the rain that left him sopping as he tipped the plesiosaur paddle bones onto his piece of oilcloth. How he scurried after those geologists, desperate to be seen and heard.

He remembers this willowy gentleman, Mr Henry Thomas, in particular. How apologetic his expression had been, and how he'd looked as if he might dissolve in the downpour.

On every occasion of seeing one another here in Bedford Street, Mr Thomas has held Adam's gaze just a little too long. Adam has felt each time the heat of this scrutiny, nettled by the thought that perhaps his identity has been rumbled. Here now, he runs a hand through his short hair, pushing it away from his forehead. He draws breath, steadying himself as Mr Thomas stops upon the stairs and turns to regard him.

'Good evening, Mr Gray.'

'Good evening, Mr Thomas.'

It seems that Adam's voice comes from some cave within himself. He has practised this with his friends, and knows not to try too hard. There's no need to be something that he isn't; he only has to mine a deeper stratum of who he already is.

'I'm very much looking forward to hearing from you,' says Thomas.

'Thank you,' says Adam, doing his best to look the man in the eye.

'And I've been wanting to say for some time now, that I'm very delighted you made it here, you know. Very delighted indeed. You do deserve it.'

Mr Thomas shakes Adam's hand and nods a slow, certain nod.

They continue up the stairs together and enter the meeting room that is draped with the molten gold of the summer evening.

They greet their colleagues and exchange the necessary pleasantries.

The chair opens the meeting as Adam busies himself with his papers, spreading them out across the polished table: his own notes and Isaac's drawings. He gathers his thoughts, heart kicking, waiting to be introduced.

And then he begins to speak.

AUTHOR'S NOTE

The genesis of this novel was a single enticing snippet about the life of Mary Anning of Lyme Regis: how this talented early palaeontologist nearly died as an infant after being struck by lightning. How she was believed to be dead, but was plunged into a bath of water and revived. How, it is said, she had been a sickly child up until that point, but after the lightning strike she became full of a bright inquisitiveness – a peculiar child who would come to be regarded by many as a peculiar woman.

Interest piqued, I went on to read about Anning: her talent as a 'fossilist'; the rejection and sidelining of her by the Geological Society of London; how this single woman, living in privation, dedicated herself to the newly emerging science of palaeontology. Immediately, I knew I needed to write a novel inspired by this important scientist and the tumultuous world in which she lived – a time of food shortages and social unrest, of Romanticism, self-education and the proliferation of the written word, of a burgeoning industrialisation, the rise of empiricism and the challenging of religious doctrine.

In all directions there was change and innovation. Certainty was, in many corners, being replaced by a bewilderment: how on earth to make sense of the world? I veered away from a strictly biographical novel about Mary Anning, because I wanted to bring a wider lens to the story overall. The outrage I felt about Anning's exclusion, on the grounds of her sex, from the early nineteenth-century scientific world to which she longed to belong, rippled out even further when I read the story of William Smith: son of a blacksmith and of simple yeoman stock, but (like Anning) somewhat stubborn and visionary, highly motivated, and more or less self-taught in the area of geology. Plagued by debt, uncertainty and public humiliation, Smith singlehandedly created the first geological map of England and Wales – an astonishing and invaluable piece of work. He, too, was deemed unworthy of membership of the Geological Society of London, and, just like Anning, had his work passed off as the achievement of others. It was only at the very end of his life, by then considered 'the father of geology', that he was finally granted membership.

Mary Anning was never offered the same acknowledgement, despite undoubtedly being the mother of geology – having discovered some of the finest complete skeletons of ichthyosaurs and plesiosaurs, and the first pterosaur to be found outside Germany, all of which helped to shape scientific understanding of prehistoric life. She died in 1847 from breast cancer, aged forty-six. In 2010 she was recognised by the Royal Society as one of the ten most influential female scientists in British history.

ACKNOWLEDGMENTS

A huge thank you to the wonderful team at Sphere: Katya Ellis, Nithya Rae, Lucie Sharpe and Hannah Wood. Special thanks to my brilliant editor, Rosanna Forte, for your insight, guidance and encouragement.

Thank you to Ella Kahn, truly the most wonderful agent that a writer could hope for.

Thank you to my beautiful family: to Lance, best friend, constant companion, science advisor and patient first reader – I couldn't do it without you; to Elfie for listening with such care and for your extremely insightful character analysis; and to Jack for your creative inspiration, for all those years of beachcombing and collecting, and for your wonderful ammonite drawing – it means so much to have your illustration alongside my writing. Thank you, too, John and Anne, Mum and Dad and the whole Chambers clan.

Loving thanks to all my friends who support me through the tumult of writing: Angela Argenzio, Imogen Ashby, Neil Berry, the BKS gals, Bex Bonner-Wallace, Anna Caig, Anton Cannell, Jeanette Caw, Blossom and Chris Chambers, Charlotte

Cooke, Shirley Davison, Karen Dunn, Annie Garthwaite, Ann Gornall, Merryn Gott, Cate Hammond, Sophie Hunter, Liz Hyder, Christine Kelly, Elizabeth Lee, Caroline and Angus McLeod, Sarah-Jane Page, Nara Rumford, Renuka Russell, Simon Seligman, Sarah Thompson, Jamie Voce, Ceris Vroone, River Wolton, Richard Wraight and Lou Wright.

I am indebted to the many books I relied upon during the writing of this novel: Deborah Cadbury's *The Dinosaur Hunters*; Tracy Chevalier's *Remarkable Creatures*; Jo Draper's *Lyme Regis, Past & Present*; John Fowles' *A Short History of Lyme Regis*; Christopher McGowan's *The Dragon Seekers*; Patricia Pierce's *Jurassic Mary*; John Rattenbury's *Memoirs of a Smuggler*; George Roberts' *The History and Antiquities of the Borough of Lyme Regis and Charmouth*; and Simon Winchester's *The Map that Changed the World*. Thank you to Caroline Lam at The Geological Society for advising on access to the *Transactions of The Geological Society*, which informed Ada's letter on pages 213–14.

I would like to acknowledge Maya Angelou and Brené Brown as inspiration for Ada's realisation that she belongs nowhere, and everywhere. And thank you William Buckland for Dr Moyle's line, *'The rocks stared me in the face, they wooed and caressed me, saying at every turn, Pray, Pray, be a geologist!'*